COLLISION

Blue Blooded Brothers Book 1

Sofia Aves

II

First Edition

Cover Art by Vibrant Designs

Editing Services provided by A. Strom - Edits with a Coffee Addict

www.redpensandcoffeebeans.wordpress.com/

www.facebook.com/redpensandcoffeebeans/

Published by Little Quail Press

www.littlequailpress.com

ISBN 978-0-6486947-3-1

IV

Contents

Dedication

To any writer who thinks they can't;

you can.

VIII

Blue Blooded Brothers Series

Collision

Politics & Paperwork

Blindsided

IX

X

CHAPTER ONE

MILA

Tiny feet pattered the worn carpet, glitter coating it with false splendour. The little girl wended her way between patrons. Some were blessed with stars, some with promises of happiness and love; others became apples and bananas. Too much *Ben and Holly*, I recalled from when I'd been forced to babysit for my best friend.

I tried not to look over to my left, the red shoe that– I spun away, and refocused on my task. The man behind me shuffled his feet. I flinched as he dug the pistol into the small of my back, and shivered — skin prickling.

The small office of Central Bank was being held up, and no one outside had noticed. Business operated as usual in the main street through the broad, glassed front as it did every day.

"Oooh, sweetheart, you cold there? I'll warm you up." Fetid breath beneath a rough growl assailed me. I repressed the urge to turn away or vomit, knowing it would only provoke him further. Clammy warmth rubbed my side. My stomach clenched, fighting the numbness that spread through me until I was ice.

A beep sounded at my last keystroke. It was a welcome distraction from my self-analysis. As the thug moved away, I squinted at a screen I'd never seen before.

"It's asking for a password." My voice was husky from lack of use, or maybe it was from screaming silently inside.

"What? No, ...Oi! Nerd! You never said nothin' 'bout no flamin' password!"

Black wire glasses appeared above the divider between the teller cubes. A tuft of dark hair wobbled above a brow furrowed in concentration.

"Seriously, already? Hang on, how far has she got?" Glasses grimaced at me theatrically from his seat at the opposite counter, rolling eyes in the direction of the stale-breathed thug. I returned the sentiment, if only mentally. There was no way I wanted any of these aggressors believing I sympathised with them.

"I'm as far as the login for the manager's screen," I snapped, short breaths puffing through a clenched chest.

Get it over, quick and easy; then they'll be gone.

2

It was the mantra that had been running through my head for the past twenty minutes.

Get it over, over.

Behind the partition, another patron was being turned into a banana.

We thought we'd been well prepared for an armed robbery. The thin booklet on personal safety was required reading. Give them what they want, and they will leave. Sound the silent alarm behind your terminal.

Karen had tried to do that.

I refused to look at her desk again, my stomach heaving. HR's strategy hadn't worked this time. Maybe I should send them a memo on it, come Monday.

If I was still breathing then.

"Only the login? That's disappointing." Glasses' brow furrowed deeply. "She should have passed that, already. I gave you the codes for those, before...well," he waved a hand behind himself, where a body lay: Karen — the teller who had manned the desk where Glasses now sat before she was yanked from the line of hostages. A swell of emotion blurred my eyes. I blinked tears away angrily.

Don't think, don't think. Over. Get it over and done.

Focus.

Tapped the keyboard, wiggled the mouse. Breathe.

Don't engage. Don't.

"Passwords?"

I was proud my voice didn't shake. My logical brain informed me it was shock and nothing that was under my control. The emotional part didn't answer; it was as numb as the rest of me.

Glasses raised his eyebrows.

"Yes, ma'am."

He flicked a brief salute. A scrap of paper fluttered from his fingers, landing beside the keyboard.

"*Fluffy22?* Really?" I couldn't help commenting. "Cat or dog?"

"Likely the goldfish. Some people have no idea, truly," Glasses responded with a roll of his eyes. We shared a look. I realised what I was doing and quickly returned to the screen: Staring, willing tunnel vision.

Don't, don't.

Heavy footsteps reverberated behind me where the bank manager's office sat. A heavy hand clapped down on my shoulder. Too hot, too overly familiar. His thumb rubbed the sensitive spot on my collarbone, forcing an unwelcome shiver through me.

I willed myself still, to not react, desperate to return to the blank nothing that had consumed me only a moment before, though the urge to jerk away lingered when he spoke. Deep and cold. The same voice I had heard beside Karen.

Before.

"How're we going, we in yet?"

"Not yet, boss; gotta put these in," Glasses indicated the passwords, "Then we should have full access."

I still couldn't believe it. These guys were going to bungle their own robbery. My screen had no way to access the electronic locks for the safe, and anyway, it was such a small branch, surely nothing they held would be sufficient to risk years of incarceration. Reflex had my mouth open to say as much until my brain kicked into gear. My mouth closed with a snap. The three men turned to look at me, and I started guiltily.

"Something you'd like to add, lass?" The question was delivered with some small humour and a touch of annoyance. I shook my head mutely.

"Right, let's get this show on the road."

I chanced a glimpse up at the man behind the robbery: tanned skin, longer-than-average dark hair, hard jaw. Tall and lean. You were supposed to remember details like that for the police, right? His face swivelled my way, displaying ice-cold eyes, unsuited to the rest of his handsome frame.

The devil within, I thought numbly. That wasn't a face that would be easy to forget. I'd have no trouble describing him later, I knew. With hands beginning to tremor from the proximity of the man responsible for the death of my friend, I entered the passwords as the prompts came up. A tiny box popped up in the centre of the screen that I had never seen before.

"...And we're in." Glasses leaned over the divider, meerkat style. "Thanks, love." He winked at me, tapping furiously on a portable keyboard he'd rolled out on the desktop. "Ta-daa."

With a dramatic flourish over his head and the tap of a final keystroke, my screen winked, flickered to blue, and reopened. The little cursor moved around with a mind of its own, opening areas, changing settings. Glasses was manipulating my computer remotely.

More tapping, a little head bobbing, and a clunk came from the rear of the office space — *the safe.* The lights flickered briefly, and I looked around. The three men moved away in a synchronised motion that made me wonder if they'd practised it. Suddenly left alone and grateful for it, I exhaled a long breath that left me more empty than before. One of the men sauntered back out, standing beside the last person in the row of hostages.

Every one of them tensed, and I wondered if they were thinking of the same sound as I did as it ricocheted around my head. Clangs and swearing came from the rear of the bank. I realised I knew less about the bank I'd worked in for three years than I had thought.

Distracted by a swirl of glitter, I looked over at the rows of patrons lining the wall opposite my station: the little girl tracing invisible pictures on the neutral carpet with a sparkling princess wand; a lone, glossy, red shoe, involuntarily discarded upon impact. A stockinged foot, partly visible, protruding behind a cubicle. I dragged my gaze away.

Sit still. Don't think. Don't.

A shadow flitted across the windows that looked out onto the street from the front of the small bank. From their positions on the floor pressed against the wall opposite the teller stations, customers — hostages — shifted uncomfortably, attempting to appear insignificant. Up top, I was exposed, the downlights above me driving sweat around my collar, though it ran down my back cold. I wasn't sure if it was fuelled by fear or heat.

My water bottle cooled my palms, and I slugged down water like a thirsty camel, placing it back on the desk. I shuffled pencils in their holder, ordering them neatly by height. It gave my hands something to do. I took a long, deep breath and tried to settle, to be calm. Letting my eyes close out the rest of the office, I focused on my breath, trying to ignore the sounds behind me. It took a few tries, but I almost had it down, the panic beginning to recede, until I remembered that Karen was the one who had taught me the technique.

My heart pounded anew as I tried to erase the image. Numb fingers fumbled my water bottle, slipping on the condensation coating the clear plastic. It spun in the air, too fast for water to escape, though its movement seemed slow enough to me.

I almost had one hand — who was I kidding; it was the tip of my finger — on the bottle when a loud clang startled me. I fumbled the bottle a second time, wide-eyed as it hit the floor, emptying its contents. I jerked as a small, black wooden box appeared in the corner of my vision and slid forward.

Tanned hands attached to thick forearms reached across my desk. I would have loved them if I hadn't known who they belonged to. I was a sucker for well-muscled forearms, but not at this moment. Fine, white linen sleeves, rolled to the elbows, looked so out of place — an involuntary glance once again gave the impression of a wealthy businessman, not a bank robber.

Murderer.

Gaze fixed, he cradled the box, caressed the lid. It was such an intimate gesture; it felt as though I was intruding on a personal moment. I inched away discreetly until the edge of my chair bit into the backs of my thighs.

Fear permeated the thickened air — from me, and the gallery on the floor. The man behind the robbery stared at the dark, little box with greedy eyes. Glasses appeared, hovering in my peripheral vision.

He annoyed me, and I wanted to bat him away. A twitch in the robber's shoulder left me thinking he felt the same.

Stop sympathising with them.

Reluctantly, one tanned hand released its prize, extended in a beseeching gesture. A tiny tremor quaked through the limb. With no small amount of ceremony, Glasses produced a minuscule key, placing it into the hollow cup of his upturned palm.

The little, silver scrap glinted dully — antique looking — until the tip. I squinted and leaned forward, trying to discern the markings at the bottom of the filigree blade. The end curled upward, screwlike. The inserted key would have to be twisted or wound, like an old music box.

Reverently, the key was lowered to the lock, almost touching. Silence reigned; within the little cluster, no breath escaped.

The moment shattered abruptly, along with the glass of the large, street-front window. A dark shadow blasted through, into the foyer of the bank, showering everyone in glittering shards. Scarlet and indigo lights reflected in the glass littering the carpet. Voices cried out — a high, thin shriek piercing above the rest.

"Daddy!" A little sob accompanied the cry. The group surrounding me broke up, the small, black box forgotten in a surge of movement. The two men who had held the hostages at bay accompanied their leader toward the mess of glass, weapons fluidly drawn as one.

These men have worked together before.

I studied the changed scene before me as though I were the one behind glass; a shiny, black Jeep protruded into the cavity that used to be the front of the bank. Blue and red lights hung slightly lopsided, the odd flash blinding and disappearing in a staccato motion, adding to the surreality of the image.

Lots of extra attachments I was sure wouldn't be on a regular, stock model hung from the vehicle. A loud whoop came from within the open-topped cab, the flashing lights turned off, and everyone in the bank froze.

Two heads emerged from behind the black utility dash. One, a shag of blonde hair bearing a cheeky grin out of place in the sombre atmosphere. The other, a weather-worn face, covered in a beard that looked more suited to a motorcycle gang. He bore a resigned expression.

The shaggy-haired driver hoisted himself onto his seat in full view of the three men, who aimed their guns at him. His mouth moved, some throwaway line I missed.

What a cowboy. The thieves evidently agreed; from my view of their backs as they moved forward, their leader shook his head, his fine shirt barely creasing with effort as he raised his weapon.

"Hold on there, John Wayne," he drawled with a tinge of sarcasm, "this here's my bank."

Shaggy gave a cocky, lopsided grin. "I've always fancied myself more as Wyatt Earp. At least he could shoot."

He held out a hand — rather pompously, I thought — and the man still seated in the passenger seat of the Jeep tossed him a long firearm. No expert on guns, I watched the exchange with fascination.

"Oh, let him have his small moment of glory."

Shaggy drew and aimed, managing to pose at the same time. I fought the urge to roll my eyes, unable to feel the fear I knew I should — entranced by the drama unfolding before me. Shaggy's firearm was matte black, matching the Jeep. Clean and pristine.

"And I half expected it to be a six-shooter." The dark man tilted his head briefly to the side. "Step aside, now. Your time in the limelight is over." A sideways glance to his team, speaking just loud enough that I could hear him, "It's time to go."

"Hold it, gents!" Shaggy seemed surprised he had lost control over the situation — if he'd ever had it. His partner started to stand also, groping the bench seat behind him when a sharp report broke the unreality of their playacting. The hostages ducked in a wave as the man to the left of the posse's leader fired a single shot.

Shaggy's partner disappeared beneath the dash. The young cop attempted to do the same, but seemed to slip, teetering comically sideways for a moment before toppling over the back of the driver's seat with a short yell. There was a thump as he landed. The moment the cop was down, the three men in front lowered their weapons, advancing towards the newly-created exit in unison.

Glasses scurried up, collected the key with a quick wink, and followed the team outside, flanked by the man with bad breath. A white transit van drew up to the curb, and the men disappeared inside.

The van moved off. I sat, frozen completely, unable to process the situation. Sirens approached from the opposite direction. Lights lit up the bank interior like Christmas, reflecting off broken glass scattered on the floor in a kaleidoscope of colour.

Reversing, the Jeep disappeared back through the hole it had created in the bank's only window, following the direction the white van had taken. Emergency vehicles rushed past in a string of flashing lights.

It's like something out of a movie.

Dazed hostages paused, watching. Glances were exchanged, though no one spoke. Fear and uncertainty still hung in the air. After a moment, the spell was broken, and movement resumed. Customers stirred, no longer cowering beneath armed aggressors. Soft chatter filled the ruined bank.

I knew I should ask them to sit alone, quietly, so their stories wouldn't be confused by each other's interpretations of what they had just endured. My training kicked in, my brain screaming at me to move, but I couldn't.

Glass tinkled as it was brushed from clothing. Swivelling slightly, I made to stand. On the desk behind me, stood the wooden box. Wouldn't the thieves be furious when they realised Glasses had taken the key but forgotten the box? One of the patrons who had been cowering against my counter leaned over to me.

"Looks like they left something important behind," he said with a sad smile. I nodded, still staring at the box, lost in thought. A tiny sob broke the murmur from the hostages, and we both looked up.

The little girl stood in the centre of the wreckage, her glitter wand drooping to brush the faded carpet, covered with a different sort of sparkle.

Eyes wide, I turned to the man who had spoken, recognising him as the owner of a local grocery store.

"I think they left behind more than one thing."

Silence fell, heavy as a shroud. Heads turned to the little girl who wandered aimlessly in the centre of the deconstructed bank, tears coursing down a face partially covered by dirty-blonde locks. Dust motes danced around the small figure in the afternoon light as brightly decorated police cars drew up along the bank front. Men swarmed toward the window.

The wand dropped to the floor.

"Daddy?"

CHAPTER TWO

MILA

FIVE YEARS LATER

The air conditioning in my car died on the hottest day of the year, so far, though it was only early spring. Inside my car was so humid, I was swimming in sweat. Dark hairs plastered over my eyes. I swiped at them, crawling forward with the rest of the traffic.

Opening all the windows to let in what little moving air there was, I glanced up in time to catch the change in the traffic lights. Heat reflected through the windscreen, the road a wavering mirage.

A hard jolt from behind shunted me out of my daze. I slammed forward, pain radiating across my shoulders, down my back. Sultry air was replaced by the hardness of the steering wheel, hidden beneath the deceitfully soft sheepskin cover Gran had always insisted I use.

I'd kept it as an extra thing to reminisce over, but it failed its main purpose. A loud *crack* reverberated between my ears as my forehead connected with the solid steering wheel beneath.

Time halted, and I wondered if the crack was the car or my head. I folded forward, suspended by the seat belt, pressing the heel of my hand against tender skin.

"Ow."

It was the only coherent thought I had.

"Oh, my god. Are you okay?"

I jumped at the voice beside me, not expecting it. Still clutching my head, I peered into the wing mirror, not game to raise my chin in case it increased the throbbing that consumed me.

"I'm fine," I mumbled, staring at the long-haired man bending to look in through my window. Blonde dreadlocks framed the bronzed face of a minor god.

"Ma'am?"

A worried look strained his perfect features, and ridiculously I jumped to answer, not wanting to cause any further stress to the earth-bound deity standing beside me. I nodded energetically and immediately regretted it.

"I'm fine," I repeated, leaning low as blood dripped from my nose. I stuffed a tissue against my nostrils to stop the flow. The heat trapped in the car thickened around me until I could barely take a breath. "Ohh."

"Ah."

The door to my remarkably unsexy Ford Fiesta was ripped open, screeching on tortured hinges. A slim, long-fingered hand matching the bronzed face above wrapped around my arm, tugging gently.

"Ma'am, I need to get you to stand. Can you do that?"

I nodded again, my vision blurring at the edges. My heels found the ground, and I put weight on them, expecting to stand as any rational person would do. Instead, my knees collapsed from under me. Waiting to hit the deck, I braced for the drop.

Suddenly finding myself curled on the ground was a decidedly ignominious moment. I studied my shoes. Scuffs decorated the toes of shiny, patent sandals. For a moment, that seemed the most important thing in the world.

Then the pain returned, crashing against the front of my skull with a vengeance.

Weight bowed my shoulders. I looked around with bleary eyes to find a blanket wrapped about them. Liquid, brown eyes found my green ones. I stared, lost for a moment in the golden flecks that streamed like sunlight from the centre.

"Ma'am. Are you okay?"

The blanket was warm, and all I wanted to do was sleep. Would this earthbound deity let me rest on him for a moment?

"I'm fine," I murmured, wriggling to make myself comfy. Maybe I could use a different word, spice up this limited conversation. Hands set me upright. I struggled for a moment, then gave up with a disgruntled sigh. "I'm fine," I repeated myself, not certain who I was trying to reassure.

"Oh, god. You're bleeding!"

I tried to stop his flapping hands, protesting to deaf ears. He bent down, trying to press into my side where it was covered in red. Far too bright to be blood, but he didn't appear to have registered that.

I placed one hand on either side of his face, drawing him up to look into those warm eyes. Thick lashes surrounded them, perfectly framing an aquiline nose and strong jaw.

I desperately wanted to paint him.

His brow dipped — in concentration or concern? I lost his gaze as he refocused on an injury I didn't have.

How come the boys always got the best lashes?

"No. No, I'm fine," I said, yet again. *Original, Mila.* Then, a little louder, "I'm fine. It's just paint."

"Paint?" Sceptical. "From what?"

"My paints. I paint." *This conversation is not going so well.* "It's okay," I repeated, sliding my thumb over his lips to shush him, palms still framing the art in front of me. "It's paint. I mean, I'm an artist."

He looked down to where the red stained my shirt and then back up.

"Paint?" It came out a trifle weak, but relief was evident in his eyes. His lips split in a wide grin, eyes twinkling. Doubt clouded them for a moment. "You're sure?"

I nodded, my soggy shirt warm where his hand had rested. I realised how close he was and dropped my hands, taking a quick breath that strangled a little in my throat. Pain blossomed across my chest as panic began to cloud in. This perfect-looking man was a total stranger, and here I was touching him like we'd woken up together. Plus, he had rear-ended my car.

I groaned, thinking of the damage. Being late for my next appointment could be an issue — this client was very particular about tardiness. *Not something to look forward to*, I thought, sweat prickling my arms. I shrugged off the blanket, recalling it was a warm spring, and folded it. It was plucked from my hands as I sighed. I hated being late.

"I have to get to an appointment. Ah– shouldn't we swap details? For insurance purposes," I added in a hurry, lest he assume I was hitting on him.

Someone who looks like that probably gets it all the time.

I smiled into those brown eyes, surprised to see him shifting from side to side; hands dug deep into the pockets of his jeans. His eyes slid from mine. I took in the breadth of his shoulders, shirt straining across his chest, sleeves rolled to expose forearms that came with hours of manual labour. Pale dreads hung down his back, an errant few drifting over his shoulder.

Damn, but he was fine.

His fidgeting didn't stop as I edged around him to glimpse the damage. My little bubble was crushed: plastic bumper crumpled, boot half ajar, one corner folded in on itself. The lights on one side dangled sadly, attached only by their wires.

"I was wondering if we might, er, keep this to ourselves? A cash job."

I jumped, brought back to reality with a rush. I hadn't realised he had followed me around the car. Cash job? Though his tone was light, flushed cheeks belied the casual words. He looked away, avoiding my gaze.

Super dodgy.

"You don't have a license? Or no insurance?" I couldn't keep the derision out of my voice as I guessed his reasons, but I didn't really care. It was petty; I wanted to make him as uncomfortable as I could, determined not to be taken in by a scammer. "*You* ran into *me*, remember?"

He nodded, running a hand through his dreads.

"Sure, and I totally understand how that sounds — I do have a license and insurance and all, I just don't want work to find out."

He half mumbled the last part. I looked over the low riding sedan: wide tyres and lots of chrome. Fresh paint made the car glow, and the heaviest looking radio antenna I'd ever seen adorned the bulbar. It looked as though it would take a Brahman bull to knock it over.

Compensating for something?

Chiding myself for being nasty, I checked my watch. *Really* late, now.

"Company car?"

"Sort of."

Wow, he was really making me work for it.

"So...what do you do? I get they'd be upset about an accident, but I can't imagine you'd lose your job over it..."

I trailed off, staring. He held out his leather wallet, flipped open. There, clear as day, was a police ID card. A small photograph in the bottom corner depicted a much younger version of the man standing in front of me.

"Oh."

I couldn't think of anything better to say. The god with dreads was a cop? A tiny giggle escaped me. He peered at me suspiciously.

"Were you on the radio? For work?"

Was that how cops worked? I had no idea.

"No, I was uh..." The shifty look back again, he cleared his throat. "I was on my phone. Texting. Uh, ex-girlfriend. I've been trying not to have contact with her." He groaned when my eyebrows shot up. "That came out really bad. Break up was a shocker. I'm trying to get away from it. But if work finds out..."

He looked at me expectantly. For sympathy, perhaps? I tried, but couldn't keep the corners of my lips from curling.

"You ran up the back of me because you were texting your ex?"

He nodded.

"And you can't tell work because they'll rib you for it for the next year or so?"

He nodded again, looking slightly put out. Well, he *had* run up the back of me, not the other way around.

"Pretty much."

I began to laugh, a giggle at first that quickly became full-blown hilarity. He stared — concern written across his gorgeous face, likely wondering whether I'd lost it. I flapped at him, grasping my side where the paint had dried into a thin crust, itching my skin as crinkles flaked over my fingers. Still laughing, I bent over, and plopped back to the gutter, taking short breaths as pain returned in my chest, throbbing dully.

"Look, I can make it up to you," he towered over me, "happy to pay cash and I have a mate who could fix– no, that sounds terrible. You pick the repair shop, and I'll pay for it. I just don't want to report it."

He kept rambling as I stared up at him, hand to my head which was playing its own symphony of pain.

"I know it sounds bad, but I can promise you I can pay for the damage, I– oh, hell. Can I take you out?"

My mouth dropped open, staring up at the sun-kissed god leaning over me while I sat in the gutter like a trollop.

"I–I don't even know your name," I whispered.

The smile that graced his face turned him from beautifully bronzed to blindingly bright.

"Callum. Dane. Cal. Cal is fine." He was stuttering as much as I was in my head.

I smiled in reply and forgot to answer. He still stared at me until finally, I remembered to speak.

"Yes."

I arrived at the café five minutes early. Cal had messaged me a few times after we had exchanged numbers, organising for my car to be repaired. A quick and easy fix, thankfully. It was good to have my car back — I hated being without it.

Cal was happy with the results, thanking me for letting him sort it out off the books. His last message about taking me out was hesitant, and I hadn't wanted to appear too eager in return, but my curiosity won out.

Five minutes early was a little later than I would normally turn up for an appointment, but in this case, I didn't want to appear overly eager. And it wasn't an appointment, really — more like a date.

Or a bribe.

Tonight was the only time I'd been able to find in my week that matched his RDOs. He'd suggested a café on the corner of Eat Street; one I'd seen in passing but never been into before.

I hesitated as I locked my car, uncomfortable in the crowd that filled the trendy area well away from the comfort zone of my own home deep in Melbourne's suburbs, and wondered if I was doing the right thing. Recalling the golden glow emanating from Cal, his perfect face and muscled arms — I was always a sucker for those — the discomfort reduced enough for me to leave my car.

Settle down, ovaries.

Approaching the café set on the corner of two main roads, I noted couples bent over steaming cups, and small tables with their chairs tucked together to create an intimate setting. My tongue stuck to the roof of my mouth when I tried to swallow. It had been a long time — a *very* long time — since my last date. If that's what this was. Shoving my doubts to the back of my mind, I tugged the heavy doors open, releasing a cloud of warmth.

The scent of chocolate hit me in a wave: dark, earthy tones, mingling with a fruity zest. I closed my eyes for a moment, breathing it in. Cal had chosen a chocolatier, and I hadn't even known. This was definitely a man to keep.

Get your head out of your hormones, Mila.

Looks aside, I wondered what had made the ex-girlfriend so irate. A small part of me said not to pry, but my mind couldn't let it go. *Miss Nosy Parker,* I thought ruefully, scanning the crowded room for his head of blond dreads.

There were no long-haired men in the room, though, not even a man-bun present. The last date I'd been on had turned up half an hour late, which had irritated me. The rest of the evening hadn't gone well, either — a friend had set me up with a workmate who turned out to be rather pasty and allergic to everything on the menu.

He'd watched while I picked uncomfortably at my solo dinner until a waiter tripped over his chair, dousing him with prawn laksa. The last I'd seen of him was in an ambulance that rushed him away, red-faced and still swelling. I hoped tonight wouldn't be a repeat.

I sighed and headed for the only empty table near a single man; head bowed over his phone. He, like Cal, sported a gorgeous tan. What was it with golden, sexy men this week? My hormones couldn't take much more of this. I noted his freshly-shaven head; a tan line around the side of his face and neck made it evident.

As I hesitated, the man looked up, brown eyes staring into mine. He rose quickly, gifting me with a blinding smile.

"Cal?"

"Mila."

His voice was soft, just loud enough to be heard over the constant murmur inside the cafe.

"What happened to your..." I gestured to the top half of him. His smile became a broad grin.

"Case is over. I won't miss them."

"Oh?"

"Mmh. Too itchy with the sand." He grinned when I raised an eyebrow. "Lots of surfing."

"There's a story there, I'm sure." I paused, studying him. Without the dreads to frame his face, he was more open, more relaxed-looking, if that was possible. Still amazing, though. Out of the sunlight, his glow dimmed, but only slightly. He still drew the eye. I tilted my head, considering. "I liked them."

The words were out of my mouth before much thought went into them. Embarrassed, I plucked a menu from the stand in the centre of the table, sliding into the only other chair, opposite him. My knees bumped his long legs as

I shifted, attempting to stuff my oversized tote beneath the table discreetly.

"Sorry," I mumbled, sweeping hair away from my face, a little flustered. My heart rate rose, thumping uncomfortably. It was as though I couldn't settle around this man.

"I hope you don't mind the place...I didn't know if you were a health food fanatic, or–" He stopped, reddening.

"I'm not," I rushed to fill the awkward space, noting his discomfort. "A fanatic, that is. I'm not one, I mean. Or that healthy."

Oh, this is going great. Awesome conversational skills, Mila.

Cal grinned at me when I emerged from behind my menu.

"That's good."

"So...what's the case you were working on? The one that required the dreads." I grasped the only thing I knew about him, but I genuinely missed the long blonde hair. "They had some good length. How long were you undercover for?" Is that what I should ask? I had no idea.

Cal's expression darkened. He placed his menu carefully on the table, pressing the edges down with firm hands.

"It didn't quite turn out the way I wanted, though we got the result we needed. Still, the bastar– the bloke got away. Again." He ran a hand over his head, dropping it down as though searching for dreads that weren't there anymore. "Nineteen months, most of it wasted. If he's out of state, I'll have to pass it to another department."

Well, that explained the length of the dreads.

"Okay, so you do...undercover work and um...?" I tried to piece the story together. Not much of a crime or police fan, I wasn't sure what to ask. "It sucks that you lost him."

"Yeah, it does. Undercover for too long...but it's good to be back, wear real clothes again. More than board shorts, anyway."

I imagined him bare-chested, stomach and chest rippling with muscles, and immediately wished I hadn't. The boy was too hot to start with.

A waitress appeared beside us. I ordered the largest coffee on offer in a takeaway cup, though I didn't think I'd need to use the emergency exit tonight. Or hoped. It was my standard order, though I eyed off a tasting platter. Would it be presumptuous to suggest it? I was too out of touch with the dating scene. I opened my mouth, preparing to jump in when Cal did it for me, even requesting extra strawberries. He shot a quick glance my way.

"I hope you don't mind?"

I shook my head with a smile.

"I was looking at it too."

"Great minds and all. You like to paint?"

Nodding, I hid my pleasure that he had remembered. Recalling the red paint incident, I guessed it was a pretty memorable thing.

"I do portraits in oils and some landscapes. Bright colours, right now. I was on my way to an appointment when…"

"Ah, bugger. I'm so sorry for that." He winced, realising. "I made you really late, right?"

"It's okay," I shrugged it off, not wanting to bring the tone of the evening down, "I got there in the end."

Mrs. Nolan hadn't been so accommodating, but I didn't say anything. I'd taken an earful from the old bag but kept my peace, letting the woman rant righteously. Though I didn't need the money, I hated confrontation of any sort, and actively avoided it.

Our order arrived, the tasting tray a lot larger than I'd had expected.

"Wow."

We shunted the menu box to the side to fit everything onto the small table. A tiny chocolate fountain sat between us, resplendent in the centre of the table. Dark chocolate flowed over the tiers, pooling in the lowest level. My stomach rumbled just looking at it.

Tiny fondue forks skewered berries, and strips of fine toffee and honeycomb were coated with a golden, caramel sauce.

"Dig in."

I held a strawberry under the flowing chocolate, mesmerised by the motion. Cal poked me gently with a raspberry.

"Penny."

"Oh." I realised I had been ignoring him and straightened, blushing for my lapse in manners. "I was just watching the way the chocolate moved. I'd like to try to replicate it, put that sort of movement into my paintings. It's the little details that...anyway, you didn't come out to hear me gab on about painting techniques."

"I don't mind." Cal leaned towards me, eyes dark. "It's a nice change from the worry you've fu– screwed up, that someone knows who you are. When you're constantly on edge. Talking about something that doesn't involve analysing a person's behaviour, hoping you're not going to have to witness some random act of violence because an idiot with a gun thinks it gives him the right to play God." Cal took a deep breath. "Sorry. I haven't talked about it with anyone for a long time. I want to hear about what you do."

"You're never away from it, your work?"

Cal shook his head, twiddling his fork between long, slender fingers.

"Not on undercover jobs. I lived there the entire time, as a flatmate. A friend." He stabbed a strawberry right through with a skewer, so the end of the metal hit the plate with a dull clang.

"That's tough." I wanted to reach out, to touch him, but I wasn't sure we were there, yet.

I opted for the non-contact route for a person in distress: distraction. Launching into a description of my day, I watched him while I spoke. Tense shoulders softened, slouched a little, as I recounted stories of past clients, of their idiosyncrasies. He leaned back, laughing, no trace of the stress of his time undercover remaining on his face, and I smiled.

"Mrs....um, Portrait," I hesitated, not wanting to divulge my clientele in the event it got back to me, "Gave me a solid talking to on punctuality. Next time, I am to arrive at least fifteen minutes early and remain well after my allotted time slot to make up for the disaster of this afternoon. Naturally," I wiggled my eyebrows at Cal, "She was wearing a red shirt, and was completely horrified when I painted her in royal blue."

Cal raised his hands in mock horror.

"Oh, the indignity."

"Indeed. So, I will be returning with a range of reds which she shall choose from tomorrow." I watched Cal settle back, tension visibly reduced from his lean frame. My gaze kept drifting back to his forearms. Those muscles...with effort, I dragged my attention back to his face. His gaze was already on me, and I knew I was sprung. Heat crept up my neck, but he was just wonderful to observe.

His white shirt, unbuttoned just at the top that said casual, was set so well against his wonderfully tanned skin. Ink peeked from beneath his rolled sleeves. I admired the lean muscle of his forearms, imagined painting them — smooth strokes where long hours of labour had defined their shape, leading to the metal band of his watch, just loose enough to be comfortable. Tanned skin beneath it told me he hadn't worn it out in the sun for some time.

A hell of a life, never stopping. Maybe this was why the ex was an ex. A stab of sympathy shot through me as I twirled the fork between my fingers. It reminded me of the gamble I'd taken, moving into Gran's house after the funeral. Not really a place of my own, but a home, none-the-less.

I paused, listening to the silence that had fallen over the table, and realised it was mine. Cal stared at me, a small smile decorating his face. One hand rested beneath his chin. I loved those fingers, slim and long, so similar to an artist's. My gaze drifted back to liquid eyes that never left my face, so intense. And that face. It should be in a gallery. Lost in his gaze, I just looked, open-mouthed for longer than was socially acceptable. I closed it with a snap.

Cal regarded me with an amused grin.

"What?"

It came out aggressive, even for me.

"You're...it's wonderful to watch you, see what you do. I'd love to see your paintings."

I was filled with a glow at his words; sure it wasn't just a line. It had been years since anyone had said that, outside my professional life. Cal leaned back, stretching one arm over the long, quilted booth seat that ran the length of the café. I felt the weight of his gaze, assessing, but not intruding.

"You have a—a magic about you, when you talk like that, about your painting, I mean. You glow with it. Something incredible lives inside you." His voice was low, sending shivers along my arms.

I looked down to the table, surprised to find my hand clasped in his. Long, work-roughened fingers wound around my finer ones. I ran my fingers over his knuckles, mesmerised that something so strong could also look so elegant.

I wanted to get a pad out and start drawing them right now, fill in the colours later. He squeezed back, and my eyes shot to meet Cal's, locking onto them. His fingers brushed gently across mine, but I didn't dare break his gaze, scared the moment would be over.

My breath came in soft puffs. I wondered if he would be able to hear my heart beating, drumming hard in my ears. A smile creased his tanned skin. He stood suddenly, drawing me from my seat, into him. His arm was around my waist before I realised I was standing, my hands pressed lightly against his chest.

"Let's go for a walk."

I nodded, taking a moment to breathe him in as he strode to the counter, paying quickly. Heads turned, following us as we passed, but I knew they weren't looking at me. The waitress smiled at Cal, her eyes wandering over him as she processed his card. I realised belatedly that I should have offered to pay. Then I remembered he had wrecked my car — just a little — and this was meant to be compensation.

I'd enjoyed tonight far more than I had expected. I'd even spoken about myself, which was rare. No friends meant no disappointment when they left because I was still so broken inside. I'd have to get the next dinner, I thought, looking down at his fingers wrapped around mine, casual yet firm, like he'd never let go.

When had that happened? It wasn't like me to go on one date, let alone plan a second. I groaned to myself — here I was getting all gooey over a man I'd known for less than a week and only spent an hour with– oh. I checked the wall clock over at the waitress's station a second time. How had three hours gone so fast?

The waitress smiled at Cal again, handing back his card. Her gaze dropped to our joined hands, then to me. I smiled back, but her face hardened. She muttered a quick "good evening" and walked away, hips sashaying dramatically.

A tug on my hand had me looking up into Cal's beautiful face.

"What?" I murmured, startled to be caught out. A small smile lit his face.

"Come on."

"Where are we going?"

"Somewhere quiet." He waved a hand at the people clustering around us. "Away from all this."

"Please. The crowd isn't really my thing," I sidestepped a mob of teens socialising in the middle of the street. "And it's not very private," I added softly. Cal looked down at me and gave my hand a gentle squeeze. My heart pounded — I never shared this much with anyone.

"I think we can find somewhere like that," he murmured, drawing me into his side.

Cal turned at the corner the chocolatier stood on, away from the crowds. He squeezed my fingers again, and my heart gave a little jolt. I couldn't remember the last time I had reacted this way to anyone. Then a pair of ice-blue eyes slammed into my mind, dragging up memories I couldn't — wouldn't — deal with right now.

Not tonight.

"Are you okay?" Cal shifted, letting go of my hand.

I withdrew mine sadly, wondering if I had driven him away with bad memories. Instead, his arm slipped around my shoulders. At that moment, I felt safe, for the first time in many years. I wasn't watching every car that sped past, wondering if they would pull over and I'd be faced with *him* again.

The chance to breathe Cal in again was welcomed. Warm and spiced, like an early autumn fire. He broke into my reverie.

"I thought we might do the beach? There's a decent length walk there."

Still wrapped in my reflections, I didn't answer, enjoying being relaxed with another person. I only experienced peace when I was painting.

"But if that's not a good plan, we could..." Cal trailed off, uncertainty glinting in his eyes. It took me a second to work out what had happened, and I hurried to fix my lapse.

"Oh, no, the beach is fine, beach is great! I love the beach." I closed my mouth, cursing myself as an incoherent fool.

"Oh, good." Cal eyed me warily, as though wondering when I might next become a rambling maniac. I laughed, possibly adding more fuel to the fire.

"No, I was just..." How did one explain to one's date they were just enjoying the moment without spilling their life's story? I tried to fix it but only seemed to make it worse. "I really do—"

"Like the beach. Yep, got it." Cal grinned at me.

I leaned into him a little, and his arm tightened around me. Pressing my head back against his shoulder, I stared up at the night sky. More stars became visible as we started down the steps that led to the promenade. Waves crashed onto the shoreline, deafeningly loud but welcome, almost rhythmic in their relentless pounding, drenching us with their salty sweetness.

We were silent as we walked, content in each other's company. I had no desire to fill our time with words that didn't matter. If Cal was going to be around more, there would be plenty of time to talk.

The promenade curved out over the rocks, drawing us away from city lights. No cars rumbled by, disturbing the sense of serenity. The crashing waves matched my own heartbeat, thundering and rolling as Cal stopped, turning me to face him. Butterflies overpopulated my stomach when his fingers brushed my chin, tilting my head back.

His eyes took up my world, encompassing everything. His lips touched mine, pressing gently — slow, firm movements. I slipped my hands up his shoulders, around his collar, arching into him. His palm cupped the back of my head, fingers massaging the nape of my neck in tiny circles. A small noise escaped me.

Suddenly, his kisses weren't so gentle. His mouth crashed against mine, tongue thrusting deep, exploring, tasting. Weightless, I clung to his shoulders, fingers curling into his shirt as though worried I would be swept away without him. My tongue danced with his when he deepened the kiss.

Everything in me tensed as he set a rhythm as hard as his frame, and suddenly I knew — *I knew* — what he would be like in bed. I gasped, his hands tightening on me, lifting me off my feet before he pulled away and set me down gently, pressing my head against his chest. I wrapped my arms around him, breathless, palms flat against the planes of hard muscle beneath his shirt. His heartbeat pounded in my ears, and I breathed in his rhythm, matching it.

After a time, he drew back a little. I looked up at him, dazed.

"God, you're beautiful, Mila."

My name was like caramel dripping from his lips. I shivered, sliding my fingers across the stubble framing his chin, brushing over the lines that made him so fine. Perfectly proportioned, the man still resembled a god, regardless of the shorn hair. Tanned, with a light shadow creeping over his jawline, he could have been from Hollywood, or a model — not someone you'd meet every day. Or any day. Certainly not someone you'd go on a date with. I swayed a little, barely able to keep my thoughts straight.

He captured my hand, kissing my fingers, his hand still tangled in my hair. Cal drew me in again, mouth sweeping gently over mine, stealing my air. His lips remained soft this time, releasing me after only a moment. That same small sound whispered its way up my throat in protest before I could stop it.

Cal's chest rumbled in response. I squeezed his arm, breathing in salt as the waves crashed behind us.

"Don't laugh at me," I grumbled playfully.

He just drew me into his side, turning us back the way we had come.

CHAPTER THREE

CAL

It hadn't taken us long to reach her car. Mila let me ramble on about the boys at work, my last case, and far too fast she was gone, waving a slender arm from the driver's window as she pulled away from the curb.

I ran a hand through my hair, still surprised when I encountered fresh stubble. Glad the dreads were gone, though, as the bloody things had itched abominably. Mila's car disappeared in a line of traffic, leaving me with a different sort of ache. My hand missed hers already, tiny and gentle, but strong beneath my fingers.

The night air was cool, and I appreciated it as I walked back to my apartment. It was only a block down, around the corner, which was how I'd known the chocolatier was such a good spot. I'd been taking Ashley there for years — our regular Sunday date. She ordered the same thing every week — a strawberry Sundae with no nuts and extra chocolate topping.

I smiled at the memory of her dark head bent over the dessert while she devoured it. She'd look up with a huge grin, joy filling eyes that didn't resemble her father in the least.

I stuffed my hands deep in my pockets as I walked, sucking down cold air. The night edged into a chill that promised a late frost at some ungodly hour. My thoughts returned to Mila — the delicate features of a much stronger woman than her petite frame had initially shown, though I'd known as soon as she'd gotten out of the car the day I'd run into her that she was something special.

A grin crept over my face, recalling her rambling and uncomfortable speech, the tiny mewl she'd made when I stopped kissing her. The asshole that I was, I enjoyed replaying the moment. She'd been so cute trying to explain herself. I wondered if she would make similar noises in my bed. It had taken all of my control not to reach down to see if her gorgeous ass would fit in one hand.

Lost in my thoughts of her, I wasn't paying attention to my surroundings. A screech of tyres brought me back to reality, high beams stinging my eyes even with my back turned. As the vehicle swung up, onto the gutter, I dove sideways into a hedge on instinct.

By the time I'd detangled myself from the shrub — *who makes a bloody hedge of roses?* — the car was nothing but a set of tail lights disappearing around a corner. I chased it, limping, but lost it in a second. I cursed loudly. A small dog yapped at me from behind a low fence. *Suburbia.* Looking down at the dog, I stared at the remains of my favourite shirt, its tatters barely covering the scratches on my arms.

Get it together, Dane.

I checked the area, yanking out my phone to take photos of the rubber left on the road. It was doubtful they would turn up as anything specific — the vehicle had been a lowered black sedan, likely chopped to bring the springs down, rather than get it done professionally. Just like a thousand other similar vehicles in the city.

I called it in, getting Steph at dispatch. I knew she covered day and night shift occasionally to bring in extra cash, but the thought of her pulling double her hours soured my thoughts. I needed her at her best at the desk during working hours. If a small raise would increase her productivity, I'd see it done.

She made all the right noises, promising to send a car by the area. The room must have been occupied because her voice lowered as she asked what was on her mind from the beginning of the call.

"Do you think it was *him?*"

I inhaled sharply through my nose, as I'd been wondering the same thing.

"Not sure, Steph. Not likely, though, huh. Just some drunk on his way home."

Maybe, but not likely.

"Okay," Steph sighed. "Night, Dane."

I ended the call. If everyone got called away on duties, Steph could talk all day. Or night. Stowing my phone back in my pocket, I jogged the rest of the way to my apartment, keen to wash the blood out of my shirt. Picking out a few thorns still embedded in my skin, I admitted the tatters could never be saved.

Cold, sweaty, and frustrated, I went through the rigorous security procedures my very nondescript but highly secure apartment block demanded. For the few minutes of delay, it afforded me total privacy, which suited my paranoia — and my obsession. I doubted there was a more safeguarded residence in the city.

Finally unlocking my apartment door, I disarmed the electronic lock Steph's boyfriend had installed a few months back. It was meant to be state-of-the-art, which had appealed to me at the time, though I supposed she wanted everyone at the station to know how great it was. But every decent cop knows if a perp wants in, nothing will stop them.

Stripping off the ruined shirt, I discarded it in the kitchen bin on my way to the shower. I turned the temp up to just below scalding, letting the heat soak into my muscles, washing away the stress of the evening. Mila's image drifted into my mind — minus her clothing, and how she'd felt when she'd arched into me. Damn, but she'd tasted fine.

Shuddering as each muscle relaxed, my thoughts kept turning back to Mila, and that fine rump of hers. I was still itching to get my hands on that, but I also didn't want to scare her. Strong and passionate as she was, there was something skittish lying just beneath the surface. I didn't want to push her too far, too fast.

I growled, realising I had a raging hard-on. I turned off the hot water, letting the icy chill sink through me. I'd need focus to do tonight's job, as always. Nothing else could distract me, not even Mila. When it was all over, I could give her the attention she deserved.

Drying off, I threw on a pair of old, grey sweats, the most comfortable thing I owned. My phone buzzed as I headed to my study, ready to work. A stupid grin slid across my face. I knew I looked like a maniac, but the thought of Mila texting me already got me going again.

I wondered whether she had a naughty side I could play with at night...then I saw who had sent the message — Mandy. When would she bugger off? I wanted her as gone as she'd clearly shown me that night. My thumb hovered over the button. If I responded every time she messaged me, she'd never let go. Another message flashed up on the screen. I closed my eyes, but they kept coming.

Mandy: I really need to speak to you. Will you please answer?

Mandy: I know you're reading these.

Mandy: Please Cal. I miss you.

The last one boiled my blood. After everything that had happened, *she* had the gall to tell me she missed *me?*

Me: I'm tired of your games. Don't message me again.

Mandy: I'm so sorry. Can I come around?

The message came through quickly, and I read it before I could stop myself. I wasn't a booty call for the woman who'd trampled my heart only weeks ago. I threw my phone across the room with a curse, an ominous crack telling me I'd smashed the screen.

Damnit. HR wouldn't be happy to have to issue me a new one.

I inspected the screen. A thin crack lined the screen top to bottom. Frustrating, but everything seemed to work so I could ignore it for a while. I deleted Mandy's messages and switched it on silent. The door to my study was ajar. I slid inside with the lights still off and placed my phone onto the desk beside the entry, face down.

Nothing would interrupt me this evening.

I nudged the light switch with my shoulder, lighting the room.] Dozens of ice-cold eyes stared at me from the walls. Logan watched me from several angles as I set up for the night. My home laptop sat on the desk, unhindered by clutter — a standalone, and untraceable. A little gem Micah had provided me with as thanks for adding him to the team two years ago. I greatly appreciated the gesture.

A pair of screens flanked the main one. I downloaded the day's recordings onto a flash drive, then plugged it into the standalone. Hours of footage from three cities popped up — I'd been working with the federal police and ASIO long enough to know which of their feeds were most accurate.

Facial recognition software scrolled commands through a dialogue box in the corner of the screen. I flicked through reports contacts had sent me that day — what I didn't have the time — or privacy — for in the incident room. Everyone has their obsession, and hunting Wayde Logan was mine.

The time I allocated scouring the feeds for Logan out of office hours had been called unhealthy more than once. I wasn't going to kid myself — I knew how bad it had gotten; the urge to hunt, to take him down, had increased recently, as we had made little headway on our investigation. Operation Niffler wasn't going well, though Liam kept most of the jackals at bay.

For now, at least.

I knew he had our backs — our success was his after all, but it was more than that. My boss had mentored me through the academy years ago, helping me resurrect a wreaked career after I let Logan escape the first time.

Which was no small thing.

Partial face shots, side profiles obscured by pedestrians and traffic popped up on the triad of screens, but I discarded them with a flick. Logan worked in specific patterns, which greatly reduced the amount of traffic I had to scroll through. Being predictable was a criminal's greatest gift to a cop.

Now, all I had to do was catch the bastard.

CHAPTER FOUR

MILA

Spring was always my favourite time of year. Colours seemed brighter, and everything was growing, throwing off its winter skin to burst out with new life. The back of Gran's old house opened out into a large veranda, complete with enormous cement balustrades topped with equally-giant spheres.

The look was typical of the period the house was built in, though I was used to it by now. Heavy enough to squash a person, I'd tried many times as a child to knock the spheres off. Finally succeeding, I'd terrified the cat sleeping in the sun nearby as the weighted ball dropped straight through the floorboards of the veranda, into the cellar beneath.

Light filtered through the unkempt garden behind the house, creating a dark labyrinth of colour full of shadowy twists and turns. As a girl, I used to hide in the back corner of the yard, sketching silhouettes as the sun coursed across the sky.

Already set back from the street, the old house was reasonably secluded in Melbourne's inner suburbs. The garden had always been cluttered with life — the perfect place for the imagination of any child to run wild.

When I'd lost Gran, the garden had stayed. With no good reason to change, it reminded me of her; relaxed, imaginative, just a little crazy, so different from other women of her generation. She had been the last of my family, but living in the house left to me, I didn't feel as alone as others — really, just Teddy — expected me to be.

With the heavy, wooden doors at the front of the house closing out the sounds of the street, and my easel set out across the length of the boards at the back, I had seven hours of unadulterated light to capture spring's birth. Selecting a grevillea about to burst with unfurled blossoms, framed by a scarlet bottlebrush behind it full of chattering Swift parrots, I lifted a brush. The vibrant colours glowed against a clear sky, so it was easy to get to work.

Several hours later, I stood, shaking out my toes. Pins and needles shot up my legs from being stuck in one position for far too long. Stepping back to look over my work with an impartial eye, I knew my stasis had been necessary. The pale-headed rosella I'd envisioned poked out at me, his head cocked cheekily, ready to dive back into the ambrosia the flower offered.

Limping, I paced the veranda, trying to encourage circulation to return to my limbs. Stretching over the railing, I breathed in the warmth of the day, afternoon sun still blazing for a few more hours, yet.

Thoughts of last night intruded, though they weren't unwelcome. My date with Cal had been amazing — talking in the café, walking along the foreshore, the salt of the waves clinging to me...kissing him — my god, that kiss. I was halfway through a detailed exploration of how he'd felt; the planes of his chest, the fire he'd ignited inside me, holding me hard against him, when a sound intruded on my daydreams.

I blinked, but the buzzing was insistent. It took a moment for me to realise it was the front door. I trotted through the enormous, old house, hoping whoever it was would be gone before I reached the other end. I was disappointed to see a wavering figure behind the stained-glass panel.

The door handle rattled, and I jumped, then called out as I fumbled with chains and locks. Gran had always been careful with house security, but I'd added more when I'd moved in.

"I'm coming," I yelled, fingers stuck in a safety chain, "Coming! I'll be right," I untangled the knot of fingers and metal and succeeded in yanking the door open, "there." Panting a little, I stared at the slim man on my patio, holding a box. Startling grey eyes shot with brightest blue stared back, thin lips curved in amusement.

I glanced down at myself, suddenly understanding how I must appear. Hair whipped up in a messy bun with a spare brush stuck through it, red-faced and covered in splotches of paint from neck to ankle; I looked like a younger version of the crazy cat lady.

"Sorry I took a while," I apologised, "I was just..." I gestured back down the hallway behind me. The delivery man's gaze followed my hand then back to me, the sharp smile still on his face as though frozen there. I swallowed.

"Coming. Yes, I heard you."

The innuendo wasn't lost on me, nor was his sweeping gaze of my body. I shivered, warnings tingling against being near this man — or was it just near any other person? Still, I reached for the box.

"Your name?" He pressed the screen on a handheld scanner.

"It's on the package," I said pointedly.

"Of course." He held out the scanner for me to sign. "Thank you, Miss Davenport."

Hairs that had settled rose on my arms again. I instantly hated that this man knew my name and where I lived. Thanking him, I retreated into the house, glad to have the stout, wooden barrier between us. The shivering began, and my breath came short.

Those *eyes.*

My mind screamed as another pair of eyes — cold and hard — stared down at me from the face of a devil hiding beneath the facade of a god. For a moment, the bank returned, the acrid tang of gunpowder and cash notes slamming into me. The room swam; people lined against the wall, terrified. A pale leg protruded from behind a workstation, a ruby shoe discarded, lay on its side–

No.

I wanted to scream, to beat the memory away, but instead, I curled against the closed door, finding myself on the slate stones. Cold tendrils reached beneath my shirt, caressing my lower back like an unwanted lover. Footsteps retreated from the front porch until I knew I was alone.

I shivered, unable to move under the onslaught of emotions. Beneath the closed front door, frigid air stroked my skin. Every muscle clenched with fear until I was shaking with exertion, as well as the cold. The parcel lay discarded beside me on the floor. I was nothing more than a shuddering, sobbing mess in my own home.

When is this going to end?

Eventually, my paralysis passed. I rose unsteadily, scraping my hands on the slate, their coolness reassuring. In the kitchen, it took several tries to slit the tape securing the box, but by the time I managed to open it, the shaking in my hands had reduced to a slight tremor.

Placing my craft knife carefully in the centre of the old wooden bench, I inhaled through my nose, though I knew my anxiety had nothing to do with the box. Sloughing in deep breaths, I tried to find the calm my last therapist had suggested. They never lasted long, saying I should be "over it all" by now after just a few weeks with them.

It wasn't a particularly helpful mantra.

Staring at the back of my eyelids, I sought something that made me feel safe. Painting was good — I was calm and could get engrossed in it, but it didn't make me any less anxious. Fear enveloped me constantly; even with my eyes shut, panic edged its way into my consciousness.

I inhaled again. This time the salt of the sea filled my nostrils, along with the sensation of warm, strong arms surrounding me. It was just a memory, but a powerful one. I tried to pin down Cal's scent — warm and smooth, with that underlying element that screamed *male* — whiskey mixed with spiced honey. I smiled, opening my eyes. The kitchen bench was cool beneath still hands, my breath even.

I rolled tense shoulders. My chest unclenched, and I could focus. Flipping back the edges of the box, I unpacked a set of fine-tipped Japanese pens with handmade inks I'd been keen to experiment with. Making a mental note to message Cal later to thank him for our date last night, I submerged myself in a world of colour until I lost the afternoon light and the air turned chill.

Covered in paint and ink from the afternoon's session, I was determined to be clean. The new inks had worked beautifully, though I'd rationed my use of them, unsure what their major project would be. They highlighted contrasting sketches best — quick scenes of people in the streets, or crowds, with the stark white of the canvas set with deep strokes of darker hues.

My hands were covered in red and black splotches, giving me the appearance of a deranged ladybug. A bubble bath seemed like a good idea. I poured myself a glass of wine on the way to the ancient, claw-footed tub, checking my diary for tomorrow's appointments: Only two slots in the morning on portrait work — one to unveil a project to the family of an older generation and one of a treasured pet. The portraits wouldn't take long, and if I could get through the midday session quickly, I'd have the rest of the afternoon free.

Though they weren't as interesting as people in terms of complexity, I always tried to convey the emotion, and personality house-pets demonstrated during our sessions. Often, a furry face didn't give as much expression, so I spent most of my time speaking with the owner and tried to instil the love they felt for their creature instead.

Pets didn't usually sit quietly while I worked; I was a new person, and too exciting for them to be sedate. Finishing up with — I checked the name — Dolly's portrait would likely take me a week or two in total, depending on how often the owner was available.

I sank into the bubbles, dipping low enough to let the water soak into the ends of my dark hair. It would take ages to get the paint out from today's session. I massaged shampoo in, enjoying the bubbles before they dissolved, dunking my head several times. Clean, I leaned back. Phone on one side of me, and wine the other, I finally, totally, relaxed.

By the time I got out of the bath, little ridges pruned my fingertips. Rivulets of water fell from me completely ink and paint-free, the water a swirl of murky rainbow, staining the tub. I resolved to clean it in the morning, but playing with the inks had been worth it.

I was half-dressed when my phone buzzed. The lock screen showed one in the morning. I must have fallen asleep in the bath, which was unlike me. I crossed my fingers that it was Cal; who else was likely to message me at this time of night?

It was. I was grinning like a madwoman as I read his message.

Cal: Thanks for letting me take you out last night. Hope we can do it again?

I smiled; it was cute that he used the question mark, but I was glad he hadn't assumed we were on just because of that kiss. Oh, my god, that *kiss*. I'd been glad we were in public at the time; otherwise, that surely would have developed into something much heavier pretty fast, and I didn't want to rush this with him. He seemed too good to be true — gorgeous, sweet, sexy as hell.

Was he a devil in disguise?

Cal: You're probably asleep. Just wanted to say thank you.

Me: You're welcome.

I pressed send, organising my thoughts as I finished dressing.

Me: I'd love to see you again.

Cal: You are up! Shouldn't you be sleeping?

A winking emoji ended the message, making me smile. The cheeky face suited him. My bed called to me and I slipped between the sheets, already typing out a reply.

Me: Just got out of the bath.

Cal: ...

Cal: ...

Me: what?

Cal: I'm imagining you in the bath.

Cheeks flaming, I swallowed.

Cal: Have I scared you off?

Me: Not yet...why are you still up?

Cal: Working.

Me: You're at work?

Cal: I do some casework at home.

It wasn't there, but I sensed the hesitation in his message. I'd accidentally touched on a nerve. Hmm. I wanted to find a way to ask about it but maybe after midnight wasn't the best time. My whole body tensed as I thought of him lying next to me in my bed. Well, maybe not next to him...

Me: Would you like to grab a coffee sometime?

Cal: I'm off day after tomorrow, want to catch up then?

It was so casual, but my heart was pounding. *Settle your hormones, girl.*

Me: Sounds great.

Cal: Cool. Message you tomorrow?

Me: Okay.

His last message had three small x's in it. Kisses. I turned the phone over to avoid its glow and lied down to sleep, but it wouldn't come. I couldn't shake the thought of him with me, to feel his weight bearing down on me...I buried my head in my pillow and tried to sleep, hoping the next day would pass quickly.

CHAPTER FIVE

CAL

I hadn't gotten a lot of sleep, but that wasn't unusual. Wakefulness haunted me after messaging Mila, thinking how fine she'd felt in my hands, those startling, sea-green eyes that held a depth I could lose myself in. The image of her haunted my wakefulness — a new obsession, and a welcome one. Stifling a yawn, I trawled through the pages on my desk with bleary eyes. My coffee was stone-cold, but I drank it anyway. I could use all the energy I could get.

"Dane, need your eyes on this, man."

"Give me a minute." I waved to my ex-partner at his desk just across from mine in the small, fishbowl of an office the team shared.

"Boss, the girl you ran into–," I shot him a look, and he lowered his voice, "The girl, Mila, she's here. On Logan's tracking feed."

It took me two go's to focus on what Theodore Black was saying, but eventually, Mila's name registered.

"Wait; what? Say that again." I was on my feet, charging towards his desk before I realised what I was doing.

Black spun around in his chair, heavily-muscled arms up in defence with an alarmed grin on his face.

"Whoa, dude. Slow down." He edged his chair back a little from his terminal.

"Tell me."

Black didn't react at my growl, just assessed me with shrewd eyes, scratching his beard.

"She's got dark hair, five foot six, give or take, and paints. Comes up whenever I put in a search on Ashley. She's always been there, going back a while. You screwing her?"

His tone was casual, but his shoulders were tense. I canted my head to the side; somehow, this was personal to him. Should I poke the bear? The big man did resemble one, after all. No, I decided dourly. Screwing around with Ashley's safety was more than even I would push.

Instead, I returned to the usual, stressed me. My impatience came through with Black, though I rarely let it show with the rest of the team. We'd worked together for too long, knew each other too well.

"What? How did we miss this? What is she, a regular visitor?" I leaned over his shoulder.

Black shrugged, still watching me. I was missing something, which with this case, irritated me to no end. I frowned, wondering what his game was.

"See for yourself."

"Who's screwing who?"

Danny Woods and Micah Rivera walked into the office looking as haggard as I felt, though they had a better excuse, coming off graveyard shift. My exhaustion was self-imposed, after all, but I ignored them, anyway.

"Pull the data and make a file. Go back as far as you need." I slapped the back of his chair. Black didn't even jump.

"Sure, boss."

Black gave me an odd look, covering it with a sigh, and returned to his screen. I wondered again what was going on with him — this wasn't normal behaviour for the man I'd been partnered with for three years before taking point on the task force, overseeing the manhunt for Logan.

Being my ex-partner's boss wasn't the easiest of jobs — Black sat slightly outside our chain of command, though we weren't structured as a typical team. Every one of my team had their strengths — and weaknesses. We overlapped in skill to cover each other's asses, making us one of the most elite teams on the force.

A small, dark figure decorated the corner of Black's computer — Operation Niffler had been named after the small, thieving creature of JK Rowling's magical world. Ashley was a huge fan, and the irony wasn't lost on me that it was her father we hunted.

"You two headed home?"

"Yeah." Danny popped the top on his water bottle, gulping down as much as he could until air sucked noisily through the straw. Ink crept around the back of his hand, the tails of chess pieces depicted there. He'd explained the moves to me once, from a recent grandmaster, a queen dominance. But chess had never been my thing — I was more about control than patience — though I admired the younger man's commitment to crafting his physique. Often underestimated because of his brawny appearance, Danny's finest-honed muscle was his brain.

Built *and* ripped, I knew the hours he put in at the gym were solid. Damn fine sparring partner, too. I might have to call in a few rounds if I needed to get Mila out of my system. I was still having a hard time believing she was connected to Wayde Logan. Was she a plant? It niggled that he might have surveillance on us — when we'd struggled to locate him at all.

Running my fingers over my hair, I waved to the boys, who headed for the door.

"You up for a few rounds tonight?"

Danny nodded. Micah didn't.

"Nah, I got to look after the missus."

My eyes narrowed. It wasn't up to me to pry into their family affairs, but if one of my guys wasn't on the ball, we'd miss something.

Just like we'd missed Mila.

Breath hissed between my teeth as I straightened.

"Alright. Just...look after yourself, yeah?"

Micah nodded, pressing his cap over a swath of brown hair, and followed Danny out the door. As soon as I heard the stairwell door slam, I turned to Black.

"They alright? Micah and his woman?"

Black wiggled his hand in the air a few times.

"They've been on and off for a while now. It's coming. Just gotta let go. He'll be fine, man. He's focussed."

I nodded and returned to my desk.

The next hours were filled with keys taps and curses.
I tried to get into my work — small data hacks on banks that
might have been Logan, but nothing huge, and refrained —
just — from leaning over Black's shoulder every five minutes.
Eventually, he stood, stretching.

"I'm going out for food. You want something?"

I shook my head, still trying to work out how Mila
was connected to Logan, ignoring the hacks. Black shoved
my chair to get my attention. I glared at him.

"What?"

"Check the screen while I'm out."

I frowned as he left, scooting over to his terminal. My
hand was on the mouse to jiggle the little bastard when
Rogers walked into the room. I spotted him in the reflection
of Black's screen and didn't bother to turn around.

"What do you want?"

"Ah, such a welcome from the Great Dane," he scoffed.

I winced before I'd thought to hide it. I hated that nickname.

"What do you want." It wasn't a question anymore, though my hand was still on the mouse. I wanted to rush the bloody thing, get the man out of my office, but he seemed determined to stay.

"I wanted to see how our resident *protected species* was faring."

The snide note in his voice wasn't lost on me.

"What do you *want*, Rogers."

Third time.

Fourth, and we'd find out if safety glass held up under the weight of an eighty-kilo man. Rogers was slight in build, like most of the pencil pushers upstairs. More business than police work, and for a greater paycheck, but I let Liam deal with the politics. Usually.

Rogers caught my expression reflected in the glass.

"I know Liam is watching out for you. Always has been, hasn't he? Maybe he's looking for a fall guy, for later on, hmm? Looks like he's climbing the ladder again. Wonder what it will be like when he's not around to have your back?"

That comment alone would have garnered the man an instant dislike. I snorted. Regardless of where Liam promoted to — it was inevitable, the man was a powerhouse — he would always have my back. The fact that I knew Rogers' brownnosing history made it worse. I stood, towering over the smaller man.

The smaller they are, the worse their bite.

I didn't usually use my height for intimidation, but I did when it was called for. Rogers definitely qualified. He took a small step back as I leaned forward, crossing my arms.

"We work for our pay here, Rogers. Maybe you should leave before a decent work ethic latches on to you."

He sneered, trying to disguise his retreat, slamming the glass door on his way out. The entire office rattled as I glared at the closed door.

Parasite.

Irritated, I watched him make his way past Steph and take the elevator back to the snake pit on the level above us. No stairs for a soft-bellied man like him.

Swallowing my frustration, I woke the screen at Black's terminal and was confronted with a picture of Mila as a younger woman. A *much* younger woman, with white-blonde curls. Memory stirred as I stared at the picture. It was undeniably her; the same green eyes, those soft lips that always seemed to be on the edge of smiling.

But the woman — girl — I looked at now, wasn't smiling. Her eyes were haunted, wide, and so vulnerable. I knew when this photo had been taken because Black and I had been getting our asses roasted while she was looked after by some of the older guys at the local station.

Mila had been there the day Logan had robbed Central five years ago.

I'd been so wrapped up in finding Logan that I'd missed something so vital right in front of me. I'd kissed her, for fuck's sake.

I stared at the screen, picking out the name beside her photo. *Annie Sommers.* She'd changed her name — that wasn't a surprise. A lot of our witnesses had, moving to new places, never speaking about what happened after that day. Logan hunted most of the witnesses down. As soon as we'd worked that out, a cop had been assigned to each one, a minder. I wondered who Mila's had been.

Or was now.

The niggle that said something wasn't right about all this was back. I'd put it down to paranoia before, but this — how had it slipped past me?

I drained the cup of old coffee on the desk before I realised it wasn't mine. Not that Black would care, he'd know I was good for a fresh one. I puffed my cheeks out, letting my eyes shut. Mila wouldn't appreciate me barging in on memories she had probably worked hard to forget. If I was right, she had been a teller in the bank, had direct contact with Logan. Muscles across my back tensed at the thought of his hands on her, how terrified she must have been — especially after watching him kill one of her co-workers.

I scrubbed a hand over my face.

Concentrate, Dane. Thinking with your cock got you into this in the first place.

I still couldn't believe I hadn't recognised her when I rear-ended her car. While I sat across from her, thinking how beautiful she was. There had been a lot sloughing around my mind back then, though. Mandy's texts had put me in a foul mood to start with.

A paper bag slapped the desk in front of me. Since I was occupying his, Black took mine, waving a matching bag.

"Thanks. What'd I get?"

"Bagel with salmon. I know you're on a fish kick. You've got no chance of beefing up like Danny with that shit. Yeah, I saw you looking." He waggled his eyebrows at me, "got that bro crush going."

"Yeah, yeah." I pushed away from the desk, letting Black have his terminal back. "Keep it running in the background; find out what happened during those years in between. And get a hold of whoever her case manager was at the station. I want to know everything."

"Are you going to tell her?"

Black stared hard at me. I shrugged, not willing to explain the confusion in my head. There was no way I wanted him to see I'd already attached myself to a woman who could be exactly what we needed to find Logan. I turned back to my laptop, ripping the paper bag open.

"No."

Danny was already in the ring when I made it down to the gym, only a few minutes after six. Sweat plastered his shirt to his chest, defining muscles I'd never build up. He might have the extra pounds on me, but I was faster — I had to be, to keep out of the way of those heavy fists. Tense from a day that had yielded fuck all results, I was glad I didn't have to wait for him.

Punctuality was something I drilled into the team. Even though I led it, we worked along the same model as Seals did — everyone had an area of expertise — their obsession, we joked regularly — and took point when needed. I was just there to keep our caseload on track, maintain morale. That was a huge thing when we'd been chasing a fugitive for five long years.

Danny stood in the ring, watching me with lazy eyes. Though he looked relaxed, I knew this was his kill look – the man had something on his mind tonight, and I was likely to wear it in the form of bruises and aching muscles tomorrow.

I changed quickly into running shorts and a muscle tee, bouncing on my toes to get my circulation going.

"You warm?"

Danny smirked at me.

"Yeah."

I nodded, stretching out muscles that had bunched into knots after a day hunched over the computer, running through file after file Black had pulled up for me. Muscles popped in my shoulders as I rolled them. Nodding to Danny, I stepped up into the ring, flicking my towel over the rope he held up. He let it go, and it twanged behind me. I frowned, looking around.

"Where's Micah? I thought I saw him earlier."

"Yeah, he had a call to make."

A quick shuffle was the only warning I got as Danny swung first. The air moved beside me, and I ducked on instinct to avoid the blow. Spinning, I dropped while he was still off-balance from the mishit; I read the surprise in his eyes and realised the bastard had meant to clock me with my back turned.

I swung out a leg, sweeping it around in a long arc. Danny grunted as he thudded to the mat. I rose, adrenaline coursing through me at the cold start.

"What the hell, man?" I glared at him. "You got something you need to say?"

Danny shook his head, rolling to his feet and prowled towards me, arms loose. His hands flexed at his sides. We danced in a circle, feet crossing to avoid getting inside each other's reach. I didn't want those meaty fists to smash into the side of my head today. Exhaustion pinged the edges of my energy, and I was already frustrated.

"Mandy."

I stopped, staring at him, nonplussed. My ex's name wasn't what I'd expected to hear from him.

"What about her?" The words came out cautiously; Mandy was wild and unpredictable, and still a thorn in my side, even after the breakup. What the hell had she done now? I wanted to say as much, but the look on Danny's face gave me pause. "What's she done?"

"She came to me last night. Said you'd been around, picking a fight with her. That you hit her."

If I hadn't been paying attention before, I bloody well was now.

"What the fuck–" I ducked the fist that swung wide, over my head. "Man, she's a stirrer. This is the sort of shit she always pulls. And no, I didn't fucking hit her. What sort of an asshole do you take me for?"

The circling resumed. I was kind of glad he hadn't answered — tired as I was if he'd started on the verbal sparring, I might hit him harder than I intended. We traded a few punches, my arm quickly sore from blocking. I shook it out, switching feet, and tried a few kicks, ending up with a numb thigh in return.

Focus.

"When was this, that I was supposed to have attacked her? I know you don't believe that shit."

The shadow of a grin lifted the scowl from his face.

"Well, I didn't want to. But it was a messy breakup, these things happen." He shrugged. "She said the night before last."

I blinked, then roared with laughter. Danny cocked his head, watching me.

"Something funny?"

"Yeah. I was on a date. That's why she's pissed."

Danny eyed me speculatively.

"So, you're finished, right? Over her?"

"Oh, man, don't go there. It'll end in heartbreak. Believe me." I shook my head, turning my back to him.

Whatever game Mandy was playing, I wasn't buying into it. Not anymore. I grabbed the towel off the ropes, wiping my face down. I was surprised by how much I'd sweated during our short fight. I turned back to Danny just in time to see him send me a shit-eating grin before his fist came flying at my face.

The ice pack had melted. I kicked the coffee table back and swapped it for a new one in the freezer. *Fuck.* That still hurt. Danny and I needed to have a solid conversation. Social lives and professional ones should never mix — I wanted to warn him away from Mandy, but he'd likely discover her charms in his own time.

I hoped he hadn't been taking his frustrations out on anyone else. Having a go at me; I could take — once. Cracking into the rest of the team, not so much. Maybe I needed to look into his caseload. See if there was something there that could be a distraction, or that might be overloading him. He was a cracker in undercover work, but too memorable to do it as often as he liked. Plus, he was an excellent hacker.

I pressed the fresh pack to my jaw, wincing. I probed the area. A decent bump was forming, even with the ice — definitely going to have a bruise there tomorrow. I wanted to message Mila but held the urge in — taking work frustrations out by sexting her wasn't a smart move.

Working on her trust would take time, especially now I suspected — knew — the root of her anxiety. I grabbed a beer — no chance I'd be able to focus on Logan tonight — and returned to haunt my lounge, mulling over the puzzle that was Mila.

CHAPTER SIX

MILA

Dolly turned out to be a guinea pig who slept a lot. Either that or terror had paralyzed her. Sympathetic to the tiny creature's plight, I took out a small canvas, setting up my oils.

"Oh, no." Mrs. Schmidt fussed over Dolly, then rearranged my supplies for me. My OCD nearly sent me into a fit, but I restrained myself. Just.

"What's wrong?"

Had the poor critter died? God, I hoped not, though it would make painting it all the easier.

"Oh, no, dear." Mrs. Schmidt fussed some more, finally diving into my bag of supplies. That was my limit.

"There are delicate...um, items in there." I closed the bag firmly, shooing her back. She retreated but hopped from one foot to the other. "What do I need to do?"

I'd found asking clients what they wanted the fastest way to get what *I* wanted — to be painting.

"Dolly deserves a much larger space, don't you agree? She is a champion, after all." Mrs. Schmidt fondled the creature's ears, apparently hitting the spot as Dolly stretched in her sleep, tiny paws flexing. She rolled onto her back. Mrs. Schmidt gestured to a line of fancy framed documents with coloured seals that decorated one wall. "Quite the pedigree, my Dolly has."

I didn't but withdrew an assortment of canvases for Mrs. Schmidt to choose from. As expected, she chose the largest possible. I explained the price difference which she flicked away with a sweep of her arm, nearly dislodging everything I'd rearranged while she'd been speaking.

Somehow, I knew the price would be an issue at the end, and determined to ask her to send me half now, when her phone — an actual-to-goodness wall phone — rang. She answered it, cooing over the person on the other end.

I shook my head and got stuck into painting Dolly, who hadn't so much as moved. I fervently hoped she hadn't died.

I was nearly finished the first pass on her coat when I realised there was someone standing behind me. I jumped, my nerves giving me a delayed reaction, managing to pull my brush away before I added a new feature to Dolly's championship hide.

"Ohhh, she does look beautiful but...isn't she a little...pale?"

"This is just the first round, Mrs. Schmidt. I'll take more time to do a portrait this large," I replied, surveying Dolly in her five-times-larger-than-life likeness. She looked good, in proportion, and the morning light was perfect for her plethora of reddish-brown hues.

"Oh! Of course. I'll see you the same time tomorrow morning, then?"

I groaned internally. Tomorrow was my date with Cal, and we hadn't set a time yet. Plus, I didn't want to arrive covered in paint. But, work was work...and I'd agreed to do this, so I couldn't just back out.

I nodded, suddenly weary as I packed my things, hoisting my satchel over my shoulder for the walk home.

"Sure, Mrs. Schmidt. I'll see you tomorrow."

"Oh, good!" The frazzled little woman perked up, collected her guinea pig, escorting me to the front door. "My nephew will be here then. You should meet him; he's a lovely boy..."

I left her talking about her family member and hoped the boy wouldn't make a mess of my paints or Dolly's portrait while I wasn't there to protect it.

I loved the walk home — it was hilly, and I was puffing by the halfway mark. The exercise was great, especially after spending the previous day parked on a stool. Plus, it cleared my head to get outside, after hours of working on the coat of a champion hamster. Excuse me, guinea pig. Not that I minded, but it was mind-numbing stuff. I needed a challenge.

Cal's face drifted across my mind. That jawline, the strength in his neck...relaxed on the outside; I could see the rage that boiled beneath. Something was eating him from the inside, but when he had been with me, that rage had dissipated somewhat, softened.

Thinking had slowed my pace, and I became more aware of my surroundings, noting something had changed. It took a moment to work it out — a steady drone just behind me. The hairs on my neck rose, alarm triggering a small adrenaline rush. As I approached my corner, I turned, just enough to see over my shoulder.

A black car travelled slowly along the road in my peripheral vision. When I turned, it pulled away, speeding up. I jumped back as it swerved, as though out of control. *Idiots*, I growled in my mind, thinking of the car accident that had stolen my parents away so many years ago.

I turned the corner and headed for home, hoping Cal would message me soon, wondering if it would be presumptuous for me to message him, first. I was *so* out of touch with the dating scene.

In the end, I found messaging Cal too daunting. I'd look at the tiny screen, wondering what to say. Giving it up as a bad job, I cleaned. I was plating my microwave dinner — *what was the point of cooking something fancy when you were only feeding yourself?* — when my phone vibrated across the counter. I grabbed for it with one hand, the other catching soggy mushrooms that escaped off the sides of my plate.

Cal: How was your day? I'm glad my RDO's are coming up.

Me: I painted a hamster.

Cal: ...

Cal: ...

Me: Well, technically a guinea pig.

Cal: Really? Still on for tomorrow?

Me: Please

I followed it up with a smiley face.

Cal: You want to do breakfast?

My heart plummeted. Breakfast was my favourite meal — sometimes my only meal. I actually stopped, ate food, enjoyed coffee. Or tea, I wasn't picky.

Me: I'd love to, but I'll be painting...

Cal: The hamster again?

Me: Yep.

Cal: Can I pick you up in the afternoon? Dress casual.

I sent him my address and finished making my dinner. I wanted to read, but the lines blurred. Everywhere I looked, red hairs streaked my vision. Bloody guinea pig had given me retina burn. I put music on instead, sorting my bag for tomorrow. More Dolly. The sky was only just darkening when I fell into bed.

Dolly refused to sit still. It appeared her stasis of yesterday had been replaced with a possessed guinea pig, rampaging from shadow to shadow. I sighed, dragging up a photo I'd taken of her in yesterday's natural light, saving it to my lock screen so I could keep working until she decided to stop.

My fingers curled around my teacup. I knew straight away it was ice cold. I sighed and sipped it anyway. It had lost some of its aromatics with the heat, but it was still therapeutic.

"Oh, dear, I've let that get cold on you. Let me freshen you up!"

Mrs. Schmidt bustled off with my cup. I mumbled my thanks, studying the photo I'd taken earlier to compare Dolly's fur to where she zoomed in the shadows, chasing dust bunnies. My head was beginning to ache. Browns and russet tones fanned out around me, various mixes numbered from yesterday.

My cup was replaced, warmth radiating from its spot next to my easel on a small side table.

"Thank you," I murmured, adding a fine stripe of grey around Dolly's muzzle.

"You're welcome."

It was a deep voice that answered, and I cricked my neck, looking over my shoulder. A pair of black jeans stood behind me. Definitely not Mrs. Schmidt. I looked up, and up. Deep brown eyes stared back, twinkling. I gaped. *This* was her nephew? I flew from my seat so fast Dolly nearly became an albino.

"Cal!"

I was hugging him before any rational thought crossed my mind, arms wrapped around his neck. I was surprised by how much I'd missed him. His arms tightened around me, light stubble brushing my cheek as he drew back. His eyes found mine again, dark and intense. A spike of electricity shot through me. He lowered his head, breath hot against my skin, adding to the heat that rushed over me. My tongue wetted the edge of my lips as I pressed into him.

"Oh, Cal, thank you for taking that out to Mila. Now– oh, I see you have met our resident artist?"

Cal's arms loosened. I slid down and away from him, flustered. I couldn't look at Mrs. Schmidt, so I stared at the hamster instead. Dolly sat still.

Probably worn out from all that racing around, I thought snidely.

"Mila had dinner with me earlier this week," Cal addressed his Aunt.

Mrs. Schmidt flashed me an unreadable look, collecting my teacup from beside my easel where Cal had placed it. She shooed us out onto the veranda, which overlooked the city.

"Well, off you go, then. Here's your tea, Cal. And yours, Mila. Enjoy the fresh air!"

She bustled us out the door, closing it loudly behind us. I looked at Cal with raised eyebrows.

"What was that all about?" I noticed bruising around his eye. "And what happened to you?"

Cal grimaced, trying to cover it by sipping his tea.

"Sparring with a mate. Don't worry about Aunt Lily; she means kindly. She's been trying to get me to socialise more, since..." he trailed off, looking out at the city. The view truly was magnificent. A muscle clenched in his jaw, but he said nothing more and continued to drink his tea in silence. He shook his head. "She doesn't always approve of my choices."

A grin that could have been a grimace slid over his face, eyes piercing. I swallowed, wondering if he meant me, or the ex. A shadow passed over his face. I tried to decipher it, but he looked away.

Following his gaze, I traced the streets with my eyes, from the bottom of the hill to the promenade, where he'd kissed me.

The memory of his arms around me only moments ago flooded back. My face heated, and I turned to him, almost shouting apologies. Cal waved them away.

"It's fine. She won't think less of you, especially since you're painting Dolly."

That hit a chord with me, and I slapped him lightly on the arm.

"When did you know?"

"That I'd see you today? As soon as you mentioned painting the hamster. Who else would commission a portrait of a guinea pig?" He swivelled to view Dolly in all her splendour on canvas, the life model curled on her side beneath it, peddling madly in her sleep. "You've done a remarkable job. The silly thing usually won't sit still."

"She's been darting about all morning," I confessed. "Though she slept through yesterday's session."

"Cheeky thing," he murmured, liberating my unfinished tea. Protests were half-formed on my lips when he stepped into me. Slipping his arm around my waist, he pulled me against him. The honeyed scent that was all-male filled my senses. I swayed, tilting my head back as I rose onto my toes, stretching up to him. My fingers curled into the material of his shirt, tugging him closer.

His mouth came down hard on mine, sending every inch of me tingling. I gasped softly and his tongue swept inside my mouth, tasting, thrusting. Then suddenly, he slowed the pace, kissing me deeply, but sweetly. I melted against him, his arms winding around me until he was my entire world.

His fingers dragged through my hair, rubbing in tiny circles against my scalp. I moaned against his lips, feeling his response, a deeper growl, rumble inside his chest. He turned, pressing me against the railing, one hand trailing down my back, hesitating at the top of my jeans.

I arched into him, unknotting my hands from his shirt, reaching up to link them behind his neck. He took it as a signal, his hand leaving my back to slide lower, over my ass and he pulled me into him, groaning into my mouth.

"Be glad we're not at my place right now, sweetheart." His voice was rough with desire. Bolts of anticipation tore through me.

"Why would I be glad?" I whispered against his lips, my heart in my mouth. I'd never been so forward in my life. Cal groaned again, slowing the pace. His fingers delved beneath my shirt, palms flat against my skin.

Finally, he drew back, looking down with such an intense stare, it sent tingles all over me. I swallowed, not trusting myself to say anything yet.

His fingers traced the corner of my jaw, across my lips, stroking lightly. My eyes closed, he kissed me again, barely touching his lips to mine. The slightest brush of his mouth sent shivers across my skin. I breathed him in, the spiced honeyed scent that was all *him.*

"Cal, we should..." I whispered, finally remembering where we were.

"Don't worry about her," he murmured, dragging his mouth across my jaw, down the sensitive part of my throat.

I wanted to close my eyes, to let him, but I couldn't.

"Not here, Cal. Please." My lips moved against the stubble on his chin. He drew back, studying me, and nodded.

"Okay."

He slid his hands down my sides, larger, rough hands catching mine. He drew one up for a quick, hard kiss on my knuckles, then let it go, still clasping my other hand in his. Cal drew me back through the glass doors, Aunt Lily nowhere in sight. I packed quickly, hoping she wouldn't mind I hadn't quite finished Dolly yet and did a quick clean up.

"Need a ride?"

I nodded. I'd walked like the day before.

Cal led me back to the front door, calling downstairs that we were leaving. A faint call came back, which I took to be okay, as Cal led me out to his white Ford Ute. The thing was enormous. While he stowed my bag in the back, I clambered up, hoisting myself into the passenger seat.

Relieved I was wearing jeans; I tackled the seatbelt. Cal slid into the driver's seat, then turned to me, draping his arm across the back of my seat. Wherever he touched me, my skin reacted, aching, until every inch of me was hyper-responsive, tuned to him. His eyes dropped to my lips, and he leaned forward, then closed his eyes, breathing in hard.

"Do you want me to take you home, get you cleaned up? Or can I take you out for the lunch I'd planned."

I looked down, surprised to find myself quite clean and presentable. Without a mirror, I couldn't check the rest of me, but I hoped I looked okay. I had a feeling the moment he walked into my house we'd end up in the bedroom — if we even made it that far.

"Lunch sounds great."

I needn't have worried how I looked — I'd forgotten Cal had said to dress casually for our date this afternoon. He squeezed my shoulder, then withdrew his arm. My skin cooled quickly, and I missed the warmth of his touch.

We drove in silence for a few moments. It grew awkward, but my conversational skills had abandoned me.

"Do you have any other clients at the moment?" Cal asked, tapping the steering wheel, looking as nervous as I felt. I smiled, appreciating his attempt to keep things smooth.

"No, only the ones you already know about. I finished up a family portrait earlier. So I have time to play around at home with new ideas, projects I want to try." I looked sideways at him. "The portraits keep me social. Otherwise, I'd never leave the house."

"Being out makes you that uncomfortable?" Cal's hands tightened on the steering wheel, his knuckles whitening. Shadows brushed across his face and were gone. I shook my head.

"No, I—" my mouth dried as I thought about the bank, how to explain it. "I'm just not good with people, sometimes. At all," I mumbled the last part, studying my hands that twisted and turned on each other.

Cal's hand squeezed mine quickly, and he flashed me a smile that lit up his entire face. I returned his smile, my mood lifting easily. His brightness was contagious, bringing me back to myself so fluidly.

"You do just fine, from what I've seen."

"You're pretty comfortable to be around." The words slipped out, and I was surprised to find they were true.

"Everyone has something they struggle with, something they can't get around. Obsessions," he murmured, staring at something I couldn't see.

He parked behind a wide, old shed. I slipped down from the cab, Cal's hands around my waist before my feet hit the ground. He closed the door and squeezed my hip gently, my shirt riding up a little as he pressed me back against the truck. Then his mouth was on mine again.

Sometime later, I came back to myself. Cal alternated light kisses against my lips with gentle nips along my jaw. I fought the desire to moan aloud, both conscious of our public display, and needing him in my bed in the same instant.

CHAPTER SEVEN

MILA

Sea breeze hit me in the face, welcome and relaxing. I had always loved the smell of salt in the air. It reminded me of summer and Christmas. The waiter placed a seafood platter between us — share dishes were quickly becoming our thing.

Salt and pepper-crusted mud-crab took up half the plate. I studied a selection of tools for dismantling the shell that lined the tray, looking for all the world like a surgeon's instruments. Crab was something I could flick across a room with ease, a talent many years in the making. I winced at memories of redecorating my family dining table with crab and shell and quickly filed the painful thoughts aside. Prawns surrounded it, garlic grilled scallops in their shells piled in one corner. The platter was tastefully done — not overloaded, and the patterns appealed to my OCD.

I studied the small patio that hung over the water. It was clean and sparse, nothing fancy, though it suited the atmosphere of the marina. Cal leaned back in his chair; his white, linen shirt stretched over relaxed shoulders. He was comfortable here, I realised, his face clear of the lines that so often gave him such an intense look. I was glad to see the shadows that had obscured his face were absent, for now. Whatever caused them, I was determined to keep at bay for as long as I could.

A glass of white wine I hadn't ordered was placed in front of me. I raised my hand in protest, but Cal smiled at me, and I relented, nodding my thanks. The waiter patted him on the shoulder, passing him a schooner of beer. I'd always loved the honeyed colours of the ales but couldn't stand the taste.

"Thanks," I murmured, taking a sip from my glass. I eyed the waiter speculatively. "He doesn't usually look after everyone this well, right?" I looked back inside the Fish Co-Op where utilitarian-glassed counters were laden with fish on ice.

Cal grinned.

"Nah, I've been coming here for years. Dad and I used to fish off the rocks..."

The shadows were back. I tried to think of something to say.

"You love the ocean?" It was a poor offering, but when Cal's eyes connected with mine, I knew he appreciated the gesture.

"Yeah. Boating, swimming...anything to do with it. I love being out there, nothing around but open sea. No land, nothing."

"I've never been out that far."

Cal shot me an amused look.

"Maybe we can fix that, then. Next time."

My heart flip-flopped in my chest. It was all so new, and I hadn't done this in...well, forever. I'd been alone for so long I'd forgotten how it all worked.

"Next time," I echoed.

I watched him shell some of the prawns, then move on to the crab. I snavelled a scallop from the corner of the platter closest to me. Those tanned forearms still got me — sleeves rolled to expose hard, toned muscle. Either he worked out, or worked outside — I didn't care much which one it was.

He deftly flicked crab into a neat pile onto a small plate and passed it to me. I took it, surprised, but relieved not to have to display my enthusiastic crab deconstruction skills.

"So, what sort of things are you working on right now?" I paused, unsure. "Wait, am I allowed to ask that? I have no idea how this works," I apologised, flustered. How was I supposed to be dating a man like this when I couldn't even hold a basic conversation with him? I wanted to run and hide, but his smile was open and genuine, relaxing me.

"It's fine. I wouldn't expect you to know what to ask, not yet." His eyes were dark as he talked, something in them not quite matching his words. I smiled cautiously as he continued. "I've been working on the same case for years now, a few others in between, like when I first met you. But always linking back to this one...all bank robberies, or supposed to be, if I don't get them first. I never fail."

It wasn't said with arrogance, just a statement of fact. Cal was good at his job, and he knew it. But his words sent me spiralling back, to carpet patterned with shadows and light from outside, Ashley years younger, prancing about. It had taken her a long time to work through what she'd witnessed, try to deal with abandonment.

As far as I knew, her father had never come back to claim her. She had a new family, now, and I enjoyed the few days a month I saw her. I knew it was something Cal would understand, this being his job, but I couldn't bring myself to talk about it.

"Mila. Hey, are you okay?"

His words returned me to him, the salty air reminding me where I was. I pushed the bank firmly away and sat mute for a moment, collecting myself.

"Sorry, just reminded me of...something." I couldn't say some*one* as the words got stuck in my throat. Cal frowned, holding his glass, but he didn't lift it to his mouth. I watched water condense around his clenched fingers. "So, this is a long-term case? Is that...normal?"

"Not really. I don't usually let them drag on this much. Always some new idiot thinking he can get greedy and take what doesn't belong to him. Or her. But that's pretty rare, a woman involved in a bank heist, statistically speaking." His fingers tapped a rhythm on the base of his glass.

"Oh." I didn't know what else to say, grasping about. "What's holding this one up?"

Cal was quiet for a minute, eyes hooded.

"Bastard is smarter than me."

I studied the faint lines around Cal's eyes, the way the corners of his mouth turned down. Whoever this was sat heavily on him, and had for a while. It must be hard when you're used to being able to catch them all. He caught me watching, and the frown disappeared.

"Sorry," he murmured, taking a sip of his beer, "my obsession, I guess. Everyone has one."

My breath caught, ice-cold eyes slamming into me, haunting. I supposed he was right, in a way.

"Or something they can't let go of." The words tumbled out before I could catch them, but Cal didn't seem to notice.

"True. What about you? Brothers I need to watch out for, family?" His eyes twinkled at me. I shifted in my seat.

"No family."

His eyebrows rose. "No one? Only child?"

"I live in my grandmother's house. I lost my parents young, in a car accident, and lived with her until I lost her three years ago, too. I just paint." It was the truth, but it sounded pathetic, even to my own ears, though Teddy and Ashley flicked through my mind. I wasn't ready to share them just yet. Cal frowned.

"What about friends? Someone to watch out for you, an ex?"

I shook my head with a smile. "No ex."

"Just painting?"

"Yup."

"Do you do exhibitions?" He studied me with a blank face, unreadable. I shrugged. Letting him into my life wasn't easy.

"I've done a few. One is lined up for next year. I like doing portraits; it shows who people really are in one glance, like a snapshot. But you can put so much more into it."

"You're a people watcher."

I raised my glass.

"Guilty."

Cal grinned appreciatively. "People are predictable. Well, most people. There's the odd few exempt."

Conversation flowed easily after that. It hadn't looked like much, but by the time the share plate was clean, I was so full, I swore I would never eat again. The waiter returned to take the plate. Cal stopped him, with a hand on his arm.

"Marcus, this is Mila. I met her...when I ran into the back of her car last week." Cal paused and sent me a lopsided grin. "I was thinking of taking her out on the water next week, maybe with Liam? I hear he's back in a few days."

Marcus turned to me, a broad smile creasing weathered skin. He proffered a hand from beneath the enormous platter, and I took it gently, not wanting to upset the load on his arm.

"Mila, good to meet you. I have heard a lot about you." His smile to me was warm, but the look he sent Cal had an unreadable quality to it. "You are always welcome to take the boat, my boy. Liam will be back in a few days, but you don't need to wait for him."

Cal shrugged. "I thought he might like to take Selena. She loves the water."

"Ach, I know boy, but she won't be pushed. Best let her make up her own mind."

I looked between the two, wishing I had a relationship with someone like this. I'd made the choice to be alone, and stayed that way for so long I'd forgotten what it meant to have friends...to have a family.

Marcus headed back into the shop. A silence fell over us. I looked out at the water, not sure what to do, and covered it by sipping my wine.

"Liam works with me. My boss, actually. We've been friends since the academy. He was two years ahead of me. I mucked up early in my career, and it cost me a promotion. Liam got it instead." His eyes were pensive as he turned them on me. "He's like a big brother to me. Looked after me when Dad passed. We were fishing on the rocks, and he...he had a heart attack. It was hot, and he'd given me his hat to keep the sun off."

Cal stared over the water, seeing something I couldn't. His shoulders were a tense line, as though bearing the memories by physical force alone. The table was too wide for me to reach across. I rose, stepping around the table to stand behind his chair, hands sliding down his shoulders. He squeezed my arms, and I leaned my cheek on his head, the bristles softer than they had been a few days ago. I closed my eyes and breathed him in. Cal's cheek rubbed against my arm.

"Walk?"

I tried to pay for lunch, but Marcus waved me away with a grin, giving Cal that same hard look as before. We headed down the wharf, away from the Co-op. The wind had come up as the afternoon progressed, blustery gusts whipping my hair around. Whitecaps decorated the seascape. Cal's arm slipped over my shoulders, pulling me into him, his lean frame providing shelter and I nestled into his side. His fingers tensed around my shoulders as we walked, the headland coming into view.

It was a steep track, waves crashing mercilessly into the cliffside below us. Mutton birds scuttled about in the bracken fern that edged the path. Salt sang into my face as we reached the peak.

South of us, water rose in a spout, and we both exclaimed, watching for any other sign. It only took a few moments before the water shifted, the hump of a whale gliding through the water. We were rewarded for our patience when the whale's flukes lifted from the ocean, crashing down with a great show of white water.

"Not the best day, sorry," Cal said into my ear, the wind so bad I struggled to hear him. I turned beneath his arm, pressing against his chest.

"Are you kidding? This has been amazing. Lunch with you, walking, whales…" I gestured around us, "this."

His fingers caught my chin, bringing my face back to his. My lips parted, but when he kissed me, it was the sensitive skin around my jaw his mouth brushed. He tilted my head back, his fingers still firm on my chin, dragging his lips down my neck, nipping my collar bone. A strangled cry broke free, my hands pressing against his shoulders. My heart pounded from his ministrations. His fingers slid to the back of my neck, pulling me hard against him as his mouth found mine.

His tongue slid past my lips, and my entire body clenched with need. I wanted to gasp, but he was relentless, his mouth hard on mine, our kisses coming faster and faster. My fingers curled on his neck, and some rational part of me hoped I hadn't scratched him. His hands tangled in my hair, tugging just a little, drawing my head back, completely controlling the kiss.

I arched into him as his other hand slid down my back, over my hips. His fingers ran over my ass, between my legs, pressing up hard. I moaned, driven by the need to be closer to him as he lifted me off my feet, dragging me over his belt buckle, where he pressed against me. I wrapped my legs around his waist, my jeans feeling terribly thin as he pushed me down onto him. His groan echoed my own. I forgot everything: the wind, where we were.

Eventually, our mouths slowed, though his hands were still wrapped deep in my hair. He held me to him, pressing his forehead to mine. I breathed, eyes closed, trying to still my heart. I was glad we were alone on the headland — I felt slightly obscene, never being into outward displays of affection in such a public manner. But with Cal, it was all so *easy*.

And I didn't want him to stop.

CHAPTER EIGHT

CAL

I set Mila back on her feet, only just holding back the urge to tear every scrap of material from her body and fuck her right there on the path. How the hell had this woman gotten into my head so fast? She felt so damned fine, kissing her was like a drug. But it was more than that — I hadn't felt this close to anyone for a long time — she'd blown memories of Mandy away in a matter of days. And when I'd spoken about Dad, she'd wrapped her arms around me. I'd nearly lost it, then, tears ready to flow.

I crushed her against my chest, resting my chin on top of her head, looking out at the ocean. The wind still blew in a gale around us, whipping her hair into my face, but I didn't care. My fingers were still tangled in her dark strands. All I wanted was to hold her, lose myself in her, and never let go.

She made a little noise, and I loosened my hold, worried I was suffocating her. She stared up at me with those huge damned eyes, every emotion exposed, raw. I ran my fingers over her cheek, and she whimpered again. I frowned.

"Are you okay?"

She nodded, releasing my shirt where she'd been clutching it, sliding her hands up my neck. I shivered as she pulled my head down, soft, pink lips brushing over mine so tentatively, so gently, I could have died. Cradling her against me, I let her in, all the way. I didn't care if she was connected to *him.*

We would make this work.

She whimpered when I tipped her head back, deepening the kiss, but gently this time. Like she was glass that could shatter beneath my hands. She felt so small, but I knew she was strong. A survivor, even if she didn't see herself that way. Thoughts of fucking her here left me — I wanted to have this woman in my bed, at least the first time. After that...I smiled against her mouth, her breaths short and fast, thinking of ways I could get her to make those tiny noises again.

Her arms wrapped around my neck, and she buried her head into my shoulder. I stroked her hair, giving her time to settle. There was something flighty about her, and I knew that if I rushed this, I'd lose her.

And there was no way in hell I was going to let that happen.

Back at my truck, I hoisted her into the passenger bench seat, the curves beneath her jeans mesmerising me. I stepped back before she caught me staring, the urge to strip her bare back with a vengeance. She shifted around as I watched her, surprised a tiny thing like her didn't look out of place in the cab, seeing as the truck should have dwarfed her. She turned back to me, eyes wide, like a deer in headlights.

"What?"

I smiled, and shook my head, closing her door. It was perfect. She was perfect. But surely no one was that good an actress.

What the fuck are you doing, Dane? Get your shit together.

MILA

Cal's fingers trailed the bulbar as he walked around the front of the truck. He stepped up into the driver's seat, sliding easily inside, making me feel rather short. The engine started with a guttural growl, which suited him. Clean and hard on the outside, rough on the inside. There was some quality about him that was...damaged wasn't the right word. Worn, maybe?

His side profile in the dying light was thrown into sharp relief, though that golden skin and sharp jawline still turned my heart over. The man looked like some kind of god sent to earth, to walk amongst mortals. I felt decidedly frumpy next to him.

Smoothing my jeans, I pressed my hands into my legs. Cal slipped the truck into gear, and reached over, wrapping my fingers in his. I rested our clasped hands lightly on my leg, remembering the way his hands had pressed into me on top of the headland. A small shiver shook me, and he squeezed my hand, eyes on the road.

"Do you want me to drop you off?"

It was a loaded question and my breath caught, suddenly unsure. That I wanted this man was undeniable. But for someone who hadn't been on a date since my second semester at university, this was moving fast for me. Too fast.

"Yes—" I started in a whisper, looking down at our joined hands.

"It's okay, Mila." He sent a reassuring glance my way. "I won't push you."

I nodded, nerves roiling in my stomach as I gave him my address, then remembered he already had it. Flustered, I barely registered where we were as he turned down the next street, winding his way through the suburbs with ease. The sun dropped steadily behind the tree-lined streets, the light dying with the day. Streetlamps flickered on. When we turned onto my street, I pointed out my house, and he pulled into the drive.

The old house was set further back on its block than more modern ones, the garden obscuring the front door. I liked the privacy it afforded me, plus it kept out street noise and headlights. Cal cut the engine but left the keys hanging in the ignition. He turned to me, indecision warring in his face.

"Mila, I—"

I leaned forward and kissed him, making the decision for both of us. His hand came up to cup my face, then he drew back, studying me. His brow furrowed, and I reached out to smooth the lines. No man that looked this amazing should have lines like that. I leaned into him again, but again he held me back. My hands slipped to his chest. I looked up in confusion.

"Love, are you sure? If I come in with you..." he trailed off, eyes dark and fathomless. Beneath my hands, I could feel the moment his heartbeat picked up, racing as he held me at bay. I swallowed, nodding.

Breath hissed between Cal's teeth as he pulled me against him, his mouth pressed to mine. He tangled his fingers in my hair, but I could feel the reservation in him, still holding back. If I thought about this any longer, I knew I'd jump out, stop because I was too afraid. But the way he asked, cared, made me feel safe — it had been that way with him since the first time he'd kissed me.

I slid my tongue across his bottom lip, stroking his tongue with mine. His movements gentled for a brief moment before he exploded against me, pushing me back against my seat, mouth hard on mine, hand fumbling at my seatbelt.

His fingers slid down my neck, pressing a little against my collar bone. I gasped, pleasure shooting through me, my eyes on his. I arched into him, pressing against the hand at my throat. He growled, fingers curling gently, possessively, as he leaned in to kiss me again.

I moaned, hungry for his touch. I wanted — needed — him everywhere. He released me, fingers drifting down the side of my breast. Sensation flooded through me. I wiggled, trying to get closer. My fingers curled in his shirt, tugging him down to me.

Cal wrenched his mouth away, cupping my face.

"Not here, Mila...I want to–" he broke off, staring over my head. I frowned, twisting in his arms.

"What?" I could barely see in the darkness. I turned back to see his eyes on me.

"You live alone, right?" His eyes were dark as night, completely unreadable.

I nodded.

"Yes. What's wrong? I can't see a thing."

"Your door is open."

I craned around him, peering through the trees. Even though I knew where everything was, shadows concealed anything farther than a few meters from his truck. My area had a lack of street lamps, and I'd always been happy with that. Cal must have had incredible eyesight to see in the dark like that. He reached over me, flicking open the glovebox, and withdrew a handgun. One hand pressed lightly against my chest.

"Stay here."

Cal left the truck silently, not quite closing his door. He slipped away into the shadows, leaving me alone.

Long minutes passed, and I began to fidget. Maybe I'd left the front door open? It seemed to be something I would do in my frazzle of getting out the door each day. I checked my keys, trying to remember if I'd locked the door when I headed out to paint Dolly this morning. Had it only been this morning? I hopped out of the cab, shivering as the chilled air hit me after the warmth of the truck, unsure what to do. It was a big house; it would take Cal a while to check the whole thing, right?

I slipped down to the drive, closing the truck door gently. I couldn't see or hear anything out of place but didn't dare call out. Cal seemed to take this far more seriously than I was. I had taken a single step toward my house when Cal materialised beside me, fingers wrapping around my arm.

I yelped in fright, and he pulled me against him. It took a moment of trying to pull back from his grasp that turned into a small game of tug-o-war, until I breathed him in, realising he wasn't a random intruder.

"I *told* you to stay in the truck." His voice was soft, but his words held an edge to them.

"It's okay; I think I was in a rush this morning when I left to go to your Aunt's. I probably didn't shut the door; I'm a bit hopeless that way–"

Cal's fingers pressed against my lips. I stopped talking, searching his face with wide eyes.

"You didn't leave the door open."

"What?"

"Mila, who would want to get into your house? Someone who might want to hurt you?" His fingers closed tight digging into my flesh. I whimpered, Logan Wayde's face flashing before my eyes.

But Teddy said I was safe, that he wouldn't be able to hurt me, to find me...I stared at Cal, my chest heaving. The world around me narrowed to a point, Cal's eyes drilling into me.

"Mila. *Mila.*"

Cal's voice was far away. I stepped back, pulling away until my back hit his truck. He stalked towards me, eyes narrowed. His gaze was so intense, so different to the Cal I knew. I froze, my fear transferring to him.

"Talk to me." He placed one hand on either side of me, caging me between him and the cold metal of his truck. The space seemed so small there was nowhere to move away from him. My chest closed up as I struggled to draw breath. Logan's eyes replaced Cal's, and I shrank away from him as he leaned into my space.

"I don't–"

Headlights shone too brightly into my driveway as a black car pulled up behind Cal's Ute, lurching in its haste to stop. Footsteps pounded the concrete drive. Cal disappeared from my view as he was shoved aside. Cold air swirled around me be before I was enfolded into enormous arms I'd known for years.

"Mila. Girl, you're okay. I've got you."

I pressed my head into Teddy's chest, his long beard tickling my ear. My breath steadied almost instantly; I was *safe*. A hand slapped the truck beside me, and I jumped, shrinking into myself just a little more. Teddy's arms drew tighter around me.

"What the hell?" Cal glared at both of us as I huddled in the safety of Theodore Black's embrace.

"Settle down, man. She'll be fine." Teddy looked down at me with kind eyes unsuited to his rough face. His tone softened as he looked at me, "Right?"

I nodded, unable to speak. Then the world spun around me, and I shook my head.

"Breathe, girl. Remember, he's not here. We are. He can't hurt you. He'll never hurt you. Not now, not ever."

I kept nodding; sure I looked like a bobblehead doll. Cal stared between us, running a hand over his head.

"Black's your minder."

I sat on my lounge, staring around at the mess that had been my living area. Whoever had been in my house had destroyed most of my furniture. Shards of Gran's china and crystal littered the carpet, pillows sad and limp, their stuffing discarded on the furniture — what little that hadn't been torn apart.

Cal and Teddy's voices reached me in soft murmurs from the kitchen, while I assessed the damage to my home. I rose to begin the clean-up as Cal emerged.

"Don't touch anything." He passed me a cup of tea, fingers sliding around my elbow, leading me back to the front door. "I saw a swing under that big tree in the front yard. Can we talk while Black sorts a crew out to look at your house?"

"What for?" Cal frowned at my question, fumbling around the doorway for an outdoor light switch. I leaned past him, flicking it on. The floodlight illuminated my entire front yard. Some of the tightness in my chest released as the shadows scampered away. I brushed against Cal and started, not liking how the intimate contact made me feel. What had he asked? "Why would they need to look at my house, I mean."

"Fingerprints, any evidence or traces the intruders might have left behind."

My stomach clenched, a shiver passing through me.

"You think there was more than one?"

"Yeah." His hands slipped around my waist, lifting me onto the swing. I started at the contact, wriggling out of his grip quickly. I curled numb fingers around the old ropes as he began to pace in front of me. "Mila, can you start from the beginning? I need to know everything you do. What's been going on, anything different. Has he contacted you? Approached you, anything at all?"

I watched him pace, hands visibly shaking though he tried to hide it by clenching his fists. My heart rate settled. Suddenly, I wasn't as panicked; I knew what I needed to do. I knew because I was looking at myself five years ago, pacing and desperate to get the man out of my head who wouldn't leave.

I patted the seat beside me.

"Cal, sit down." He glared at me, mouth open to argue. I raised my eyebrows. "Sit with me. Please."

He frowned when I extended my hand, making as though to rise. He paused for a moment, as though thinking the better of it, then shook his head. Ignoring my hand, he lowered himself onto the swing gently, as though not trusting it to hold both of us. I grinned inwardly; if the swing held Teddy, it would definitely hold Cal.

I took his hand in mine. He flinched at the contact, fingers stiffening, then relaxing. I held my breath, but he didn't pull away, just looked at me, waiting. I held on, letting him settle, his fingers tightening around my hand to the point it was painful, but I didn't move. He needed this, just as I had. When his breathing slowed, and his grip became gentle, I nodded.

"Tell me."

Cal looked at me with wide eyes, clenching my hand as he forced the words out.

"I've been hunting Wayde Logan for five years. And I've failed."

CHAPTER NINE

CAL

Everything came out — Wayde's escape from Central to right through to every damned bank I'd been at too late ever since. It was like rewatching an old movie you knew had a shitty ending. The bad guy was never supposed to get away; justice was meant to be served.

I leaned forward, elbows planted on my knees, glaring at the ground. I was an absolute idiot for not trusting her, for not knowing what my team was doing. And I'd scared the shit out of Mila.

Though she was taking this well — I risked a sideways glance. Her face was hidden in the shadows. Pale, but calm. I kept waiting for the storm to break. She sipped her tea, mug straight in still hands. That inner strength I'd known was there. Just as she'd seemed to know how broken I was, recognised it in herself, perhaps.

"I'm sorry. I shouldn't have jumped on you like that. It was..."

She nodded, staring back toward the house. Faint, red marks decorated her arms where I'd grabbed her. It hit me like a kick in the guts. Sickened, I reached over to her, to apologise, hug her. Anything. She flinched away, slowly bringing her eyes up to meet mine.

"Cal— it's all mixed up. In my head." She took a breath, knuckles white around her mug, and started again. "I've been terrified of him for so—so long. And now, looking back at who you were then, the way you behaved..."

She trailed off, my heart clenching at her omission. I blinked, and suddenly I was back in the bank, hands on the rail of Black's old Jeep, mouthing off instead of doing my job. Being a drama queen, thinking I was all that. I'd completely screwed up, and Logan had gotten away. Which was why we were here now.

This is my fault.

Nauseated with having to live in my own skin, I floundered for something to say that might make this right. It didn't matter that I'd managed to recover my career, with a huge dollop of Liam's help, and it wasn't just that I'd let Logan escape. I stared at Mila, fear still crinkling the edges of her eyes. She would be so much safer if I'd never come near her, but now, I didn't want to leave. She swallowed, her eyes on mine, as though she couldn't look away.

I knew that look, had seen it often in victims who'd experienced violence at the hands of some arrogant fuck, often one they knew, and trusted. *I'd* done this. She wasn't safe with me. I nodded and rose, the swing moving gently beneath me.

"I'll get your house sorted as fast as I can, so you can get some rest."

Mila didn't speak, just watched me. My chest closed up. I nodded curtly to her and walked away.

It was all I could manage without falling onto my knees and begging for her forgiveness.

By the time we'd collected what little evidence there was to find — if you could even call a few scraps with partial prints *evidence* — Danny and Micah had arrived. The house was enormous compared to my stunted apartment, but we managed to get most of it organised, amassing garbage bags full of broken things to trawl through later, just in case.

Micah collected the lot, tossing them into the back of his enormous, blue truck. The thing was bigger than mine — he used it for monster truck competitions — and covered with sponsorship logos. But, it was road legal. Just.

Black stood at the edge of the porch, a sentinel staring into the darkness beyond the reach of the floodlight. I wanted to do one last walk through, secure the place myself, though I suspected the intruders were long gone. It wasn't likely they would return tonight, not with us trawling through the scene, but I didn't want to leave Mila unprotected.

Black turned hard eyes on me, and suddenly I was back in the station after screwing up Central. That mistake haunted me. I couldn't help the sneer that ran through my chest, knocking him with my shoulder as I stepped past, though it barely moved him. The old bastard was wired with solid muscle.

"Above and beyond, right, *brother*."

Black followed me inside, closing the door behind us.

"Man, I get you're pissed with me, but I've spent five fucking years looking after that girl."

"Looking after her? Or screwing her?" I couldn't keep the derision out of my voice.

Black levelled a cold glare my way.

"I've taken that girl to counselling *every month*, sat through meditation classes, let her paint portraits of me so she could have someone to practice on when she was too afraid to leave the house. She is *completely alone*. Perfect

122

target for an asshole like you to come in and take advantage. That girl is like my sister."

I snorted, folding my arms, but he wasn't finished.

"I've tried to encourage her to go out, but she can't trust anyone. You attacking her like that? She'll take fucking forever to forget tonight. Put your ego down man, and see the damage you've caused with this. Yeah, I wanna catch him too, but not at the expense of the people we're meant to protect."

I raised my hands, stepping back. It was the longest speech I'd ever heard Black make, and every word rang true. I let out a long breath.

"You're right. I was an asshole. Now she's terrified of me." I swallowed hard, clenching my fists to do something — anything. Everything seemed so far out of my control. I turned away, disgusted with myself.

You're a fuck up, Dane. Same as you always were. A huge hand landed on my shoulder, breaking me out of my pity party.

"You wanna fix this? Tell her what she means to you. *Show* her she can trust you."

I shrugged his hand off, fighting back the tears prickling the corners of my eyes.

"I don't know how."

Taking one last look through the house, I headed out to the back patio. Canvases scattered the wide space, a cupboard where they must have been stored busted open. I sighed, stacking them in a neat pile. If Mila saw her work so carelessly strewn about she'd be heartbroken. When I reached the ones farthest away from the cupboard, I stopped. The lines on these canvases weren't painted, they were sketched in graphite. Light, basic and unadorned, but the face was easy to recognise.

It was mine.

She'd drawn me angled, looking away from her. Relaxed and smiling, something I never saw in myself. From our first date, perhaps? The one beneath was more detailed, still me but sporting the dreads from the day I'd wrecked her car. My heart ached. She was so fucking incredible. And I'd screwed up what we'd had.

A loose page fluttered its way over the wooden boards. I stamped on one corner to stop it blowing into the garden. This one was me, too, but pensive. Something raw in it stood out. I was stripped bare just looking at it, as though she'd captured a part of my soul and exposed it on paper. I traced the lines of my own face, uncomfortable and sad at the same time. I folded it quickly, sliding it into my pocket.

I left the veranda, locking the door behind me.

When I got to the front door, I paused. Black must have left it open while he watched Mila; I could see the two of them sitting on the swing beneath the tree. Her eyes were red and puffy, cheeks glistening in the harsh light. She leaned her head on Black's shoulder with a familiarity I envied. His hand stroked her hair. So, she'd been able to cry in front of him but not in front of me? I'd really busted the trust we'd developed.

In a few short days, what we'd had was over.

Black was speaking to her, but she looked up, straight at me as though she'd known I was there. Or had been waiting? I hoped it was the latter. Black nodded to me as she straightened, jumping off the swing. He said something to her, reaching out, but she shook her head. Black's hand dropped to his side, and he followed her slowly at a distance as she approached the house.

I shoved my hands deep in my pockets, watching her as she walked up the steps, so slight, arms hugging around herself. Her eyes never left mine. I started to ask if she was okay, but the answer to that was pretty obvious. She probably wouldn't feel safe for a long time.

"Do you want me to stay?" I wanted to take the words back as soon as they left my mouth. They hung in the air, a fragile thing that could shatter at the slightest resistance.

Those gorgeous green eyes got wider, if that was possible, her mouth open just a little. I huffed back a laugh, knowing how it had sounded, then hated myself for it.

Idiot.

"I meant, out here. I can stay here, outside," I put emphasis on *outside*, "so you know there's someone here. You're safe; you can sleep. Or, Black will hang out for the night if you prefer. Outside."

I happily volunteered the ass that had been sitting with my girl for the best part of an hour while I sorted through all her private stuff, then winced at my attitude. She had never been mine.

Wallowing, Dane? Grow up.

"You."

It came out as a whisper, and she looked straight at me as she said it. I was glad I saw her lips move, or I might not have believed what I'd heard. My heart leapt a little.

"Okay." Biting back the impulse to yell and leap in the air, I leaned against a veranda post, looking out over the garden.

Black enveloped her in a huge hug, speaking quietly in her ear. Jealousy consumed me. I could see nothing more than Mila comfortable in another man's arms, and I turned away, spotting a piece of wall that looked good to spend the night with.

"Night, bro."

I pivoted on my heel, finding Black a step too close, his eyes hard. I held his gaze until he nodded, satisfied. He left without another word, striding to his car still parked behind my truck. The engine of his black sedan purred softly as he backed down the drive. He had a passion for Japanese imports, the only one of us who didn't drive a truck, and I was reminded of the black sedan that had almost run me down. I opened my mouth to ask Mila, but she was gone, and the front door was shut.

I frowned, but it was my own damn fault. Flicking the floodlight off, I waited a few minutes on edge for my night vision to adjust, but nothing came at me out of the darkness. I was the only terrible thing out tonight, it seemed. I'd just settled against the wall when the door opened again. Mila held a blanket, an arm full of pillows, and had balanced a shot of amber liquid in a fragile-looking glass on the top.

"Would you mind?" she asked, clutching the tower, the glass wobbling precariously on top.

I tried to smother a smile but failed woefully, by the reproaching look in her eyes. It just made it worse. I scooped the glass from the top of the pile with a broad grin. I freed her arms of their offering with my other arm, putting it all in a pile where I'd chosen to spend the night.

"Thanks," I said softly, holding the glass out, "yours?"

She shook her head.

"It's for you."

"I don't usually drink on duty."

She cocked her head.

"I don't think one shot is going to stop you, Cal."

I missed most of what she said, just focusing on the fact that she'd used my name. I gripped the thin glass, never breaking away from her gaze and drained the thing. It was sweet and raw when it hit the back of my throat, the burn that followed, welcome.

"Thank you," I said softly. She looked up at me but didn't back away. I reached out, waiting for the flinch, the moment I'd know we were truly done. Damn, I was pushing my luck with her.

She stayed stock still. I cupped her cheek with the lightest touch, almost no pressure in between her skin and mine, leaned down and kissed the top of her head. When I stepped back, her eyes were closed. She swayed a little, and it hit me how exhausted she must be.

"Get some rest, honey."

She opened her eyes, and I was startled to see tears there. I ached to touch her again, to hold her, but stupidly,

the fear of rejection stopped me after how I'd behaved
tonight. I still had no idea where I stood with her for now,
but even if I couldn't offer physical solace, at least I could
provide some sort of protection while she recovered.

I settled on the pillows, blanket over my shoulders,
staring out across the yard. The door closed with a soft
click, but I could have sworn I heard her whisper *goodnight.*

CHAPTER TEN

MILA

The door clicked shut behind me. I closed my eyes, the energy draining from every limb. I wanted to sink to the ground and sleep right there, on the other side of the door from Cal. When he'd touched my face, I'd frozen — expecting to be afraid of him, but I wasn't. No matter what had happened tonight, what Teddy expected me to feel, Cal was still my safety net.

I knew he'd protect me, even though I wished I was there to protect him, right now. He was hurting badly; anyone could see that. But I couldn't be there for him, not just yet.

My house had been wrecked; I had nearly passed out in fear of a combination of the man I was dating — *had been dating?* — and the man who had haunted me for so many years. Our obsessions. I laughed as I walked into my room and snapped my mouth shut. No. I wasn't giving into this.

Cal was right; I needed sleep.

My room was full of shadows, but I breathed, the regular patterns easing the panic a little. The boys had checked the house; I was safe. Safe. If I repeated it enough, it might, one day, be true.

I collapsed on my pillowless bed and was able to close my eyes, knowing he was outside.

It wasn't quite light when I woke, covered in a film of cold sweat. Something seemed wrong as I opened my eyes, blinking in the pre-dawn light. Shadows flitted above my bed in odd patterns. It took a moment for my sluggish mind to figure it out — my cupboard was on the wrong side of the room. The boys must have moved it when they tidied everything up.

I lay still, letting yesterday wash over me. I didn't want to think of the bad, not just yet, though I knew I'd need to face it — him — soon. I remembered painting Dolly, the rush I'd felt, seeing Cal standing above me. He'd lost it last night, but never in any of the times he'd kissed me, had he been too rough, or cruel.

132

Still, would he do it again? I wanted to think it was okay, that things could go back the way it was before, but my heart was racing, and I turned to bury my tears in my pillows before I remembered I'd given the lot to Cal.

Would he still be there, waiting outside the door? I slipped out of bed, realising I'd been so out of it the night before, I hadn't put my pyjamas on. I grabbed fresh jeans out of the cupboard and pulled a long, knitted jumper over the top. It was black and silky, and my favourite. I flicked away specks of paint clinging to the hem and went to make two cups of coffee, hoping I wouldn't be drinking both of them on my own.

I nudged the door open with my foot, having successfully juggled the locks and mugs without dropping anything, peeking outside. Cal sat propped against the wall, blankets puddled around him, staring out at where the sun would soon rise through the trees.

I slipped out the door, sliding down the wall next to him.

"Thank you for staying all night." I passed him one of the mugs. He accepted it with a grateful smile.

"Did you get some sleep?" He didn't look at me, just stared out at the yard still dark where the sun hadn't spread its warmth to, yet — the ultimate protector.

"Yes. I think because I knew...you were here. That I was safe." I felt silly saying it and stumbled over the end of my sentence. Would I ever feel safe again, truly? But the light that returned to his bleary, bloodshot eyes at my words was worth it. "Do you have to work today?"

"No, I have the next two days off."

I remembered he had said as much, yesterday. My memory was terrible. A bright red dot appeared between the trees, flooding the sky with orange and pink hues against the deep blue of night holding on for just a few moments longer.

"I love sunrises."

"More than sunsets?" He looked at me over the rim of his mug.

"Better colour," I considered, closing my eyes to absorb everything I could, "and it's quieter. There are too many people awake at sunset. Too much chatter."

"I usually run at sunrise." Cal gave a short laugh, gesturing to his clothes. "Maybe not today, though." He looked at me speculatively. "Not a runner?"

"Nope. I walk everywhere I can. That's my exercise."

"Good enough." He leaned back, closing his eyes. It took less than a minute before his cup tilted in his hands. I'd been watching for it, and grabbed it as liquid slopped against the rim. He must have been awake all night long, as he'd promised.

I bit my lip, contemplating him. His skin appeared even bronzer in the light of the rising sun, but for now, he was more relaxed than I had seen him before. At least he found peace in his sleep. I waited for the sun to fully rise before I nudged him.

"Come on. You can't sleep like that; you'll be horribly sore."

Bleary eyes blinked at me. Cal tucked his legs under himself, trying to stand, and laughed, though it came out painfully.

"Damn. Everything's gone to sleep."

I collected pillows, leading him inside.

"Lounge. Don't get any ideas. I'll be out there." I pointed to the veranda, but Cal held up a hand. "What?"

"Mila," his voice was rough with sleep, and I loved how my name sounded on his lips. "Honey, your paintings, they were pulled out of the cupboard. I stacked a few..."

I raced through the house before he could finish, fumbling the lock on the back door, finally yanking it open. The paintings were outside the cupboard, which usually held my paintings locked up tightly, so mildew wouldn't get in. I hated the smell of paint inside the house.

Flicking through the pile quickly, I noted Cal's on top, then a stack of Teddy in a series of ridiculously serious poses. I counted as I went. But in the end, I didn't need to; I could see which ones were missing.

My coffee rose in my throat, but I swallowed it back down, gasping. I blinked rapidly, my mind stalling as panic speared into me. Now I knew what Cal did — that *he* or one of his people — had ransacked my home.

"Mila. Honey, talk to me." The urgency in Cal's tone washed over me as he crouched on the floorboards. I was on the floor. When had that happened? He reached out, then drew back, looking scared. "What do you need?"

I tried to gasp the words out, but they lodged somewhere around my heart. Finally, Cal settled for rubbing my back in long strokes. "Breathe," he whispered. I nodded, inhaling through my nose, still clutching the pile of canvases with white fingers.

"I did pictures of h-his eyes," I whispered, tears filling my eyes. "It's what I see when I panic, any time I close mine. At night. A therapist suggested it, drawing them. So the image would leave my head. Teddy stayed with me while I did them, and usually, it worked. But they're gone. There were three of them. That means it's him, right? Not just some random person vandalising my house."

I stared straight at him, terrified beyond anything I'd known for so long. *You're safe now. He can't hurt you.* Teddy's words rang hollow in my eyes as my tightly packed, compartmentalised life fell apart in a single moment. I knew the truth of my words, but saying it made it all so much more real, and the tears overflowed.

Then I was back in Cal's arms, safe against the hard chest he put between me and my nightmare. The prior day hit me like a slap, and I pulled back. Pain etched Cal's face. He searched my eyes, but after a moment, he dropped his hands.

"Is he—is he chasing me because you're here? You said you'd been hunting him for years, right?"

Cal scrubbed a hand over his head, and I almost smiled at the familiar gesture. He shrugged, slapping the floorboards with frustration. I jumped a little, and he had the grace to look apologetic.

"Honestly, I don't know. Could it just be some fu— fool that likes your paintings and took them? No, sorry, not that your paintings are bad. I love them, actually." Guilt crossed his face. "Not that I—"

I waved away his apologies. "It's fine, Cal. Honestly."

"Though that picture of Dolly..."

I laughed, hiccupping. "Don't you bring that hamster into this. Blasted animal never sat still!"

Seeing Cal smile made a huge difference to me, like something heavy had been lifted away, the sort of weight you don't know you're bearing until it's gone. Then his smile vanished, replaced with a frown.

"Wait, I forgot to ask you last night. Have you seen a black sedan hanging around your house? A new one that doesn't usually live around here?"

"No," the lines on his face relaxed minutely until I shook my head, "maybe? One followed me home two days ago. I wasn't really paying attention, I was thinking about, um, you..." My face heated. Cal raised an eyebrow, and I rolled my eyes at him. "Something *was* odd; I turned around, and there was a black car idling just behind me. When I noticed them, it took off, swerved madly around the corner — not mine, the one you took yesterday, when you dropped me home. It wasn't my street, so I didn't think– I thought they were just drunk, or something."

Cal's eyes were intent on me — this was him in full work mode, and it was a trifle scary. I hoped I'd said it all right.

"You said 'them' in the car. Did you see more than one person?"

I closed my eyes, imagining the scene with an artist's eye, looking into the interior of the car, recalling the shadows in that momentary glance over my shoulder, and shook my head.

"No, the windows were too dark."

Cal frowned, then nodded. "Even the front one? Okay, what about the number plate? Did you see any of it?"

I began to shake my head, then closed my eyes and watched the scene again. While I'd only glimpsed the front of the car for a moment, the back of the car had been visible for a lot longer.

"Um, B, J...something, something, X...one. I think? Black and white personalised plates. Sorry, I can't see any more."

Cal looked surprised but happy.

"No, that's great! But are you sure? That sort of detail isn't usually easy to pull back to unless someone's invo–" he cut himself short and I hurried to reassure him.

"No, I memorise details really easily. Practice from painting scenes and portraits for so long, I guess." I paused, my gaze narrowing. "Wait, were you about to say that you think I'm involved in this? Is that why you lost it at me last night because you think I work for *him*?"

Cal held his hands up, leaning back as I leapt to my feet.

"Mila, wait. No, that's not what I meant–"

I wasn't listening anymore. My mind cast back to our time at lunch, the questions he'd asked, the odd stare from Marcus. Teddy clearly hadn't told him he was my carer...minder, whatever they called it. My friend. But why not? Cal was his boss, from what Teddy explained last night. And Cal had taken that same turn yesterday as the black car had...

"You knew where I lived," the words came out cold. "You absolute bastard, you checked up on me! And here I was worried about not trusting you, thinking it would be okay. That I was okay with you when you haven't trusted me at all. What a bloody fool I am."

I laughed, but there was no mirth in it.

Cal rose slowly to his feet, hands out. "Mila, I'm sorry. I check everyone who has contact with him, contact with Ashley–" Cal froze the moment the words were out of his mouth, but there was no way for him to take them back. For a brief moment, I wished I could un-hear them — my mind piecing it together automatically. From the panicked look that crossed his face, he'd come to the same conclusion.

"If he was here, he knows about me — then he'll know about her!"

Guilt immediately assuaged me, but I threw it off. I could examine my own ineptitude later. Why hadn't I been more careful? Teddy had gone over the risks with me so many times they were etched into my mind. I reached for my phone, but since I'd changed, it was probably still in my room.

Cal was already on his.

"Jenny? Hi, it's– no, no, everything is fine. Is Ashley up for a visit this morning? I have some time...okay. Jenny, listen, she needs to pack, just for a while, at the very least. Just, don't– ah, don't answer the door to anyone, okay? Wait until I get there. No, it's fine, I'll be there in...oh, twenty minutes?" He ended the call to Ashley's foster mother, and then dialled a new number. One of the boys, from his brief greeting. He walked to the far end of the veranda, speaking softly. It was a quick call, and he came back to me abruptly.

"Get some shoes on. I'll wait in the truck."

"What?"

"Ashley. You're coming with me to get her, right?"

I nodded, speechless, then dashed away for my phone and shoes.

"Mila!" he called after me, and I stopped in my tracks, looking back over my shoulder. "Pack a bag."

CHAPTER ELEVEN

MILA

We were in his truck, halfway down the street, before my brain caught up with me.

"Cal, why did I pack a bag? You said we're going to get Ashley. Won't her new parents be averse to that? Aren't there laws? And why am I here when you obviously haven't trusted me!" the questions tumbled out of me, edged with frustration.

"I need to collect Ashley before Logan gets to her," his voice broke a little, "which I'm confident he will. I'm not keen to put her into witness protection as sometimes, things slip through the cracks. Like you. I can't afford to miss anything else." He gave a sharp laugh that stole my breath, staring straight ahead.

I nodded slowly, still not sure I could see the greater picture, and more questions brimmed, each more confusing than the last. I didn't know what to ask first. My hands trembled in my lap — apparently, the caffeine had kicked in. I smacked his arm with the back of my hand, which stung. Cal didn't so much as grunt. Despite his rational explanation, I was still sore about him questioning my trustworthiness. He sent me an amused look.

"Driving."

"Bugger off," I grumbled.

"Are we even, now?"

I looked over at him, copying his raised eyebrows.

"For what?"

"Smacking me. And before you rant at me, I barely knew you. And I'm *very* protective of Ashley." A muscle in his jaw jumped. "I think of her like a little sister. Maybe a niece, or a daughter."

That stopped me. I looked at him — really looked at him — hands in a death grip on the steering wheel, white showing at his knuckles. Ashley really did mean a lot to him, considering who she was, who she came from.

The odd thing was, I understood. I'd spent years taking Ashley to the park, trying to give her a life, friends. Family. She had been shunted from home to home for a long time. Until recently, she hadn't had a foster family who had invested in her.

Cal sat frozen; jaw clenched, muscles tensed in those carved forearms. Waiting for judgement. He'd screwed up that day at the bank, pretty massively. And he was still trying to rectify that through being there for Logan's daughter.

In a single moment, I understood why he'd lost it with me last night. He loved Ashley, which was a pretty easy thing to do — I did, too. That fast, he was forgiven, but I had no idea how to tell him. I nibbled my bottom lip for a moment, searching for the right thing to say. He looked over when I didn't say anything and puffed out a breath. I smiled into my lap. He wasn't a patient man.

"Cal, I think that's how Teddy sees me. Like a sister."

Cal didn't say anything but nodded after a moment.

"Yeah, he said so last night. I get it; I just wish someone had told me. It hurts to think someone I've worked with didn't trust me with...with this." His fingers squeezed the steering wheel, and he looked at me askance. "Especially Black. We have a...history."

"He was your partner, back at the bank, wasn't he? It's not your fault," I hurried to explain when Cal gave a jerky nod, "I asked him not to tell anyone. No one was to know unless something like last night happened. The officer who set it all up, Neil Jenkins, I think? When he retired, Teddy just slipped the information somewhere else, so your office wouldn't see it. So I was safe." Trees whizzed by as Cal sped up on the highway. We were only a few minutes from Ashley. I began to pray she was okay. "I hope she's okay. Cal, I'm sorry I've caused so much trouble."

Cal reached over, gripping my hand.

"You haven't," he murmured reassuringly, " I just– I wish it had been me that told you everything, explained it to you. Not Black."

I squeezed his fingers and didn't push him away. A small smile played at the corner of his lips. Veering off the highway, Cal took the next exit, taking a shorter route than I'd known to reach Ashley's foster home. When we pulled up, Ashley was in the front window; the curtain pulled back. I waved, and she lit up, disappearing from view.

"She shouldn't be there," Cal growled, not bothering to turn the engine off. "Stay here."

He jumped out before I could squawk at him about giving orders, tapping the hood of the truck as he went by. The door opened, and Jenny's blonde bob peeked out. He had a quick word, and she nodded along with him, arms folded against her chest.

I knew it was a temporary arrangement, but there were tears in the woman's eyes when she hugged Ashley tight, fussing with the backpack already strapped over her shoulders. My heart ached for her, but after last night, there was no point in denying Ashley could be in serious danger. Just because Logan hadn't come for her yet, didn't mean he wouldn't now.

Cal opened the back door, lifting Ashley into the backseat. She cuddled her backpack, a wide grin settling on her face. Once Cal had buckled her in, she extracted a stuffed crocodile, waving it at me excitedly.

"Hi, Mila! I'm so happy to see you! Were you going to come and see me this week? It's been ages! Did you watch Iron Chef last night? They had the 1995 Championship on again. It was sooo funny!" Ashley stopped to draw breath, leaning as far forward as her straps allowed. "I don't think Cal watches it, but we should, together! It would be fun since I'll be staying with you."

She unzipped her backpack again and pulled out a colouring pad. I turned to face Cal as much as I could. He didn't acknowledge me but had the grace to look uncomfortable.

"Cal, what are we doing?"

He looked into the rear-view mirror where Ashley was engrossed with her texters. Lips pressed together; he huffed a little. I grit my teeth, trying not to glare at him, while I waited for his response. Maybe I should have been more aware of what he was asking this morning, but our destination beyond Ashley's house hadn't made it to my list. Finally, my patience burned out.

"Cal..."

"You'll both stay with me– no, wait before you yell. Liam's out of town 'til Wednesday, and I've just had the best security system in the world added to my apartment. It's safe, and it's hidden, completely off the radar. We'll just need to keep her out of my study downstairs."

I frowned, taking it all in. Annoyed as I was, it made sense, sort of. But an apartment with three of us sounded...cosy. I wasn't sure I was ready for that. And Cal's boss wouldn't be back for nearly a week. Were we doing the right thing, dragging Ashley from her home? Maybe he wouldn't find her there. Maybe...

Cal touched my knee. I jolted at the contact, my eyes leaping to his face.

"Hey. It's okay. We're looking after her, and the boys know. They'll take care of it all, and I have the right to relocate a witness in danger. Something more permanent will be sorted, but Jenny–" Cal sighed, the shadows falling over his face. "Let's talk about this bit later, okay?"

He squeezed my knee quickly, pulling his hand back. My leg was cold, without his reassuring warmth. I looked forward, trying to process the situation and slow my heartbeat at the same time. The stupid thing was off like a rocket the moment he came near me. How the hell was I supposed to survive sharing a cramped living space with this sexy cop?

My hormones were already in overdrive, reminding me of my teen years. Only, I'd never been kissed by a man anything like him, back then.

Then his comment about Jenny hit through my hormone-induced haze. Ashley wasn't likely to go back. I knew she'd had readjustment issues, but Jenny really did love her. If Ashley were taken away, it would break her heart. Yet another relocation, somewhere very hidden. Cal would probably change her name, too.

Did that mean I wouldn't be able to see her either? My eyes stung. I traced patterns on my jeans, blinking. Everything was so out of control, and I had no idea who was holding the strings.

Cal pulled into a driveway that dipped beneath a very nondescript building, not much different from the rest of the street, which held a distinct industrial flavour. He swiped a card halfway along, and a heavy, metal gate painted black retracted sideways. The drive was deep, but it looked low, and I hoped we'd fit, his truck was so big. The place looked like a prison. I swallowed, wondering what I'd gotten myself into.

"It looks like Fort Knox," I murmured, as the gate closed behind us.

"It's secure."

We wound down, through several levels of parking. Cal slid the truck into a reserved spot without a number. I turned to make some inane comment to Ashley, but she was fast asleep. Cal grinned.

"She loves my truck. Says it sounds like a monster, bigger than all the others." His smile dimmed for a moment. "I was going to take her for a ride in Micah's monster truck, but I was a bit worried she wouldn't like this old girl so much afterwards."

It's always about size.

I opened my mouth to tell him he needn't worry; it was him that made her feel safe, not the truck, but he was already gone, slipping out the door as quietly as he had last night. He untangled Ashley from her car seat buckles, hoisting her gently onto his shoulder. I realised this wasn't the first time he'd had to carry her asleep and vulnerable, and I was glad she had him to look after her, like a favourite uncle.

I collected her things and my bag, slipping the stuffed crocodile on top of it all, and followed Cal to a lift. He used a key to access his floor, different from the toggle he'd swiped to open the gate to the garage. This place had so many layers of security, and we weren't even in his apartment yet.

The lift opened silently to a floor with only three doors. Cal headed to the middle one, opening it with yet another card. Just inside the doorway, he pressed his thumb to a glowing pad positioned halfway up the wall. It beeped softly and went dark. A short, narrow corridor opened out into a wide lounge, corridors, and rooms spearing off in different directions. His apartment must take up half the width of one of the floors, I realised. I wondered who his

neighbours were and what they would think of two
additional occupants.

Cal took Ashley down a hallway and into a room. I
followed, holding out the stuffed animal as he reappeared.
He placed it next to Ashley, who was quite happily asleep on
a bed with a blue cover.

I bit my lip at the thought of where I would sleep,
trying to check rooms as I returned to the lounge. I found a
toilet and bathroom, but no extra bed. The apartment was
huge, a maze of twisting corridors branching off from a
central kitchen and living area.

Standing in the middle of the lounge, I felt lost. Cal
grinned, and grabbed my hand, towing me down yet another
hallway to a pair of rooms at the end.

"My study." He pointed to the door on my right.
"Please, do NOT go in there. I'll have to uh, clean it up,
today." He pointed to the other room, motioning me in.
"You'll sleep here."

He flicked on a light, illuminating what was clearly a
man's room. Everything was dark, with simple lines. The
coverlet was black, matching a pair of bedside tables the
same colour. The bed was king-sized, though a man his
height would require something that large. I looked at it
nervously.

"I'll sleep on the lounge," Cal murmured the words
softly, his lips brushing my ear. I jumped as his arm slid

around my waist, pulling me back against him for a moment. My hands slid up, over those forearms I loved so much, holding on. I closed my eyes, letting go of everything. Cal placed my bag onto the floor, his lips grazing my cheek fleetingly. Then he let me go and left.

I leaned against the wall, wondering what had just happened, and how I would survive the week living with him.

When I returned to the living area, Cal was chopping vegetables in the kitchen. The smell of coffee hit me hard, and I tried not to race over to the counter where two steaming mugs stood on a black, stone bench.

"Mine?" I asked, pointing to one of the mugs. Cal nodded in confirmation.

"Yours."

I slipped my hands around the mug, grateful for its warmth. Black and strong, but I needed that right now. Frankly, in an emergency, I'd take coffee any way it came. I wandered around the wide breakfast bar that doubled as kitchen space, watching him work.

"You cook?"

That pleased me to no end — I loved cooking. It was just hard to be bothered when you had no one to cook for. Maybe this week had at least one more perk — though I hadn't yet decided if being in proximity with Cal was a perk, or not. Surprises I didn't like kept popping up with him. I wasn't looking forward to discovering what the next one might be.

"Ashley said you like Iron Chef," Cal murmured, not looking at me.

"We love it. Watch reruns together on YouTube when I take her to the park. She watched it the night before. They're just old episodes, but they're fun." I was a little defensive; it was a quirky TV show, but something we enjoyed doing together.

"I know."

"What?" I was saying that a lot recently.

Cal tilted his head, looking sideways at me. "I've watched it since I was eight. Dad–" he swallowed, "Dad used to put it on after we'd gone fishing. My favourite was the Sea Cucumber. Chen Kenichi made sea cucumber–"

"Ice cream!" I finished for him, laughing and grimacing at the same time. He grinned. "I loved that one, too."

I settled on a bar stool on the other side of the bench, content to watch him. Not only was I out of practice, but I also didn't want to intrude on his peace. There would be plenty of time to pay back the lunch from yesterday. That had been yesterday. I closed my eyes, suddenly exhausted, then realised Cal must be running on empty. He'd had next to no sleep in the last day.

I was about to suggest he take a nap while Ashley was sleeping when he slid a plate filled with a Mediterranean vegetable salad across the counter. I nearly squealed, salivating at the sight. Cal slid onto the stool next to me, digging into his own bowl.

"Sorry, I only have one or two of everything. I'll have to get groceries. Maybe the boys can bring some up."

"Please don't apologise, Cal. We're invading your home as it is. Thank you." I stopped, not knowing what to say. He had opened his home to not only a girl he used to date — was dating? — but to a small girl, who was regularly displaced. That brought new tears to the surface.

The thought of Jenny losing her daughter broke my heart. I blinked away the tears, suddenly angry it had come to this. All because of *him*. Again.

"It's okay; I'll go home and grab some things. I have boxes stored under the house–"

"You can't go home, Mila." Cal's voice was low, and a touch of pity flashed across his face. I stared at him, my mouth hanging open.

"Why ever not?"

Cal sighed, placing his fork carefully on the benchtop.

"He knows where you live, sweetheart. If you'd been there last night...hell, I don't want to think about it."

"I–I thought I was just here because, you know, I was a female and you needed one around a little girl, for safety and transparency..." I trailed off as his face tightened.

The idea I couldn't go home hit me hard. Ashley and I were homeless, with a madman chasing us. I grabbed my cup and drained it, wishing it held something far stronger. My mug emptied too quickly. Cal passed me his.

"Drink it; it's yours." He yawned, reloading his fork. "I need to get some sleep. If the guys come by, buzz them up," he pointed to a grey box on the kitchen wall. "I'll message Black, ask him to get some extra things for you two."

He finished his plate with efficiency and began to wash up. I leaned over the counter, tapping his arm.

"Don't. I'll do it as soon as I'm finished." I gestured at my still-full plate. The enormity of what Cal was doing struck me in full. The least I could do was to try to make as little impact on his life as possible, while we invaded his home.

He nodded, grabbing a blanket from the back of a recliner that faced the TV, heading for the sofa. I stopped him again, waving at his bedroom. He raised an eyebrow. I wished for a moment I could wipe the thing off his face.

"Go on, Cal, it's your house. Apartment, whatever. Get some rest."

I turned back to my food, ready to eat with gusto once he left the room. I was starving. I jumped again when his hand landed on my hip.

"Would you stop doing that!" I twisted around. He gave a cheeky grin that spread warmth through me. He squeezed my hip, which elicited a completely different reaction.

"Thanks, Mila."

He said the words softly behind me, dropping a kiss into my hair. When I turned around, he was already halfway up the hall.

CHAPTER TWELVE

CAL

My lounge was awash with testosterone and glitter when I emerged from my bedroom. Ashley's backpack must have contained gallons of the pink and purple stuff. It hung in the air like a unicorn had hosted a frat party while I was asleep.

Danny sat cross-legged on the floor while Ashley tied tiny bows in his short hair. It stuck up at all angles, like an over-pampered dog in an animal primp parlour. Mila passed him a refilled bottle of water, wandering across the living room to where Micah and Black had parked themselves in a pair of my recliners.

Black snagged Mila around the waist, pulling her onto his knee. She slung an arm around his shoulder, tipping her head back to laugh at something Micah was saying. The easy movement reeked of familiarity.

The green monster in my chest awoke with a vengeance, roaring his disapproval. Black spotted me over Mila's shoulder, eyeing me with caution as he continued his conversation. His hand closed around her waist, and a growl rose in my throat. The grin that grew across his face told me he was taking the piss, and my monster retreated a little.

Mila leaned forward, slapping a high five with Micah. I decided enough was enough. The boys should definitely *not* have their hands all over my girl. I was halfway across the room when Ashley stopped me, attempting to drag Danny across the room, and failing wonderfully.

"Cal, Cal, look!! Doesn't he look *sooo* pretty?"

Danny grinned, reclining on a stack of pillows while Ashley jumped on his shoulders, trying to reach me. I couldn't not smile at the madness that filled my house and gave Ashley's pigtails a playful tug.

"You've done a great job, kid."

Ashley beamed with pride. I gave her a quick hug, eager to reach Mila. Conversation ceased as I approached, three sets of eyes watching me with varying degrees of wariness. It gave me pause, realising I was far too close to letting the monster break the surface.

I forced a smile, and Micah turned back to Theo, making some snide comment. Black smirked and shifted Mila, so she straddled his leg. She swatted at him, leaning forward with the ghost of a smile, enthralled in whatever anecdote Micah was regaling them with.

It hurt that she didn't seem to notice my pain. Having someone else's hands on my girl set off an ache deep inside me. But was she my girl? There were still the same sparks, the same tension between us there had been since that first day, only a week ago. So much had happened, I wasn't sure of my place with her — or if I even had one, beyond the bond we shared with Ashley.

I leaned over, liberating the mug from her hands. She looked up at me with wide eyes that narrowed when she saw me drain the mug. The asshole in me was back, grinning at her irritation.

She slipped off Black's knee, yanked the mug from my hands, and stalked to the kitchen, ostensibly to refill it.

"You don't have to be an asshole all the time, you know." Black stood beside me, watching Mila. He turned hard eyes on me. "You could have something special with that woman if you let it happen."

I scraped one hand over my scalp, shaking my head.

"I think that boat has sailed, man. I want her, but she shies away..."

"Are you surprised?"

I shook my head sadly. "No."

"She's open to it."

"You think?"

Black considered, head cocked. As if sensing our attention on her, Mila paused mid-pour with the kettle in hand, and very slowly, looked up. She was still, for a moment. Then, with the faintest smile curving her lips, she returned to making herself a fresh cup of coffee.

"She won't run."

A hand nudged me. Mila proffered a steaming mug to each of us, and I took mine uncertainly.

"It's yours if you like?" I held it back out to her, but she shook her head with that same, enigmatic smile, and stayed put beside me.

The monster in my chest subsided, a warmth spreading through me.

The day was almost over when Black took me aside, an open beer from my fridge in each hand. I eyed them suspiciously; Black had never been a big drinker.

"Tell me."

"Logan was sighted in the city...we think." He held up a hand to stop me from interrupting. "It was a partial match. Thought it might be the brother. I doubt Logan will show his ugly mug until he intends us to see it."

I nodded; Black was right. Logan screwed with your head, that's just how the bastard worked. I knew that as well as any of us.

I looked across to Mila. He'd been in her head for that long, too, and she was coping well, considering her situation. Ashley played quietly on her lap, pushing pieces of a puzzle around as she lounged back onto the most gorgeous woman I'd ever seen. Mila stroked her hair, shadows darkening beneath her eyes. Ashley's too; they both needed rest after the last twenty-four hours. Which I would see they got.

But first, I needed to know where we were at.

"You think he's a decoy or a scout? Does everyone know?" I fired questions off. Black nodded at all, bar the last one.

"Yes. Possibly, and no, not yet. We all came in Micah's truck, so I'll brief them on the way home. It's a safe space, at least."

"Yeah, let's not get our asses handed to us like last time."

Only two years ago, we'd been so close to catching Logan I could almost smell his fear. But he'd escaped again. It took us six months to figure out why a set-up we'd spent weeks on had failed; the bastard had bugged us. It was the first time I'd realised there might be an insider amongst us.

I'd never been able to figure out how Logan had accessed our office, my paranoia developing like a canker in my brain. The bastard truly knew how to mind-fuck his victims. Which I refused to be.

Black, Liam and I had kept it mostly between us; the rationale being the fewer people that knew, the better off we were. It had been Logan's little brother, Joey, who had been sighted early on then, too. This had the same off feeling as last time, and with the girls so closely involved, I was keen to get this thing finally put to bed.

Until I spoke to Liam, the state's safe houses weren't an option. My apartment was as secure a building as any — if not more, with the added security measures — plus, I could be there around the clock.

"Keep an eye on everything outside; I'll drop into the office tomorrow, then I need a favour." My gaze connected with his, and I hoped to god this was going to work.

Black listened while I outlined my plan, a cheeky grin growing over his face. He slapped my shoulder, giving it a decent squeeze. I refused to wince, and his grin grew wider.

"Welcome back, brother."

MILA

The boys left us with a huge amount of food and kitchen items enough for a small army. Which, I supposed, they were. Ashley kicked tiredly, half dangling over my legs, pushing puzzle pieces around on Cal's carpet. There were so many sparkles embedded in it that a carnival could have camped here overnight. We waved the boys away with tired goodbyes from the floor, Danny and Micah trundling eskys along the slim corridor to the elevator.

Teddy hung back, talking to Cal outside on the balcony that overlooked the river. Small tugs and pilot boats constantly trundled along the shipping lane, bringing the bigger ships into the port to unload. It was nice to have something to look at.

I'd quickly realised we were on the top floor of Cal's apartment block. Black re-entered the room, clasping Cal's arm. I was relieved to see the rift between them healing. A rift I'd caused.

Teddy headed straight for Ashley and I. He gave the tiny girl a hug, leaning down to kiss my forehead. I wrapped my arms around his shoulders as far as they could reach, my hands not quite meeting on either side of his back. He tucked his head into my shoulder.

"Let him look after you." He drew back, and I read concern in his face. "You're safe with him, Mila. He needs someone like you. You don't have to be alone."

I resembled a guppy as he followed the boys out the door, Cal calling after him to have the alarm checked. He secured the apartment as they disappeared into the lift, their ribald comments disappearing with them.

"What's wrong with the alarm?" I asked, hoping the nerves that writhed in my stomach wouldn't show in my voice. After all, wasn't that why we were here, because of some fancy alarm? Though the rest of his building was so well secured, I doubted we could get out, let alone someone else get in.

It occurred to me I didn't know where the front door of the building was, or if there even was one, as we'd entered through the internal door connected to the garage where Cal's truck resided. I said as much, and Cal laughed at me. I shushed him quickly, pointing to Ashley who had fallen asleep beside me. He smiled down at her, and I was amazed at the peace in his face. Not a single shadow remained, and my golden god-man was back.

He covered her with an oversized knitted rug. Straightening, he offered me his hand. I eyed it warily, Teddy's words swirling in my head. I let Cal draw me off the floor, and with a gentle tug, he pulled me right into him. His fingers brushed over my hair, sending goosebumps down my arms.

"Glitter," he murmured, stepping back to inspect the rest of me. "Actually, you're covered in it."

I was. Glitter was stuck to my jeans, coating my arms and sweater.

"Just getting my unicorn on."

He motioned with his hand in a circling pattern.

"Turn around." I did, feeling ridiculous. "Ah, why don't you change those? Your jeans I mean." His gaze travelled the length of me as I turned back to face him, my cheeks heating. "Let's not get your unicorn all over my building."

I changed into a pair of pink cotton yoga pants, washing away my sparkle in his en-suite. Cal passed me a fresh mug of coffee and led me down to the ground floor, explaining which buttons to press and gave me the access code that led to the foyer. It was good to know I could get Ashley out of the building if I needed to.

Cal opened the foyer door. I expected to see a reception desk or a doorman, but it opened into a bare, carpeted space with a neat row of locked mailboxes set flush against the far wall.

The rest of the walls — and the door, I presumed, though I couldn't tell which was which — were glassed, but so heavily tinted I doubted anyone would be able to see in from the outside.

Cal motioned to the wall to our left.

"The centre one is the door." He held out a small ring of keys. "Use this plastic card to get in and out of the building, if you have to but–" he hesitated, jaw tensing, "I'd really prefer you didn't, especially not with Ashley. Not until this whole thing blows over. I know that's a pretty big ask."

His eyes shifted back to me, questioning. I smiled, squeezing his arm. He was still sexy as hell. Despite the gorgeously distracting man standing before me, doubt bloomed deep inside me, and I knew I wasn't doing a very good job of hiding it.

Cal had been hunting Logan for five years — and had never caught him. Just how long would it be before I could go home? I knew the boys were working as hard as they could — the afternoon spent settling Ashley and me in before they put in a night's work showed their dedication — it wasn't fair to ask them for more.

"It's okay; I get it. I kinda figured we would be stuck here until...well." I stopped, not sure what to say.

If I couldn't go home, where would I go? Would Cal expect me to stay with him? I wasn't sure how I felt about that and if we were in the apartment alone, with no excuse...I looked up at him and saw the moment he came to the same conclusion as I had.

"It's okay, I'll find somewhere–"

"I won't expect anything of you; you're safe to stay–"

We both babbled at each other, breaking off into a loaded silence. Cal cleared his throat, jingling the key ring.

"This tiny key is the letterbox — number twenty-six. Why don't you check if there's mail?" he offered, picking up the conversation where we had left off. I nodded, sorting through the ring of keys and cards. I got the right one the first time and opened the box.

At first, I thought there was nothing inside; then I saw a black envelope sitting dully in the bottom. It took a few tries to flick it out, and I studied it while I closed the lid, making sure it clicked.

It was heavy paper, almost card, with a luxe look to it. The other side was addressed to Cal in gold, curly letters, with no postage stamp. This had been hand-delivered. The writing was open and elegant, done by hand. *A woman's*, I thought.

I flipped the envelope over, but there was nothing on the back, no return address. I didn't like the idea of another woman inviting him to something — a party, or...I wasn't sure what and didn't have the right to tell him what to do. I really had no idea where we stood. It wasn't as easy and clear anymore.

My world had changed so much in the space of twenty-four hours. Homeless, with a child that wasn't mine, living with an incredibly hot man I wasn't with, who set me on edge just by looking at me...I was in so much trouble.

I walked back to Cal quickly, talking too loudly to cover my nerves.

"I think you got something, and no, I promise Ashley and I won't go out without you, it's no problem at all–"

"Shh!"

"What?"

I'd been rambling, but shushing me was just rude. I looked up, annoyed, but Cal was staring over my head. Tendons stood out in the line of his neck, and his arm came around me quickly, steering me away from the foyer door.

"I thought I saw that black c–" He turned to face me and cursed. I tried to smile, cover the fear that set my heart racing, but I'd never been good at it.

The keys were whisked out of my hand while I tried to crane around Cal's bulk, and the elevator doors closed before I could spot anything unusual.

"I just want to get back to Ashley," his voice was soft, but tension radiated from him. I found his hand, and he gripped mine painfully tight. He swiped the card, and I thought back — had he locked the door when we left? I knew the alarm was playing up... but for the life of me, I couldn't remember Cal locking the door.

CHAPTER THIRTEEN

MILA

I didn't want to alarm Cal further than he already was, but the elevator ride up a short seven stories to the top floor was the longest of my life. The doors began to slide open, but Cal was through them in a flash, sprinting down the corridor to his apartment.

I raced after him, watching him open the door without the key — it hadn't been locked after all — and I nearly screamed. How could we have left Ashley so unprotected? I shot through the door, hissing her name — unable to make a greater sound.

Arms wrapped around me as I barrelled from the hall, pulling me into a hard, broad chest. *Cal.* He turned me, making a shushing gesture. I nodded as he aimed me at Ashley, still curled exactly where we had left her on the sofa.

He squeezed my arm, and I heard him retracing our steps to the door, locking it, the beep of the alarm as he set it. It beeped a few extra times, and he swore, thumping the wall.

"Bloody alarm," he growled, pacing each of the hallways, opening every room. I stayed with Ashley until he returned to the lounge, jaw tense. I wanted to ask him more, but hesitated, not wanting to frighten Ashley if she woke up.

"Do you want to bring her to her room," I murmured, "and I'll get her bed ready? She doesn't need to be woken up right now. She can have some dinner if she needs it later on. It was a huge day for her — for all of us."

Cal looked like he might object, but nodded, looking down at the tiny figure curled on his sofa. He cradled the tiny child against his chest and carried her to her room. I slipped past him to turn back her covers and made sure she had her crocodile.

I closed the door gently, leaving it only the slightest bit ajar, and followed the lights back to the lounge. The shipping lane was aglow against the evening sky, flashes reflecting off the water. Cal stared out of the window, his back to me. I didn't want to break into his thoughts, but he turned, arms open, and I stepped straight into them without hesitation.

He crushed me against his chest, his hand cupping the back of my head, fingers sliding through my hair. I clung to him just as tightly. A tremor started in my hands, running over my body. I tried to breathe.

"I thought we lost her," Cal murmured into my hair, then held me back, eyes darkened with concern as he looked into my face. I nodded, smoothing my hair back with shaking hands. *Breathe.* I stared at the floor, still collecting myself. Cal shuffled his feet. "I'm sorry I scared you before."

I raised my head, finding him closer than I had expected. Tingles began in my fingers, running to my toes. I shifted against him, to retreat so I could work out what was going on. I couldn't think with him so close. Cal's next words stopped me completely.

"I thought I saw that black sedan again."

"But...I thought this was a safe place."

Cal nodded, a muscle in his jaw ticking.

"It is. You are. I think it was just a car. I'm getting paranoid about it." He stroked my back in lazy circles, his gaze darkening.

I narrowed my eyes, studying his. Deep brown, shot through with honey yellow made them almost translucent, something I could lose myself in. But I refused to be distracted, this time.

"Are you sure? If you think he knows..."

Cal shook his head, smiling, but his eyes were dull. Lines criss-crossed his face beneath the lights.

"I don't." His voice was firm, and I wanted to believe his lie. I nodded again, gesturing to the kitchen for something to do.

"Should we...should we cook something? For dinner." It sounded pathetic, but Cal nodded vigorously.

"Yes."

He launched into the kitchen, mucking around in the cupboards. I opened the fridge, relieved to see a range of fresh vegetables and foods.

"Something Chinese? Mexican? Do you like chilli?"

I nodded to everything, then paused.

"Something Ashley might like? More than just the sandwiches I get us at the park."

Cal looked guilty.

"I, uh, usually take her out for chocolate." The last part came out as a mumble, but it brought a smile to my face as I made the connection.

"Is that why you took me to the chocolatier?"

"Yeah. It's got some good memories. I–" He broke off as a bag of pasta burst open in his hands.

Tiny spirals exploded into the air, bouncing off cupboard doors, skipping across the tiles. He crouched down, scrambling for ones on the rebound. I grabbed the container he'd completely missed. Pasta pinged into the plastic, filling it quickly. A few had skittered into an open cupboard filled with cups and glasses, even a plastic one for Ashley. I took note of its location for later.

"So, pasta?" Cal sent me a lopsided grin, but it was only half there. He was still tired, despite the rest he'd had earlier, it seemed. Worrying about Ashley had put more responsibility on his shoulders yet again — I couldn't help but wonder if he was taking on too much.

I turned back to the fridge, extracting a block of cheese and fresh asparagus I'd spotted before. Mushrooms were hidden in the bottom of the crisper drawer, and a bottle of semi-sundried tomatoes was a great find. Cal eyed my collection.

"Vegetarian?"

"No...I was just thinking healthily."

"Good."

Cal retrieved some bacon and chicken pieces from the depths of the fridge. Soon, the kitchen smelled amazing.

I located plates and cutlery, trying to remember where everything came from.

"Where are we eating?"

"Let's use the table outside. It's a bit dark, but we won't wake Ashley talking out there."

I slid the door open, setting the table, thinking back to the last time I had done it. It must have been before Gran was in the hospital for a broken hip she never recovered from. Pneumonia had crept into her lungs while she was on bed rest, and I'd never been able to bring her home. Now, it was me who couldn't go home.

Cal placed two steaming bowls on the table. I made the mistake of looking at him, as he caught on to my upset right away.

"Mila...?" he left the question hanging, and I shrugged it away, unwilling to dive into my own heart tonight. But, I didn't want to appear ungrateful.

"Thank you for looking after us."

I sat down with my back to the view, so I could see Ashley if she woke. The light was bright, and I blinked a few times, getting used to it. Cal stared at me for a moment, then reached back, flicking a switch, so the internal light went off.

I smiled my thanks, but he waved it away.

"It's okay, honey. Just eat, so I know you've had something."

It didn't take long before both our plates were empty. Cal took them inside before I could object. Turning my chair, I stared out over the black river. It was quiet, and salt hung in the still air.

A full glass of wine clinked on the table in front of me. He sat beside me, a beer in his hand. He leaned back, closing his eyes. I watched a small tug boat bring in a container ship so large it looked too big for the river. The tiny tug released its burden, and headed back up the river, ready to pilot the next ship in.

"I know it must be very...different with us here. Disturbing your normal routine. I'm sorry."

"Honestly, I like it."

I looked at him in surprise.

"You like your impeccable, luxury bachelor pad covered in glitter?"

"I like it filled with people, laughter. It makes it more like a home, rather than just somewhere I usually sleep." He gave me a lopsided grin that did nothing to hide the sadness reflected in his eyes.

"I thought we might be taking up your space."

Cal shook his head, reaching a long arm around me in a quick hug.

"You'll never feel like you're taking up my space. It's better with you in it."

I leaned back against his arm where he'd left it, nursing my wine. My eyes began to close, and I yawned, the weight of the last day hitting me hard. I lifted my glass to finish it but found it empty. When had that happened? I rose to my feet, only a little unsteady.

"I should go to bed."

The moment the words were out of my mouth, I wish I could take them back — even to me, they sounded like an invitation. Cal watched me from hooded eyes.

"I'll be out here, or in the study across the hall from your room if you need me. I have to clean it up."

It was a relief he hadn't jumped on my comment. Really must work on this trust thing.

"Goodnight."

Cal's eyes were fathomless, sending a shiver through me.

"Goodnight, Mila."

I slipped back inside his apartment and into my — his — room. I closed the door and leaned against it. If I'd stayed another moment with him, I would have been on his lap. I wanted to blame the wine but knew that wasn't it. Breathing deeply was a mistake; the entire room smelled of him.

I closed my eyes, going back to the moment he'd scared me. He'd been protecting Ashley, tiny and defenseless, caught in the middle of something she couldn't control. I was okay with that.

It meant he'd do the same for me.

I changed into a pair of cotton shorts and a lace bralette that stopped at my ribs. I started at the inappropriateness of my pyjamas, wondering if I should sleep in my yoga pants, instead. I discarded the idea — Cal wouldn't be seeing me dressed like this.

I fell into Cal's bed, exhausted. It was a mistake. His scent surrounded me, no matter where I lay. I rolled over, trying to settle in the strange bed, part of me wishing I'd asked him to stay with me.

A light flicked on in the hall, opposite his room. I remembered his comment about cleaning his study and drifted into oblivion with the knowledge he was only a room away.

At some ridiculous hour after midnight, I woke with my tongue stuck to the roof of my mouth. I'd forgotten to get a bottle of water before I went to sleep, and lay awake, trying to work out if I could survive the night without going to get one.

It was far too long before the sun came up, and after a few unsuccessful attempts to swallow, I gave up, opening the bedroom door cautiously. The light in Cal's study across the hall was off. He must have gone to sleep.

I slipped into the kitchen, kneeling down to open the cupboard the cups were in, but I was wrong. Oh, so wrong. A simple search for a cup became a quest, and soon I was sprawled on the floor, arms reaching into the depths of the cupboard where I was certain I'd spotted the stupid things the evening before.

"Having fun?"

Cal's amused voice hit me, and I scrambled to my knees.

"I was just looking for a glass..."

Warm hands circling my waist, he lifted me onto the kitchen bench, stepping between my knees before I thought about what he was doing. I could barely see him, but brushed against hot, bare flesh, and realized he was shirtless.

"Cal!" I hissed, terrified Ashley would wake up and find us in a compromising position, "What are you doing?" I smelled the beer on him. "Are you drunk?"

He silenced me with his fingers across my lips. He brushed them lightly back and forth until the skin was a mass of sensitive nerves, then he pressed his fingers between my lips, into my mouth. My hand curled around his wrist, and he stilled but didn't remove his fingers. Just...waited. I squeezed his wrist, not able to get my whole hand around it, as he began to stroke his fingers into my mouth in a steady rhythm.

My eyes widened in the dark, trying to see his face, but the slow movement of his fingers sliding between my lips was the most erotic thing I'd ever experienced. It took all my effort for my hips not to match his pace. I let my tongue flick the tips of his fingers as they withdrew from my lips. He rewarded me with a low growl, pressing them back in the same, steady pace.

His gaze dragged over me, perched on his kitchen bench, half-clothed. I shivered, and he pulled me closer, heat radiating from his chest. My hand landed on the hard ridges of muscle around his torso, and I desperately wanted to see him in the light. I let my hands explore, memorising the feel of him.

Cal's other arm snaked out, sliding around to scoot me forward until I was flush against him. My legs wrapped around his hips, the soft cotton grazing sensitive flesh. I could feel every defined inch of him in his sweats as he pressed against me with the same rhythm as his fingers.

A whimper built in me. I breathed hard through my nose, but it wasn't enough to hold back, he was hitting all the right places. I tugged at his wrist, and a predatory look on the little I could see of his face told me he *knew*. A shiver started deep inside me. He pulled me closer, harder, and that's all it took.

His fingers slipped from between my lips as I gasped, whimpering. He lifted me off the benchtop, arms tight around me. I clung to him, needing to feel him wrapped around me. My head dropped to his bare shoulder, my lips brushing his skin. I tasted salt as he carried me through his apartment, laying me gently on his bed.

I could barely sit up, tremors still shuddering through me. He knelt beside the bed, drawing me close to the edge, staring right into my eyes.

"Gorgeous," he whispered, stroking hair back from my cheek.

Cal dipped his head, his lips covering mine in a deep kiss that set every inch of me on fire. I shifted, pulling him down to me, but he caught my wrists, encompassing them completely. He pressed my hands down onto my pillow —

his pillow — and I whimpered in protest. I *needed* to touch him.

"Goodnight, Mila," he murmured, releasing my hands to brush his fingers over my lips, and walked out of the room, closing the door softly behind him.

I lay in his bed, surrounded by the scent of him — who was I kidding, his scent was all over me — and wondered how in the hell he'd just given me the most powerful orgasm I'd ever experienced.

CHAPTER FOURTEEN

CAL

I had breakfast made for the girls when they emerged from their respective rooms. Ashley was still in the clothes she'd worn the day before. Mila, mercifully, had changed into jeans and a blue top. It dipped at the neckline, but not dangerously.

Thank god it was nothing like what she'd worn last night when I'd found her face down on the kitchen floor. Keeping my hands off her in those skimpy shorts that stopped at the top of her thighs had been too much to resist. Then I'd pushed the line with her, again.

No. This time, I'd crossed way over it.

I placed a mug full of coffee in front of her. She murmured a quiet thanks, hoisting herself onto a bar stool. Mila played with the handle, turning the cup in small circles, refusing to meet my eyes. My hand covered the top of the mug, and she stopped, looking up in surprise.

"Mila," I started, then had no idea what to say. She held my gaze, and I was pleased not to see fear or rejection there. I smiled, lifting my hand. She snatched the hostage back, peering at me over the rim as she took a long sip.

"I have to go into the office, try to sort some of this mess out. I should be back around five, and I'll get takeaway for dinner, so you don't have to look after everyone, all day." She made noises of protest, but I waved them away. "No buts. Tomorrow, the boys are going to come around to babysit. Micah's bringing his girl as a 'female presence'," I used her words from the day before, "and I'm going to take you somewhere."

Mila looked across the breakfast bar at me, surprised.

"Where are we going?"

I winked, hugging Ashley who had attached herself to me like a limpet. "Just something we need to do together. Danny and Micah will be here to watch you, okay, and I think you'll like Gina," I spoke to a pair of pigtails that tickled my chin.

"Okay, Cal. Can I do Micah's hair this time? It's so silky."

I snorted, but the kid was right. Micah spent more time and products on his locks than any decent man should. Then I remembered that Danny had punched me, and decided to throw him under the bus instead.

"Why don't you do Danny's nails, first? I'm sure he'd love a bright selection." A smothered laugh-turned-cough caught my attention. I raised my eyebrows, pretending innocence. "What?"

Mila waved me away, spluttering into her coffee. I grinned, slipping Ashley off my lap. She found a spot in the middle of the lounge and began to set up more ponies than could possibly fit in a regular-sized backpack. I waved at her.

"I swear she's got a bag like Mary Poppins."

"I'm impressed you know who that is."

"Is that all it took? I had a childhood, you know." I placed a set of keys in front of her, spinning the bar stool with my foot, so she faced me. "They're for an emergency. Oh, Steph's boyfriend should come by this morning, I think, to fix the alarm. Just buzz him in — I showed you how to do that yesterday, for the boys? He'll fix whatever he needs to, but you'll be fine with him. Okay?"

She nodded, but my stomach clenched. It took me a moment to recognise fear — that I wouldn't be there if she — either of them — needed me. If I didn't absolutely have to go into work, I wouldn't, but I needed everyone in one place while we sorted our strategy out. Logan's game was changing, and we had to get ahead of him. I didn't want to do that in front of the girls.

Mila wasn't the only one afraid. The more I cared for her, and of course, I already doted on Ashley, the more I had to lose if I screwed up this case. It was time to put it to bed.

Fear wasn't something I came across in myself very often, and it was unsettling to realise there were so many factors out of my control. I took a deep breath.

"Mila, please, stay up here, stay inside. Please don't take her out onto the balcony. The glass is reflective, and tinted so that no one can see inside during the day — even with the lights on."

Mila nodded again. I squeezed her arm and left before I did something inappropriate, stepping over pillow paddocks and purple ponies grazing on a carpet of glitter.

By the time I got into my truck, my chest clenched again, scenarios of finding the place empty when I got home tearing through my mind. I wanted to slap myself, to not go into the office, to stay at the apartment and play ponies on the carpet with Ashley — to just spend time with her and Mila. But before I gave in to any luxuries, I needed to work out Logan's game.

I searched for the tell-tale black sedan as I left my apartment, but it wasn't around. I drove in circles around the surrounding blocks, then conceded I was a paranoid fool.

The boys were heads down, tails in the air when I walked in. Danny sent me a cheeky grin, and I sighed, wondering how long it had taken him to hook up with Mandy. At least she was his problem, now, not mine. Providing she didn't spin any more shit to him or cause drama with the rest of my team. What she did in her own social time, I really didn't care, so long as she was far away from me.

Steph hung over the divide, chattering at everyone, though no one was listening. They were all too bloody busy to be gasbagging like a pack of old wives. A sharp look sent her scuttling back into the reception area.

I stood in the centre of the room, trying to get the cogs turning to figure out what Logan was going to do next. I didn't know where he'd been last, and it was frustrating — every day, he was several steps ahead while we fell further and further behind.

He'd broken into Mila's house, of that, I had no doubt. Ransacking it though — destroying her personal items — that was something new. Taking the sketches she'd drawn of his eyes, wasn't; it fit the egotistical bastard's profile perfectly. He'd be grandstanding, thinking she was obsessing over him. My stomach clenched. I shook my head to clear it.

Think, Dane.

He'd found her, but how? After all this time, the only thing that had changed was that she'd met me, but did that mean he had tabs on me? I doubted it; maybe the timing was a coincidence, but I was sure there was something I was missing. Her car repairs? No, I knew those guys as well — part of Micah's monster truck crew, they worked on the blue giant he drove around town, though the damned thing was barely road legal. They were good guys; rough, but good-hearted — just a little extreme with their hobbies.

It wasn't that. Think. *Think.* There was a connection somewhere.

The black sedan was his too; I guessed they'd been scouting for Mila's house when they came across her as an easy target. The question was, why hadn't they grabbed her then? They'd found me the night before — perhaps that was it — someone, maybe the brother, Joey, that Black thought had been spotted had seen us on our walk.

They were rambling coincidences, and I still didn't like it. The off feeling was growing. I'd spent hours staring at the pictures of Logan; filtering through data, basically throwing pins at the map and hoping my guesses were accurate because that's all we had right now. Liam would be

back in a few days, and I wanted to have a few decent leads
to work forward with.

Now that Mila and Ashley were involved; finding
Logan was becoming a time-critical venture. The girls
couldn't live with me forever — what we were doing wasn't
technically above board. It tugged at my heart to think of the
big space empty, except for me and my obsession. No glitter
in the carpet, no Mila in my bed. *Damn it.* I growled,
yanking back my chair.

Get it together and think with your brain.

Someone coughed, and I looked up to see the boys
staring at me, apparently coming to the same conclusion as I
had. I logged into my terminal, waiting for the info dump
that would load everything I needed. In the meantime...

"What have you guys got, anything?" Three heads
raised, then lowered. "Micah, that partial plate Mila gave us,
you got anything on it?"

Micah spun to face me with a grimace.

"Yeah, and no, boss. It's registered to an Ethel
Masters, who lives in the city. Went round yesterday and got
accosted by nine cats. Place stank of piss. Anyway, she
hasn't held a licence in the last forty years, as she's almost
completely blind. Never had a car registered at that address,
and lets the neighbour use her parking space for his yuppie
BMW bike."

I grinned; Micah hated anything mainstream. Apparently, cats made the list too.

"Okay, so that's something — the records have been changed. We need to find where and who. Danny, you got that?"

Danny nodded, his fingers flying across the keyboard.

"Alright, anything else — Black?"

Black turned to me, very slowly.

"Yeah, I think I do."

My heart jumped.

"What?"

"The brother, he's definitely around. Got this off a shopping centre feed, looks like he's been buying electrical stuff. Can't see what but we've got the time, and we can try to match the bank and purchase records from the shop."

I nodded. "Alright. That's great, man, thanks. You and I are heading down there. I'll leave you two still looking for that car and anything else that comes up. Okay?" I looked over at Danny and Micah. They may be junior members of the unit, but they were better cops than most.

Heads nodded around me. Black grabbed his jacket off the back of his chair and followed me out the door.

I paused at the front desk, leaning over it to find Steph painting her toenails on the floor. I coughed to get her attention, and she smiled widely, jumping up without managing to flash me, which I thought was quite a talent, given the length — or lack thereof — of her skirt.

"Can you get your boyfriend to check the alarm he put in the other day? The stupid thing has been on the blink, and I want to make sure it's working right."

Steph's smile was ridiculously bright for this time of the morning. Maybe it was worth having her on the front desk, after all.

"Of course, Cal! We have to keep the girls safe, now, right?"

My shoulders jerked, though I tried not to let the shock show.

"Who told you...." I didn't need to finish the sentence — her gaze shot back towards the office, right to Danny. I swore under my breath. When would the bugger learn not to shoot his mouth off? Between Steph and Mandy...oh, shit.

"It's okay, Cal, I won't say anything! They're safe there!" Steph's voice was shrill, and I cringed. Hell of a weapon the woman possessed, especially when it was used in close quarters.

Black lounged against the doorway like a hard motherfucker, though I knew he wasn't — not all the time.

He raised his eyebrows — he'd objected when I'd put Danny on the team, and I'd been on the back foot ever since to prove my choice. But the boy had skills; he just needed a bit of direction to develop his potential. I glared at Black and turned on my heel.

"Danny, man, we need to talk."

Micah was up and out the door so fast I didn't have time to move. For the biggest guy in the unit, he was surprisingly fleet when it called for it. He ducked his head as he passed me — apparently, this occasion was worthy.

"Man, you keep shooting your mouth off like that, it'll cost us the case. Or a witness. You can't tell Steph that sort of shit — she'll shout it from the rooftops. And Mandy is worse. You don't say a word to anyone outside this office, outside of this room right fucking here, from now on. Clear?"

If I had to plaster the door with a sticker that read, *What goes on in the Incident Room, stays in the Incident Room,* I would.

Danny leaned back, hands in the air.

"We're good, dude, c'mon. You said you were over her."

"It's got nothing to do with Mandy or anyone else. It's about being a fucking professional and keeping your mouth shut. I'm starting to wonder if we've lost Logan at some point now because you've said something to the wrong person!" I ground my teeth, glaring at the younger man.

"Now, wait just a—"

"You want to argue? Log it with Liam when he gets back. Tell him your sob story, and he'll tell you what I just have. Damn it, Danny. Just...get the damned job done." I stalked back to the elevator, Micah clapping my shoulder as I passed.

"I'll talk to him."

I nodded, not trusting myself to speak to anyone civilly for the moment. I was furious with myself for losing my temper, and even more pissed it had been at Danny. There were bridges to build, and I wasn't ready to burn him — not yet, anyway.

I needed to keep it cool to catch Logan, but this sort of dissent was what he was famous for. We weren't the only unit to fail to catch him — but I swore we'd be the last to hunt him.

The drive to the shop where Logan's brother, Joey, had been seen was short but silent. We parked, and I killed the engine.

"Say it."

"Say what?"

I snorted. "Whatever's eating you."

"You are."

"What?" I looked at him askance.

"I get that Danny fucked up. But you come down hard on him like that, you do it in private, with the door closed. You bust him down in front of everyone, and his confidence lags; he won't do the job, not well. The team doesn't work." Balck leaned back, drumming his fingers on the passenger door.

I clenched my teeth, wishing I had never asked. Black was right, though. I hadn't handled that well. I began to apologise, but he stopped me.

"I get it. You got a little girl and Mila in your apartment, and you want to be there to keep them safe. But we gotta get this job done, man, gotta stop him."

"I know."

The shop assistant happened to be the same one who'd served Joey. When I dragged out an old photo, the kid nodded, poking the flimsy paper.

"Yeah, him. Freaky dude, always staring. Shorter hair, though. Bought rolls of wire and tape, said he was stocking up to do Christmas lights. But what he bought wasn't for that sort of job. It was more like he was rewiring a house or a building. So much stuff, he'd never use what he bought on his own."

I thanked the kid and turned to Black.

"Where's he going to hit? You heard him — Joey bought enough stuff to wire a building, but for what? Is he bypassing security systems, or getting cameras in there? Where, though."

I scuffed the ground, frustrated. Black stopped.

"What?"

"He's back here, right? He hasn't been in this town for five years. Let's check if there's something big happening — something he wants that's coming in or being held here." He resumed walking. "Maybe check Central again."

It came out casual, but I knew by his tone he was holding back, waiting. The thought that Logan might hit Central a second time...I scrunched my eyes closed, my brain kicking in. We used to call him Lightning Jack, in the beginning, because he never hit anywhere twice. That was his pattern. His profile centred on building blocks like that. Was this time different? Something felt off, that much was clear. I nodded.

"Look into it."

I spent the afternoon trawling through the week's data on Logan looking for new patterns, for something that stuck out, something I'd missed. The boys did their jobs, Danny quiet at his desk on the far side of the room, working with his back to me. A bridge I had to rebuild that would take more time away from looking for Logan.

I resented that, but to catch him, I needed everyone at their best, with no more distractions. That didn't just mean Danny; I included myself in that list, too.

I stood, stretching, and wandered over to him.

"You training after work? I could use a decent sparring partner."

Danny shook his head; eyes fixed on the screen.

"Nah, man, said I'd have dinner with..." he let the comment hang. I finished it in my head. *Mandy*. She'd be a sore spot, as long as either of us let it stand.

"Danny. I really don't care for her. She's all yours, believe me. We good?" I tapped the back of his chair to get his attention.

'Yeah..." Danny tapped frantically at his keyboard, distracted by his screen. "Ah, fuck it!" He slammed his hand to the desk and stood up. "I gotta go for a walk. I've been trying to trace that hack, but it's fluid. Like someone's moving the target every time I aim at it."

"You're doing good, Danny. You're the best; otherwise, you wouldn't be here."

He finally met my gaze and held it for a moment before he nodded.

"Thanks."

"No worries. Walk it off, whatever. I'll leave soon, just want to download this for tonight."

"You should get some sleep. Or, maybe not sleep, but..."

I jabbed at his arm, but he dodged, faking.

"No seriously, Dane. Get some rest. You can't live on fumes forever."

I was in the elevator on the way back up to my apartment, before Danny's words truly registered. I hadn't realised the entire team knew I worked at home each night, searching for Logan in my sleep, half slumped over my desk. Uncomfortable with the thought, I added it to the growing list of things I'd missed this week.

They were the best — that's why I'd selected them. I was sure we all knew more details about each other's personal lives than was usual for a unit like ours, but an operation like Niffler that ran on so long — it was close work. I just hoped none of us would burn out before we finished it.

I opened the door and knew right away that Steph's boyfriend had been to fix the alarm. It glowed a steady green and worked when I input the code. The apartment was quiet — very quiet. Maybe Ashley was asleep? I checked the lounge and the kitchen. Glitter still decorated the carpet, but other than that, there was no sign of my house guests.

My gut wrenched, as panic hit me hard.

I checked the bedroom, the balcony, and finally made my way down to Ashley's room. I poked my head in and nearly wrote it off as empty. But a faint shh-ing came from one corner. I stepped into the room, letting my eyes adjust. Mila sat with her back against the bed, curled into a ball facing the wall.

"Mila," I whispered, leaning forward, terrified she'd been hurt and dreading checking. The day I'd run into her, the red paint staining her shirt had horrified me then, but it was nothing compared to how I felt now. Images swam across my vision as I reached for her.

She moved, shifting a little and I saw a blonde head tucked into her chest. She looked over her shoulder, eyes on my face. I recoiled in shock. Wide, red eyes stared out at me, tear tracks marring her cheeks. But it wasn't the tears that got me; it was the anger. Blazing red and hot, and directed right at me. I swallowed.

"What's happened? Is she okay?"

Mila stroked Ashley's hair, shushing her. She shook her head at me, and I saw a wall go up between us, far stronger than anything had before. I kneeled next to her, but she flinched away. My stomach sank at the movement.

"What've I done?" the words came out harsher and louder than I liked, panic tearing control from me in an instant.

Mila leaned down wordlessly, lifting Ashley's head to peer into her face. The tiny girl was asleep, but even in the dim light, I could see her face was blotched with red patches and bloated from crying. I wanted to reach out to her, but the narrow angle of Mila's shoulders told me not to. Fierce, like a mamma bear with a cub. I loved it.

She placed Ashley on her bed — the kid was never going to get a decent sleep if this kept happening — tucking her in. Leaning down, she felt around on the carpet. It took me a moment to catch on. I passed her the crocodile and saw the wall between us crumble, just a little.

Then the hardness came back at me with a vengeance. I held her gaze, not backing down either, desperate to know what had happened to upset them both so badly while I was away. Scenarios raced about in my mind, but I pushed them all back and waited. It was one of the hardest things I'd ever done.

I rose and let her stride past me. We were in the lounge when she turned on me.

"We have to leave here."

"What? Why?"

"She was looking for you. Maybe she was looking for your room to see what was in it. I don't know. She'd disappeared, and I thought she went back to her room to get some toys. Then I heard her screaming from the corridor that leads down there." She gestured towards my bedroom, and suddenly I didn't need to hear the rest. The floor dropped out from under me.

"Oh, my god, I'm so–"

"I don't think I need to tell you what it's done to her? The screaming, the abject fucking terror she experienced today..."

Mila's jaw clamped as she cut herself off. It was the first time I'd heard her curse.

"My god, Mila, I am so sorry. I meant to take it all down; I got caught up in work–"

"You're sorry? I had to try to explain to her why there is a room in her *safe place* that is covered with a thousand pictures of her father! All those eyes, staring down at her — at me – Cal, *I* nearly threw up. I think that if I hadn't been looking after Ashley, I might have."

She stood in the centre of the room, arms crossed, shivers wracking her slight frame.

"Mila, I didn't get to it, and dammit I needed to do that, I just– I never thought–"

She snorted and turned away.

"Mila, please, let me apologise. And thank you for looking after her. I'm glad you were here."

I stepped up behind her, but she didn't turn, just watched our reflections in the glass.

"It shouldn't have happened."

"No, it shouldn't have. You're right." I placed my hands tentatively on her waist, waiting to see how she responded. My heart slammed in my chest — how could I have been so stupid, so selfish not to clean it all up when I'd promised I would? But as usual, work took precedence.

Something had to change, or this — whatever it was — would break before it had a chance to develop. I couldn't bear to have that happen.

Mila stood stock still, not moving, her eyes closed in the reflection. She took a step back, into me. My heart stopped, and I wondered if it would ever start again. *She wasn't running from me.* I wrapped my arms around her waist, burying my face in her hair.

I'd been so ready for her to push back, to run...but to be able to hold her was such a relief, I could have laughed though that might have been inappropriate.

"I'll do it tonight. Right now, if you need. I'll take the lot to my truck and leave it at the office tomorrow."

Except that I wasn't going to the office tomorrow. Damn it. It didn't matter; I'd figure it out. Maybe we could drop it all back in afterwards. I'd like Mila to see where I worked. I turned her in my arms. She looked at me, eyes huge, and bottomless, full of the uncertainty I felt as I brushed the tears from her cheeks. I pulled her close, just holding her.

It was fully dark by the time she moved, stomach growling. I groaned. I'd totally forgotten the takeout I'd promised. Mila smiled shyly.

"I made something today, for us, just in case...anyway, it won't take long to heat up."

She shot into the kitchen, working with a speed and efficiency I admired. Her eyes narrowed; movements quick and precise. My phone buzzed in my pocket, and I pulled it out, remembering to ask about the alarm.

"Hey, did Steph's boyfriend come around to fix the alarm?"

"Yes! He did. It took a little while, though..."

I looked down at my phone to see a message from Mandy. When was the girl going to get that I wanted to be left alone? I opened it, scanning through quickly. It was all nothing, about being out with a guy, a nice place...was I supposed to be jealous?

Wait, wasn't the guy Danny? A grin unfurled on my face. It was his problem now — not mine. Mine was currently staring at me. I'd stopped listening.

"Sorry, got distracted. How was it?"

"He was fine, maybe a bit odd, creepy and rough looking. Is Steph a nice girl? I'd hate to think of this guy with a girlfriend. He just gave me the wrong vibe."

"Well, I'm sure he's nice."

My phone buzzed again, but I refused to look at it, trying to concentrate on what Mila was saying. It kept buzzing, and she stopped talking, looking at me expectantly. I groaned and turned the phone over in my hand — more messages from Mandy.

Mandy: Did you get my card? I wanted you to take me to that black-tie gala we'd talked about.

I shook my head, wondering what she was talking about, then remembered the black envelope Mila had fetched from the mailbox. I had completely forgotten it, but now I knew who it was from, I resolved to throw it in the bin at the first opportunity. She had to figure it out. I fired off a short reply.

Me: Why don't you take Danny instead?

I blacked the screen, sliding my phone across the counter. She could message all she liked; I had no more time for her. I turned back to Mila, taking the beer she offered, apologising.

"We were talking about Steph's boyfriend?"

"Haven't you met him when he did the alarm the first time?"

"No, I was working, so the building manager let him in. He's great with security, so I was happy for him to organise it."

"Oh. Well, maybe ask her about him? He was just a bit, um...creepy." She gestured with her hands, "I don't know, he stared a lot. And I thought I caught him looking through my phone..."

"*What?*"

Mila started at my tone, then flapped a hand, flustered.

"I'm sure it's nothing. I think he put his things on the bench and it all got mixed up; I don't know. Don't worry about it, please, Cal? I shouldn't have said anything; it's nothing. You worry about everything, and I don't want to add to that. Please?"

I nodded, brain whirring as she slipped out of the kitchen and stood awkwardly in the space between us. I was drawn to the concern in her face. Panic settled there; tiny lines etched across her forehead. I wanted to smooth them out but didn't dare to approach her.

"You've been stuck here for a while; it can make things seem out of proportion. That's frustrating," I acknowledged, "Paranoia and obsession is my hobby."

She gave me a wan smile.

"You've got enough on your mind right now. Let's concentrate on what's important."

I started; hadn't that been what Black had tried to tell me today?

"So, what's important?"

I didn't move, just waited. She tentatively moved across the distance dividing us, pausing just outside my arm's reach of her. For just a moment, she stilled. I closed the short space between us until I could feel her breath on my skin. She leaned into me, sliding her arms around my back, clinging as though she were drowning. I crushed her against me, resting my head on the top of hers. A fruity smell rose from her hair when she moved, a scent I was beginning to associate with her

God, she smelled good.

CHAPTER FIFTEEN

MILA

Danny and Micah stood in the lounge, dwarfing the room. I couldn't think of a space these two together wouldn't dominate. Gina, who I'd just been introduced to, hovered at the kitchen bench, half-turned away from Micah. Whatever their relationship was, it was clearly strained. Ashley already had a hairdressing station set up on a small table in the corner, complete with Velcro rollers and a pink fluffy dressing gown.

"It's just your size, dude."

Danny smirked, elbowing Micah, who turned on him with a benevolent smile.

"Your turn today."

Cal grabbed the robe, flinging it over Danny's broad shoulders. The shaggy pink material barely made it across his back, hanging by the edges at its widest point. He kicked the chair behind Danny's knees, and the bigger man fell into it, a dazed expression on his face.

I dropped a kiss on Ashley's head as Cal propelled me towards the elevator.

"Be good for her!" I called to the boys who responded in a chorus. Gina waved half-heartedly and locked us out.

Cal's hand wrapped around mine as we waited for the elevator. I didn't want to pull away, scared I'd break the happiness that radiated him this morning.

"Uh, Cal? Where are we going?"

The elevator door slid silently open, and he let go of my hand to sort through his keys.

"Just something I think you need."

Well, that wasn't ominous at all. I shook my head, but let him play it his way. I was just glad to see him so much less stressed. He'd even *smiled* this morning. That was a change.

As the gate opened, the shadows again passed over Cal's face. Shoulders tight, he craned at the edge of the drive, surveying the streets. I saw nothing unusual, but I knew now that Cal saw the world in a very different way to everyone else.

Finally, we turned onto the street, and I knew it wasn't himself he was worried about.

"She'll be okay," I murmured, and he shot me a grateful glance, "have you taken a step back to see the size of those two boys? No one will fit through the door to get to her."

Some of the tension left his shoulders, and his grip on the steering wheel loosened just a little. I cast around for something else to say.

"So, what are we doing? You've been all secret squirrel about...wherever it is we're going."

I expected him to evade my questions, but to my surprise, Cal actually answered me.

"I'm taking you shooting." He glanced quickly at me, then returned his attention to the road.

"What?"

"Well, to learn to shoot — I'm guessing you've never held a gun before, from the way you reacted when I pulled mine out of the glovebox the other night."

I shouldn't have been surprised he'd noticed since reading situations was a part of his job, but it came as one anyway.

"Cal, I-I'm not really a fan of guns. Ever since..."

I let my thought hang unspoken. I wasn't sure I *could* put them into words if I tried. A pair of feet with one shoe dangling from the end of a stockinged foot floated across my vision. My hands clenched together, and I closed my eyes, trying to ward off the image. The truck jerked to a stop. I opened my eyes. Cal's face appeared in front of me.

"Mila, honey, look at me." Tears ran down my face. His palm cupped my chin, brushing them away with his thumb. "This is why I want to take you shooting. So you'll have a way to protect yourself. Maybe it will help calm the nightmares, too."

I jolted, staring at him a little wildly. How had he known about the nightmares? I was sure I hadn't mentioned them and wracked my brain trying to work out if I'd had them during my short stay in his apartment. His fingers stroked my face, eyes filled with sadness.

"You cry out in your sleep, honey. I didn't want to wake you, so I sat on the bed until it stopped. It was only a guess, but I figured it would be..."

I nodded, blinking back more tears that flooded my vision. "I'm so sorry you have to put up with that," I whispered, more than a little horrified.

Cal shook his head firmly.

"Mila, I have *lived* this for the last five years. Almost every damned moment – at work, at home, when I sleep. I get it. I get *you*."

He tucked loose hairs behind my ear, giving my hand a quick squeeze and put the truck into gear. The drive across town was silent — filled with memories both of us wished we could erase. The building we arrived at was huge and took up most of the block, surrounded by warehouses and mechanic yards. There wasn't a single person on the street at all. As I slid down from my seat, I realised it was quiet. I had expected noise from a firing range.

"You ready?"

I nodded, pressing my lips together nervously. Cal keyed a code in at the foyer to access the elevator, the ping of the door seeming ridiculously loud as they closed. We went down several floors, nerves jumping in my stomach. When the doors opened, a cacophony of sound ricocheted around the small space, echoing in my head.

"It was so quiet downstairs," I remarked to cover my discomfort. The noise was a little overwhelming, and the sounds of the individual shots...I shivered a little, moving closer to Cal. I willed the memories not to flood me. Panic attacks were bad enough; to have one in public — the muscles around my ribs constricted, shortening my breath. Cal watched me, and I was thankful when he didn't push.

"Being below ground makes a difference, and the room is soundproof." He pressed a light hand to my back, rubbing gentle circles with his thumb.

Long lanes divided the cavernous room, each with a small box and a target at the other end. Cal waved, and a small, round man with an open face approached us. He shook Cal's hand, pulling him down for a quick hug, and turned to me.

"You must be Mila." He clasped my hand in his larger ones. There was a faint inflection to his words. "John Bird, Instructor. Come down to the end, this way. I've got everything set up for you; a quiet spot picked out."

Sharp retorts bounced off the walls, merging in a knot of harsh echoes. *Quiet* was a relative term, apparently. I studied Cal's back as he followed the small instructor, wondering what he had told the small man.

An arm slipped around my shoulders, keeping me moving forward. Caught up in my own thoughts, I hadn't realised Cal had stopped to wait for me. I gave him a tight smile. He squeezed my arm, concern in his eyes.

"You can do this," he murmured.

John led us to the final bay, situated at the far wall. A single pistol — at least, that's what I thought it was — lay on the small bench, next to several small boxes. John opened one, gesturing me forward as he started to point out the features of the gun, turning it over in his hands, and naming the working parts.

I tried to remember them all, but it was a lot, and I was on the verge of freaking out. I wanted to reach back for Cal, but a quick glance behind me showed him deep in conversation with another cop.

"Mila, I hope you don't mind, but Cal has shared your situation with me. I am glad he has brought you to me to learn, and I understand how terrifying it can be. In Chile, I was a negotiator. I would walk into critical situations completely unarmed. Often, a room would be full of men aiming weapons at me. I had nothing but my open hands and brain to get me through it."

He tapped his balding head with one finger, eyes twinkling. "Yet, here I am. Not all situations end as yours did, and I am sorry this has happened to you. Cal thought it best you have protection here," he tapped his head again, "and here." This time his hand lowered to his heart. I frowned, not quite understanding. John smiled kindly at me. "Being able to defend yourself might help you to conquer your fear. Sometimes, just knowing can help."

He placed the pistol in my hands, which trembled slightly as I closed them around the grip. The gun was heavy in my hands, which tried to shy away from the thing even as I clutched at it.

"Ah, not so hard. Here, like this." John lifted my hands, relaxing my wrists. "Too tight, and you will pull the shot. Hands must be firm, but not grabbing the gun. You don't need to strangle it."

He went through the sequence of loading an empty magazine into the butt of the pistol, folding my hands around the handgrip, so one overlapped the other, explaining how it increased accuracy and stability.

I jumped when he retracted the slide to cock the weapon, the sound echoing back in my memory. As if sensing it, John put a reassuring hand on the small of my back and made me repeat the process until I could do it smoothly, with confidence. He placed a printed target in a little clip and sent it barreling down the lane. It stopped around halfway down, and I was glad I didn't have to try to hit anything further away.

Positioning me, so I faced the target head-on, John fussed about, adjusting my stance, squaring my shoulders. I found the three tiny posts to aim with, but they might have been pinheads for all that I could get them to line up. With John repeating the sequence in my ear, reminding me to push forward as I squeezed the trigger, I was ready. Stance, aim, squeeze.

I ran over it in my head, hands sweaty on the grip. Stance, aim, squeeze. I breathed in.

Stance, aim, *CLICK.*

I flinched, dropped the gun, and stepped back, wiping my hands on my pants. I looked over to John.

"What happened?" My voice was shaky.

"It wasn't loaded, Mila. But it is good to get past that first shot. Most people jump the first time. It's not just you. Now, we fix the stance." John returned to his fussing until I felt like a mannequin being primped for a window. Finally, he gave a happy nod. I tried to nod back without moving the rest of me. John laughed.

"Breathe, Mila. And relax those hands!"

I tried, but nothing felt right. I was all angles; breathing and thinking at the same time was too hard, and my arms ached already. My frustration must have been obvious, because John patted my arms, signalling me to lower them.

He pointed out how to unload the weapon, facing it away from myself, or anyone else. I smiled, shaking trembling arms out with relief as I listened. A bottle of water appeared beside me. Cal leaned against the bay wall, nursing a cup of coffee. He saw my envious look and batted my hands away.

"Mine. You get one when you've fired fifty rounds, tightly clustered."

"Fifty!" I exclaimed, then lowered my voice. "I haven't even fired it properly once yet."

Cal smirked at me. I narrowed my eyes, thinking of ways I could return the favour. John clapped Cal's shoulder, sliding out of the small booth, which was ridiculously cramped with three people in it. He sent me a reassuring look when I drew in quick breaths.

"You will be fine with Cal. He is the best."

It was said so simply, I didn't doubt the truth of his statement.

John patted Cal's arm again, and with a broad grin, left us alone. I looked up at Cal, unsure of what to do. A different sort of tension gripped me as my eyes trailed up the fitted black tee he wore over his jeans. It barely concealed the muscles I knew were hidden beneath the thin material. His eyes darkened, the annoying smirk still present. I fought the urge to smack him. He knew this made me uncomfortable, but he seemed to find me amusing, anyway. It wasn't helpful.

"Tell me everything John told you."

I sighed and began to parrot everything I'd learned. Cal leaned against the side of the booth. Close, but never touching. Small comments had me straightening one arm, relaxing the other. Pulled my shoulders down, counted me through breathing exercises. Finally, he deemed me ready to fire.

My finger was on the trigger, my thoughts muddled with not snatching at it, not pulling, just pressing with the pad of my finger. The handgun trembled in my hands. I closed my eyes, unable to move.

It was too much.

I took a deep breath in — or tried to. A shallow breath shuddered in, my heart only just keeping a steady rhythm. Warm hands slid along my arms, folding around my hands.

Cal's chest pressed against my back, his knees nudging the backs of my thighs. I leaned back a tiny bit into him, but his arms pushed my shoulders down.

"Breathe with me," he murmured into my hair, his breath brushing my cheek. "Close your eyes and breathe."

I followed him, inhaling as his chest rose against my back, exhaling when he did. After a few moments, I opened my eyes.

"Thank you."

"Breathe again, but this time, let the breath go all the way out, and don't take another. Focus and fire." He stepped away.

I gripped the pistol, then relaxed my hands. Breathe in, breathe out. Empty, the world around me fell into silence.

I pulled the trigger.

The recoil wasn't bad, and I put the gun down quickly, unloading it the way John had shown me. I turned to Cal. He had retreated a few steps, resuming his post against the booth wall.

"Was that– did I do okay?"

His expression was unreadable.

"What do you think?"

I searched the target for any sign of a bullet hole, but couldn't find a single one. Maybe I'd missed the entire sheet? Cal reached over my shoulder, pressing a button to retrieve the target. He unclipped it from its peg, laying it out in front of me. In a circle of black, just left of centre, was a small hole. I touched it, a little shocked it had all worked.

"I can't believe I hit it." I grinned at Cal. Something loosened in my chest, and I was suddenly glad he'd brought me here.

"Don't get too happy. You have a lot more to do."

Cal wasn't kidding. He put a tiny white circle over the bullet hole — like a Band-Aid for the target — and sent it back down the lane. After twenty more shots or so, he replaced the target, sending the new one just little further back, showing me how to compensate for the difference in range.

An age later, my vision was beginning to blur, and my hands shook with overuse. Cal checked my last lot of shots, nodding.

"You've done well, for the first time you've ever held a gun."

I offered him a wan smile.

"I had a good teacher. Two," I corrected as John approached, a styrofoam cup in one hand. My stomach rumbled, and Cal laughed. John held the coffee out. I took it, grateful.

"Thank you."

"You are welcome any time, Mila. Even without Cal."

CHAPTER SIXTEEN

MILA

I yawned as we got back into the truck. Cal looked over at me speculatively.

"Do you have enough energy to go out for lunch, or do you want me to take you home?"

"Lunch sounds good...oh, my god, how is it after midday? You're a slave driver," I accused him. He grinned, pulling away from the curb.

"Do you have somewhere in mind?"

I leaned back in my seat and shook my head. I was too drained to even think.

"You pick."

"You did really well, Mila. Thank you for trusting me." Cal squeezed my hand.

I smiled with my eyes closed, glad to be alone with Cal and no one else for right now.

We ended up at a small Chinese restaurant, just a block away from Eat Street. Inside, the lights were dimmed. Red wallpaper dominated the small space, giving it a cosy warmth. Fans and lanterns decorated the ceiling, while concertina screens depicting mountain scenes gathered around the tables, affording a degree of privacy.

Cal spoke to a woman who greeted us quietly in Chinese, gesturing us to the back of the restaurant. My stomach rumbled as we passed by the kitchen.

I slid into the booth, flicking through the menu. Cal slipped in beside me, and I bit my lip. He shook his head.

"I just can't sit with my back to the room. I need to see everything."

He shifted beside me; his eyes were dark. I wondered if he was as aware of my presence as I was of his. Heat emanated from him. I tried not to squirm, studying the laminated tabletop scored with a million tiny scratches. Cal leaned over my shoulder, reading the menu I'd spread out, his breath tickling the crook of my neck.

The tension between us was a huge thing. I loved it, but I was also worried that was all it would be — lust. Once the honeymoon period wore off, would I be alone again? He kept doing so much: providing protection, giving me a safe place to sleep — well, an almost-safe place. I snorted softly, thinking of his fingers sliding over my lips and crossed my legs, pressing my thighs together.

I flicked over the menu, trying to make out the tiny writing. Cal's hand landed over mine on the page, pointing out a crispy duck dish, stuffed with shallots and mushroom.

"Or did you want seafood again? The duck is something special; trust me." His fingers drifted across my hand, sending more shivers over me. I closed my eyes, desperately hoping that we were more than just physical tension.

He was right. The duck *was* amazing, And we had enough left over not only to share with Ashley for dinner but something to give the boys as thanks when we got home.

"Wonder if Ashley has primped the boys up yet," I murmured, leaning back with a full stomach. The duck had been far too easy to overindulge in. Cal nodded, mirth lighting his eyes as he stretched his arms across the back of the padded bench seat.

"I'll bet she has. More unicorn puffs in my carpet, I expect."

"Well, they have to roam free. Wait, why aren't Danny and Micah at work today?" The thought occurred to me way too late. "Is Teddy holding the fort on his own?"

"We usually work seven days. No one has a break much, though sometimes we go out in the evenings to let off a little steam."

"You don't have a day off? Wait, I thought you did when I met you."

"We take time as we need it, usually when there's little going on. And when I took you out for lunch, I wasn't sure..."

I sat back into the seat, breath leaving me. When he wasn't sure if he could trust me; when he thought I was one of Logan's crew.

A spy.

Silence fell between us, a heaviness hovering, as though ready to crush everything we'd made up in the last few days.

And what is that, exactly?

I didn't have an answer to my own question.

"What do you think now? Do you trust me yet, Cal?"

"Honey, I let you sleep in my bed, I made you come on my kitchen bench…I think we're passed the trust issue now."

And we were back to sex, again. Would it ever be more than that? Cal watched me, and I knew this was a moment he wanted a reaction, but I had no idea what to do. I was always hopeless under pressure, more likely to freeze than act — unlike Cal, who I suspected thrived in it, his natural environment.

Were we too different? A little voice in my head told me to try it before I rejected what Cal offered me, but I had trouble trusting myself, let alone someone else. Trust. I looked at him sharply. Maybe he knew me better than I had thought.

"Let's save this for dinner, leave some for the boys?" I gestured at the spread left on the table. Cal leaned over, turning me to face him.

"Mila, please don't run from this, from me. You don't need to be afraid." He squeezed my shoulders, then let his hands drop, giving me space. When I sat silent, he collected everything, standing. "I'll get the kitchen to box it up."

The trip home was quiet. Cal was tense again, hyper-alert, scanning our surroundings constantly. I *was* safe with this man, and I needed to let go of all the things that held me back from him. But it wasn't easy to release a five-year habit born in fear.

I expected him to take the side road leading back to his nondescript building, but he kept along the main road, heading deeper into the city.

"Where are we going?"

"I need to drop into the office to store all the stuff that, uh, came out of my home office."

He didn't look at me, but a muscle ticked in his jaw.

"Oh." There didn't seem to be anything else to say. "Thank you. It's a huge thing, you not only taking us in but reorganising your house around us."

Reorganising your entire life around us.

But I couldn't say it, suddenly scared he would agree it was too much, and send us off...where? It stuck in my throat, knowing I had nowhere else to go, right now. Cal smiled fleetingly.

"I don't mind at all. Please, Mila. Stop worrying. I won't kick you out on your own, or Ashley. Ever. You have a home with me as long as you want it — or until this thing blows over."

But how long would that be? We couldn't stay with him forever; each of us had a life to go to. My fingers, still sore from gripping the handgun for so many hours, itched to hold my brushes. I couldn't go to get them, but maybe Cal had some paper floating around I could sketch on. Not painting for a few days was beginning to get to me. And I had appointments next week...

"I never finished Dolly!" The words shot out, jumbled together. Cal raised his eyebrows.

"That's what you're thinking about?"

"But I never even called! My god, I'm so unprofessional. How could I forget that?"

"Honey, you've had your house broken into, and needed to get away. Don't worry. I already explained — well, sort of, — what was going on. I didn't tell her you were staying. I haven't told anyone."

"Am I that bad?" I joked, not sure if I should be hurt, or not. Cal pulled into the car park of an office building.

"The more people that know, the easier it is for him to find you." He grabbed a large box from the tray, hoisting it in his arms, leading me inside.

"Can you press six? I'm a bit..." He gestured with his fingers, and I giggled at the sight of him hopping from one foot to the other.

"What, Superman, you can't do everything yourself?"

"If I were Superman, honey, this isn't where I'd be."

"No day job disguise for you?" I paused, pretending to study him. "Glasses might make a sexy change, give you that intellectual look."

"You want brains, honey? Maybe you should be living in Liam's apartment. He's got the looks *and* the smarts."

"Didn't you say he has a flame? Might have to be you after all."

I enjoyed the shocked look on Cal's face as the doors slid open. The office floor was tiled with a sandy brown look, and a reception desk stood off to the side. A woman with over-straightened, cherry-red hair sat behind the desk. An odd smell struck me, and I tried to place it. As we approached, I realised she was painting her nails.

"Steph, this is Mila. I just need to put some things in my office–" The woman raised her head, and Cal broke off. She glared at me for a fraction of a second, then it was gone, but I knew from Cal's reaction that he had seen it, too. "Is everything okay?"

Steph nodded, assessing me with hard eyes. "Sure, boss. Didn't know you were taking in strays."

My eyebrows flew up. Cal placed the box on top of the reception bench very gently.

"Steph, why don't you come and help me with sorting this stuff." His voice was sharp. It wasn't a request. "Mila, I'll be back in a minute."

He collected the box again, clenching his hands on the sides, so it crushed a little at the corners. Steph glared at me, following Cal into the glass-walled inner office with a sashay of her hips. I suddenly had an idea why she'd reacted so viciously. Cal sat at a desk, kicking out a chair for his receptionist. I turned away to give them some privacy, not wanting to watch Cal dress someone down.

I studied some of the photographs hanging on the foyer walls. One was a grayscale cityscape, taken from a distance — maybe from a crane or a helicopter. I didn't recognise which city, but even in the monochrome tones I could tell the sun was rising. Mist hovered around some of the buildings, trapped in an inversion layer. The effect of the white and black contrast made me itch to paint it.

"Brisbane. In spring," Cal spoke behind me. I jumped, not having heard him return. Ducking my chin, I checked the desk. Steph sat quietly, her head down as she typed something. Cal gave a shrug, his lips tilted but for all the façade I could see he was still annoyed.

"Who took these?" I asked, moving to the next photograph. This one was in colour — blues and yellows dominated the scene. Still a cityscape, but flat, tiny open boxes of grid highlighted the ocean on one side, mountains framing the other.

"Barcelona. I was there for a conference a few years ago."

"These are yours?"

Cal nodded. "I haven't done many in the last few years, but I like seeing cities from above. Takes out the chatter, leaves what's really there. All those people, stuffed inside their tiny space, but it's silent."

He led me back to his truck as I pondered his words. They struck me as odd, seeing as he lived in an apartment but...

"You want to live in a bigger space?"

"I'd love to. I don't have time to look after an entire house, yard...farm." Cal rubbed the back of his neck, then stuffed his hands in his pockets.

"Work takes a lot from you, doesn't it," I said, studying him with new eyes. So many complex layers and I had a feeling I'd just scratched the surface.

"Yeah."

The warm air had a chilled edge to it as he held the door of the truck open for me. Used to the height by now, I pressed one foot onto the sidestep, grabbing for the handle above the door to swing myself in. Cal's hands brushed my waist as I slid by him, leaning his arms on the roof of the truck, looking down at me.

His black t-shirt stretched tight across his shoulders, lean but hard muscle framing his arms — the tail of a sea serpent coiled around his bicep, disappearing into the sleeve of his shirt. The artist had curved it around his muscles perfectly so that even still, it undulated in the waves surrounding it. I watched, mesmerised until Cal's voice brought me back to him. There was a glint in his eye. I shifted under his gaze.

"How...how did it go, with Steph?" I had to ask, curiosity finally getting the best of me.

"I'm sorry about that. She thought I'd taken in a single mum and her daughter...which really was none of her damned business. I hope you don't mind, but I've let her think that. I didn't want to say who Ashley was. I should have been more careful letting her boyfriend into the building." He sent me an apologetic half-smile. "Guy sounds like a world-class asshole."

"It's okay." I grinned ruefully. "I think she has a thing for you."

Cal snorted. "Yeah, and half the guys in the office. She's the girl you never take home — though after today I can promise you the boys have more class than to take her out. Mind, Danny would take home anything that walks right now."

"What happened with him?"

Cal looked shifty, touching the fading bruise over his eye, and pulled his hand away too fast.

"Wait, did he, is he...is Danny going out with your ex? The one you were texting when you ran into the back of my car?"

Cal nodded, lips thin. I burst out laughing.

"Oh, my god, that's hilarious. And he punched you, because of her?" Another nod. "Wow, you guys need to get your act together on that."

"I'm glad you find it so amusing." Cal shut the door grumpily, but I was still laughing. It was better than midday TV.

We arrived at Cal's apartment with no further incidents, and I saw the moment he relaxed as Ashley came barrelling down the hall to us.

"Cal! Mila!"

Cal lifted her up onto his hip, inspecting her skin which had an odd tinge to it.

"Why are you blue?"

I eyed her critically and would have said green.

"Danny and Micah said it was my turn and covered me with tattoos! It was so much fun. They did my arms and around my feet too, see?" She kicked out pale legs that bore traces of patterns from the knees down.

Cal stopped, turning to me with wide eyes. I held back my laughter as he strode into the lounge with force. Danny and Micah were seated on Cal's rug, surrounded by ponies, a tea set between them. Both were covered in glitter, and what looked like my eye shadow. Micah sported orange nail polish. Gina was curled into a ball on the recliner, a sour look on her face.

From the side, I could see Cal's mood lift, and before the boys could move, he whipped out his phone, taking several photos. They stared in horror.

"Two words. Christmas party." He let the pause hang. "The state one." He leaned down to where the two of them sat, frozen.

"Don't ever cover a nine-year-old in tattoos again."

CHAPTER SEVENTEEN

CAL

The boys packed and left after a good-natured ribbing, Gina trailing silently after them. If her attitude bothered me, it made Micah — who I'd never seen lose his temper — furious. There was no contact and few words between them. I just hoped the inevitable break-up wouldn't send shrapnel flying around the office when it hit. We had enough going on with Operation Niffler, without additional domestic conflicts.

The girls spent a quiet night in front of the television, watching MasterChef. I spent far too long on the phone trying to sort out politics, and by the time I was finished, the lights were off, and the lounge was empty. I cursed quietly, loving the job but hating the time it cost me away from my girls.

In the end, I slept on the lounge when all I wanted was to slide into my own bed and fall asleep with Mila's head on my chest. The sofa was a shitty alternative, and as lumpy as the night before. This time, I wasn't drunk and felt every bump.

I awoke to the smell of coffee. Mila smiled, eyes bleary from sleep. She looked so gorgeous sitting at the breakfast bar, hair mussed and piled on top of her head. What would it be like to wake up next to her, to sweep the hair from her face and kiss her? Damn, I was getting soft. I snorted, rolling off the lounge. Every muscle in my back protested, and a groan escaped me.

She looked around at the sound, eyes travelling over me. Shirtless, I'd slept in my sweats, the most comfortable thing I could find without rummaging through my room and waking her. Her gaze stopped on my arm, studying the sea monster there. Her lips curled in a smile that nearly had me shooting across the kitchen, and I wanted nothing more than to kiss the hell out of her. I turned away to stretch, adjusting my sweats. Well, maybe not so soft after all.

"Morning." Her voice was raspy, still coated with sleep.

God, she was sexy in the mornings. I wordlessly passed her a fresh cup of coffee, not sure I could trust what might come out of my mouth.

"Thanks," she said inhaling. "What are we doing today?"

"I have to go back to work. Yesterday was a luxury." I busied myself making toast. When she didn't respond, I looked up. Her face had fallen, and I cursed myself as an idiot.

Well done, Dane.

"It's okay. I just...do you have any paper? Just something plain, it doesn't matter if it's got lines. A pen..."

She spoke into her cup, tracing patterns on the bench. I stared for a moment, then cursed myself twice over. She was missing her art supplies. Maybe I could drop into a shop in the city. Was there one? Google would save me. I'd make it a surprise for her when I got home tonight.

"There's stuff in the study." She looked up sharply, and I hastened to reassure her. "It's all cleaned out, just an old laptop and some stationery stuff."

Dane, stop talking. Just go dig yourself a bigger hole.

"I'll have a look. Thanks."

And just like that, the awkwardness raised its ugly, damned head. I drained my own mug.

"Have you eaten?" She shook her head, and I slid my plate in front of her. "You should."

"After the duck yesterday? I won't need to eat for a week."

I stared pointedly at the plate until she took a bite, pushing the rest back across to me. I ate it, looking at my watch.

"I should get ready. Will you be okay with Ashley for the day, just the two of you?"

"Of course. She's the easiest kid in the world to get along with."

I snorted. "Yeah, unless you're six-foot-four inches tall, and built like a tank. Then you're prime real-estate for a makeover."

"They did look cute."

"You could say that." I grinned, heading for the shower. When I emerged, she hadn't moved, still staring into her mug. I grabbed my laptop bag and paused — I didn't want to leave her. "Are you sure you– do you need anything?"

Mila spun around on her stool, shaking her head.

"Thanks, but I've got it all right here." She gestured to her mug, but I didn't believe her for a second.

"Okay. You've got my number, call or message any time..." Damn, this was awkward. I jingled the keys in my pocket. "Say good morning to Ashley for me."

Shy of kissing her, I had no idea what to do, so I left, wishing there wasn't such a barrier between us and no idea how to break it down.

MILA

Cal left. Without him, the apartment was too empty. I slipped off the stool, and padded around to the sink, wondering what I would fill the day with. The washing up was half done when a fluffy pink jumper accosted me at waist level, sleeves waving frantically. A muffled voice echoed from its depths.

"Stuck."

I tried to hold in my laughter, but giggles boiled to the surface and erupted. The voice became indignant, and I began to wrestle with the jumper monster.

"Mila, can you help me, please? I'm stuck."

Laughing, I freed Ashley from her tangle of sleeves and zippers. She looked at me, curiously.

"Why don't you use the dishwasher like Cal does?"

The rest of the morning was spent explaining why old houses don't come with modern appliances and a little education on water conservation. Ashley loved looking at the images of the Antarctic with its penguins and asked a lot of questions I couldn't answer about climate change.

By noon, we were both mini-experts on the topic, though I closed the tablet when Ashley's tummy grumbled.

"What would you like for lunch?"

Ashley stopped, thinking. Her arms folded and she fidgeted, tugging on strands of hair that had worked their way free from her ponytail.

"Ashley?" I prompted. She looked at me with big eyes. I crouched in front of her. "What's wrong?"

"I wish Cal was my dad."

The words came out in a rush, and the floodgates opened. I pulled her onto my lap, stroking her hair. My heart pounded. My emotions were all skew whiff, jumping from anger at her real father to the reality of a little girl who didn't have a family or a home. No wonder she was always climbing Cal, or jumping on my lap — the girl had five years or more backlog of love top-ups to fill.

"Oh, honey." I paused, because that's what Cal called me, and it just slipped out. But I liked the term, I decided. Ashley finally settled, lying with dry but red eyes, across my knees. I flicked on the TV – thank god, the remote was close by – and let her watch Winx reruns.

When she was settled, her attention on the brightly coloured fairies, I whispered back, "I wish he was, too."

We shared tortillas for lunch; hers stuffed with sour cream, corn, and avocado; mine with mostly salad greens. Full and satisfied, we both lay with our backs to the lounge while Ashley shot marbles at the opposing wall. She'd found them while scrounging for games and curiosities in Cal's cupboard. This box of treasures had been stored in an old margarine container, and the patterns on the tiny glass balls had entertained her for hours, enough to distract her from her upset earlier.

My phone buzzed, and I checked it, smiling when I saw Cal's name pop up.

Cal: I won't be home 'til a bit later. I want to follow up a lead. Tell you how it goes.

Me: Thanks for telling me. Good luck.

Cal: Movie when I get home? Or an old GOT episode?

Me: GOT sounds good

Cal: Thank god. If you didn't like that...

I grinned, glad I could make him smile. I still didn't know if I missed him because I *actually* missed him, or if it was because I'd been cooped up in his apartment all day. A marble ran over my toes, and I flicked it lightly back to Ashley. She chased after it, gigging when it slipped between her hands.

Cal: Have I scared you?

Me: Scared me?

Cal: ...

Cal ...

Cal: I want to take you on a real date after this is all over.

I squeezed my phone, and it cracked a little under the pressure. I put it down, not sure what to say. Did I want to go out on another date with him? I enjoyed his company, and loved that he relaxed around me, let his guard down. I had a feeling that was something he didn't do very often.

I realised with a jolt I enjoyed flirting with Cal. My phone buzzed again. Maybe this was worth the risk, after all.

Turing my phone over, I frowned. The number wasn't one I knew. I scanned the message. That one line changed everything.

It's good to see you looking after my baby.

For a moment, the room darkened, and all I could see were those words.

Logan.

It had to be him. It wasn't just a random message sent to the wrong number. I felt it, way down in the bottom on my stomach. My mind went blank. I stared at the words on the tiny screen, still as a statue. Nausea crept up my throat, and I swallowed back bile as a reflex. Honestly, throwing up might be preferable to looking at those words right now. But I couldn't put the phone down. Three small dots appeared below the message.

You will make a beautiful mother for her.

Shock dissolved into panic, my breath hot and fast on my hands, misting the screen. My brain scrambled to catch up — how had he gotten my number? Why was I a mother — to Ashley? *Were we safe?*

He's insane.

My phone buzzed again. I jumped, my skin prickling in a thousand places. Reflex had me open it.

Cal: I'm sorry if I've upset you? You don't need to answer the date question.

Some part of my brain immediately argued that it hadn't been a question at all.

Cal.

Relief hit me — someone I could trust. My hands were remarkably still as I hit the call button. The dial tone came again and again...*pick up, please Cal, please pick up.* The seventh ring chimed, and I almost hung up on him.

"Oh, thank god, I've never been happier to hear you," I babbled. Ashley surrounded me in marbles, concentric circles that trapped me in their centre. My stomach clenched, and I stepped out of the circle, pacing the length of the apartment.

"Mila? Are you okay?"

I stared at the phone, wondering why I'd called him. My brain was a fuzzy blank. I sat down on Ashley's bed, picking at the cover. My phone buzzed, and a pair of cold, hard eyes floated across my vision.

"Mila? Did you need something?"

"He has my number," I croaked the words from a dry throat, surprised I could feel anything in my state of numbness. Blinking, I wanted to take them back straight away. If I didn't say it, maybe it wasn't real.

"What?"

"He sent me messages–"

"What?" Cal's voice was sharp, cutting through the white noise consuming my head. "Mila– he– Logan? Is that who you mean?"

I nodded my head emphatically, then remembered he couldn't see me.

"Yes. I think so? It's a number I don't know. He says I'd make a great mother, that I'm looking after h-his baby."

The words sickened me. He knew I was with Ashley. He was — oh shit. He knew where I was, where Ashley was.

"Cal, he knows…"

"Mila, I'm two hours away. We all are. Stay in the apartment, and *don't* open the door to anyone, unless it's me. He can't get in. Do you hear me? You are safe. I'll get a security detail for the elevator door and station a few guys on the street. Mila. Mila?"

"Yes?"

"Is Ashley with you?"

"No."

Everything stopped.

I lurched to my feet. Why had I left her alone? Cal was still talking, but I couldn't hear past my own thoughts as I raced back to Ashley. She sat in the circle of marbles, organising them by colour. I froze, desperately wanting to hold her, convince myself she was safe, but she was so serene, playing in the maze she had created.

After this morning, I couldn't bring myself to frighten her. I sat down on the other side of the marble city; phone pressed to my ear. Cal's voice began to penetrate my brain smog.

"–honey, you need to say something. I know this is frightening, but..."

I let out a hollow bark that died as it left my throat. That I might be *frightened* was laughable. Terrified, out of my mind with fear was more like it. Red shoes and alabaster legs overrode the lounge, and I couldn't see anything more. I could feel his heat beside me — for someone so cold and hard; he had presence.

Something touched my arm, and I screamed, ripping away onto my back, feet pedalling until I hit the opposite wall.

Two large, blue eyes and a halo of golden hair appeared before me, crawling slowly forwards. I gasped like a guppy out of water, and those beautiful blue eyes filled with tears. Ashley's bottom lip wobbled as they began to fall.

"Oh, Ashley, no, I'm so sorry! Come here, please–" I held out my arms, and she leapt into them, hitting me with a force that nearly bowled both of us right over. I held on tight as my own tears began.

Calm down; you're scaring her.

I sucked air hard through my nose, and after a few breaths, my head finally began to clear. An odd noise was coming from halfway across the room. I saw my phone lying face-up on the carpet. Cal was yelling, voice tearing with panic. I let Ashley go and flopped onto the carpet, reaching for my phone.

"Cal, it's okay, I just had a fright. We're both perfectly fine. I'm so sorry."

There was silence on the other end.

"Cal?"

"Mila, you scared the shit out of me. I thought–" The speaker filled with white noise. Cal must have breathed into it. "I'll be back as soon as I can. Just…just stay inside. Don't open the door for anyone but me. Do you understand?"

"Yes. We will stay here," I parroted.

"Repeat it all back to me, honey. You've had a shock; I need to know you'll do this." There was an edge of desperation in his voice that made me want to calm him, bring him back — the same way I'd felt the first day we'd met when I'd sat in the gutter like a trollop. I gave a hiccuping laugh.

"Mila?"

I breathed, and repeated his words back to him as closely as I could, my phone buzzing in my hand.

"More messages are coming through."

"Don't look at them. Don't react. Please don't turn your phone off in case I need to call you, okay? I'll call when I'm in the garage, so you know I'm coming up."

I could hear the frustration in his voice, but I believed him. He hesitated before he hung up; neither of us knew what to say. Two hours suddenly seemed a very long time. It was the thought that Logan might be nearby, that he knew where we were *and* that he had my number — *I bet it was that little techie guy* — but that train of thought put me back in the bank, and I wasn't going there again.

I drew the blinds around Cal's apartment, flicking on the lights. Ashley packed up the marbles, storing them back into their old plastic container. I watched her for a while, wondering if we hadn't made a huge mistake in taking her from her foster home and family.

But if Logan had found me, and knew she was with me, then he would have been able to take her from Jenny. I wished I had Cal here to talk through all the things running about in my head.

My phone buzzed repeatedly, and I grabbed it, hoping to see Cal's number pop up, but the first part of a message came up instead.

Why did you close the blinds? I want to see your face.

I let the phone fall, not caring if it smashed, stepping backwards. The lounge butted against the back of my knees, and I sank onto it. Ashley crawled onto my lap, presenting me with a glittery pink book with a prancing unicorn on the cover. It was heavy and thick. She looked at me with pleading eyes.

"This is my favourite book. It has a Prince who always saves the day, and the her-o-ine," she pronounced it slowly, to get it right, "is a warrior princess. Her best friend is a unicorn. There are castles and ogres. It's my favourite."

I couldn't say anything, afraid I'd burst into tears. Ashley had the biggest heart I'd ever known. I hoped she would never grow out her kindness.

"It's okay if you don't want to read, though," she said in a small voice, "maybe I could read it to you?"

I rearranged us on the sofa, opening the book. She pulled a blanket over both of us, snuggling in.

"What don't we take turns reading a big page each?"

And that was how Cal found us when he burst through the door. Frantic clicks followed him as he secured the apartment. His heavy footsteps pounded along the corridor in our direction, and I wondered what the neighbours would think — increased security and police outside the building's front door and so much noise up above.

He appeared at the end of the hall where it opened into the lounge and kitchen, pale and drawn. The moment he spotted us, his face relaxed into a smile, relief evident, though the shadows hovered at the edges of his false calm.

I waved, but Ashley never stopped reading, determined to make me feel better, it seemed. Or herself. Either way, we were together now, and with Cal home, I felt that much safer.

He crouched down, eyes travelling over both of us as though checking for injuries that weren't there. Ashley launched from my lap, arms outstretched.

"Cal!"

"What are you reading?" he asked as he caught her, turning to the cover of the book.

Ashley rattled off an explanation of the current unicorn crisis. He laughed with her, pointing out all the flaws in the bad guy's plans, his free hand scooting under the blanket to give my hip a quick squeeze.

Tiny shocks shot through me. He sent me an easy smile I could barely return. I wanted to pull him back to me,

but I was too cautious to show him affection around Ashley.
I smiled, glad to see no hesitation in his gaze.

Ashley refused to be parted from Cal, wrapping
gangly arms and legs around his waist. I smiled at the sight,
hopping out from under the blanket. Cal deposited Ashley
on the ground, wincing as she gave him an enthusiastic hug,
thumping his back, and offered to make dinner.

"Oh, Cal. I didn't even think to–"

To his credit, his smile never slipped.

"It's okay, Mila. I want to. Gotta look after my girls."
He tossed a pony to Ashley who caught it deftly, racing off
to reunite it with its kin.

I swallowed back uncertainty at hearing Cal refer to
us — to me — as his girl. I studied his profile as he ferreted
through the fridge.

As soon as she was out of sight, he stepped into me,
framing my face with both hands. His thumbs stroked my
cheeks for a moment before he pulled me into him, crushing
me against this chest.

"I wasn't here for you. I wasn't here," he whispered,
his hand cupping the back of my head.

My arms still around him, I wriggled until he loosened
his hold, everything I'd managed to keep hidden for the past
two hours brimming over the top.

"How did he find us, Cal? How– what–"

My arms shook. I squeezed them into his sides, trying to hide it. He made a small sound, a tightness disappearing from his face as I looked up. His mask slipped back into place.

"I don't know."

The omission sat between us, a starving thing that gnawed at my heart. This time, it was Cal who put the walls up between us.

His sleeves were rolled up, exposing those amazing forearms. Cal had resumed his facade at making dinner. Shirt tucked into his jeans; he looked like a model on the cover of a cowboy magazine. There was something so relaxed about him — only his eyes told the story of the underlying intensity that drove him.

He straightened, running his fingers over his head in a familiar gesture, and passed me a glass of wine. I took it, murmuring my thanks. His easy smile was back, though I read the worry behind it. Tiny lines formed around his eyes, jaw just a little tense — he would be impossible to read if you didn't know him. It came as a shock that I *did* know Cal, at least a little bit.

We'd been living in each other's back pockets and through some pretty stressful situations too, which was when people truly showed who they were. I wondered when I would be able to see the real man underneath all the false fronts he presented.

"Any preferences for dinner?" he asked, leaning back on the counter. He raised his beer, hiding a flash of pain that passed across his face, eyes on me the entire time. I shook my head, watching him as he shifted against the bench at his back.

"No, just...I'm too, I don't know..."

Cal shrugged it off, but I wasn't going to let him get away with it.

"What happened today?"

He let out a sigh, shoulders slumping. The shadows closed in. "We found one of Logan's old haunts. Got a few of the lackeys he's used. Found the car." His shrug said more than his words, lips compressing.

"The black one?"

"Yeah. Plates like you described. Only one letter off. I'm relying on your memory from now on." He saluted me with his beer.

"Artist's memory." Cal buried his head in the fridge, but he wasn't getting out of it that easily. "So...what happened to your back?"

Cal's jaw set. "It got a...little rough."

"A little? You flinched when a nine-year-old patted your back."

"It was more than a pat, Mila."

I snorted.

"Yeah, a tough guy like you, taken down by a little girl."

"No, this tough guy was almost taken down by a shovel swung by a thin guy. Glad he wasn't much bigger." Cal raised his eyebrows in emphasis.

My mouth dropped.

"What? Let me see."

Cal looked at me for a moment, lips pressed together. I circled him, gently lifting the hem of his shirt. He didn't say anything or move away, which I took as permission.

Long muscles framed his lower back, disappearing into his jeans. Red patches started halfway up his spine, spreading across his shoulders. He sighed, shucking his shirt over his head with a barely suppressed groan.

Purple and red welts spread across his broad back, reaching from shoulder to shoulder — angry and swollen. I gasped at the damage, surprised he could move, let alone deal with Ashley hanging off him. My fingers hovered over the raised marks, but I drew my hand back, not wanting to hurt him.

"I'll get ice."

He sent me a cheeky grin over his shoulder, eyes following my hand back to my side. I rolled my eyes, scrounging in the freezer. One long, folded ice pack lay in the bottom of the tray, next to a pack of frozen baby carrots. I grabbed both, sure the icepack alone wouldn't be enough.

Cal leaned over the benchtop; forearms braced on the cool, black stone. Snaring tea towels from the oven door, I wrapped both packs.

"This might hurt."

"I'll survive." The cheeky grin was back, but when I placed the first pack across his back, Cal bowed his head with a stifled groan. Muscles twitched beneath the cloth. I bit my lip. The marks — soon to be bruises — were so extensive, the longer pack didn't quite cover them.

I laid the wrapped bag of carrots over his right shoulder, my hand on his arm, pressing down on his tattoo to balance myself. Cal didn't flinch this time. Even half bent over, he was still a giant, compared to me.

His skin was smooth under my hand; hard muscle layered just beneath the surface. His shoulders were tight with the pain, but looked as though they had been sculpted to absolute refinement — not a millimetre of skin was wasted.

He wasn't the sort of male an artist usually attracted.

My fingers brushed the muscles framing his arms before I had thought what I was doing. He just looked so perfect. I lifted the ice pack a little, but there was no improvement yet. How hard must he have been hit to sustain such damage? Had he just gotten back up and kept going?

I shivered a little, tracing the long, lean musculature of his arms. I would love to paint him. Golden-haired and bronze-skinned, I had initially thought of Adonis when we'd first met, but now I thought more of a fighting culture — Vikings, or the Norse gods, perhaps.

Perfection.

"Having fun?"

Cal watched me over his shoulder, head tilted, and I realised how close we were. His gaze drifted down to my fingers sliding along the length of his arm. I snatched my hand back, heat rushing to my face. I started to stammer, then closed my mouth, attempting to collect myself, but any prospect of serenity avoided me. Flustered, I flapped at his back. So much better than stammering. I wanted to facepalm.

"Leave those on for ten minutes. We'll alternate." I backed away a few steps, unsure of what to do.

Cal watched me steadily, the shadow of a smile haunting his lips.

"I thought you weren't into sports. How come you know how to apply an ice pack?"

"My gran had a few falls. The nurses taught me what to do for her." The timer went off on the microwave. I lifted the pack, but there was still no change. If anything, the welts were beginning to look worse. "Did you treat this at all?"

Cal shrugged, wincing.

"Didn't have time. Needed to get home to the unicorn whisperer over there...and you."

"Oh."

I couldn't think of anything else to say. I'd been in panic mode this afternoon, desperate to have Cal back, to feel safe. Which I — we — did.

Ashley pranced into the kitchen, dancing with a pair of ponies, glitter trailing in her wake. Cal rolled his eyes heavenward in silent prayer. I hid a smile, redirecting the pony party to an already glitter-encrusted section of carpet.

Must clean that up tomorrow.

Would I be here tomorrow? It obviously wasn't safe anymore. I was glad of the distraction treating Cal's back offered, but now he was home, my mind began to churn as the ramifications of Logan's messages slammed into me. Where would we go? I made a note to ask Cal later, after Ashley was asleep, to avoid panicking her with too many changes.

"I need a shower," Ashley announced at my hip. I smiled, grabbing a towel from the linen press and setting her up in the bathroom, then wandered back down the hall to where Cal was cooking, still hunched over, balancing the ice packs on his back.

My stomach rumbled. It had been a long day, and attempting anything that was a semblance of normality seemed wrong. Especially while stalking psychos were out in the darkness, waiting for us to emerge.

Exposed.

I squeezed my eyes shut, fingers wrapped around the stem of my wine glass in a death grip. Hands covered mine, squeezing gently.

"Mila, it will be okay. You're going to be okay."

Worried eyes met mine. I managed part of a grin. Fake it 'til you make it, right?

"I'll be fine." The lie came out too easily.

Cal returned to the bench, texting on his phone. The timer was ready to go off again, so I reshuffled everything, with firm orders to stay put this time.

I leaned on the bench beside him, pressing my back against it — no time like the present.

"Okay, she's in the shower. Now, please tell me what we are going to do."

"Do?"

"Don't you play coy with me." I jabbed him with my elbow. He faked a groan. "We have to move, right? We can't stay here if Logan knows where we are." I was quite proud I didn't trip over his name.

Cal shook his head.

"This is one of the safest places there is. Moving you two creates a real target — he wants us to leave here because he can't get in. We'd be doing exactly what he wants." Cal wriggled his shoulders with a grimace beneath the icepacks. "This is what Logan does, fucking with your mind."

I nodded, pressing my hands onto the bench behind me and scooting up onto it. Too late, I remembered this was where I'd been that night, my legs wrapped around him. A quick, indrawn breath confirmed he did, too.

I made to hop back down, but Cal stopped me, placing a firm hand on my knee. I inhaled sharply. "Cal..."

"Stay there. Please?" He looked at me sideways, gentling his touch.

Breathing slowly to steady my racing heart, I nodded again and tried to bring the conversation back on track.

"So...we stay here? Knowing he knows?" I tried to concentrate, but with Cal's hand on my leg, it was a little difficult.

"Yes. I can protect you here. Out there — I have no way of knowing if he's seeing us."

"Wait. What about you, each time you leave here? Doesn't that make you a—a target or something?"

Cal shrugged.

"I think he knows pretty much everything at this point, honey. If he wanted to kill me, I'd be dead by now."

He's lived like this for the last five years. Bile rose in my throat. Was this my new normal as well? I asked the question I hadn't wanted to.

"Won't your boss object to us being here?" I closed my eyes briefly, not wanting him to answer. He squeezed my leg.

"You're safer here," he replied, his jaw jutting out.

"Saying that doesn't make it so," I reminded him, but Cal just stared at me. Floundering, I tried another tack. "Why is Logan so hard to find?"

"He's unpredictable and incredibly smart. Every time I find a pattern, it changes. We keep working, trying to find something to use against him. One day, one of his crew will slip up, and we'll get him. Waiting is the killer."

I mulled over his words, thinking of the men with him in the bank. Were they still the same people, after all this time, or did he replace them, as they made mistakes? I frowned. Something Cal had said set off an alarm in my mind, but I couldn't pinpoint it. I looked at his back again.

"You found someone today though, right? Did you learn anything more from that? Anything...useful? That was worth this." I tapped a small section of unmarred skin on his back. There wasn't much left. Cal rolled his shoulders reflexively, muscles rippling.

Close your mouth, Mila. You're drooling on the floor.

"The boys are still down there sorting through the house. Micah doesn't look much better; he copped a folding chair." He stated it all so impassively, a soldier making a report, as though this happened every day. Watching his strong frame hulking over the benchtop, I wondered if, for him, it was.

"Ouch. Is he okay? Should he — or you — go to the hospital to be checked?"

"He'll be fine. Let's just say we won't be working out for a few days at least."

Cal grinned, just as I had a lightbulb moment, sitting up straight.

"You're waiting for Logan to make a mistake." It wasn't a question, and my tone was flat.

"Yes. That's always been the plan unless we get something new." He tapped his screen again, dismissing me.

"Something new. Like us." Cal's gaze sharpened, his head moving a fraction, but I saw it. He waited. "You're using us as bait." I knocked his hand away, swivelling on the bench. He shifted as though to reach out, but I swatted his hand away with a stinging slap. "You bloody bastard, you're using us to draw him here. So *you* know where *he* is. You're waiting for him to show his face. *Here.*"

Damn it, Cal. Every time I thought I could trust him, something else popped up. Frustration curdled with a huge dose of fear sank deep inside me. This time, I couldn't ignore it. He stood, gripped my shoulders in hard hands — not hurting, or shaking me, but glaring into me until I felt naked beneath the intensity of his gaze.

Anger blazed in Cal's face, matching my own. Half of me wanted to collapse into the shelter he offered; the other half needed me to stand on my own two feet and actually adult. Which I wasn't particularly good at, especially today.

Cal stared at me a moment longer, mouth tight. Then he released my shoulders and busied himself in the kitchen again.

How would I cope with living with this man for the rest of the week? A snide little voice told me that now Logan had found us, we wouldn't be able to stay here much longer, anyway.

And that filled me with an ache, deep inside.

CHAPTER EIGHTEEN

MILA

Dinner was a quiet affair. Ashley arrived in the kitchen just in time to interrupt our argument. She poked at her food, surrounded by ponies that provided a barrier between her and the rest of the table while Cal and I pretended to play *happy families* at the other end.

Cal's gaze held a dark promise that our conversation hadn't been forgotten. I swallowed hard, wishing I could escape the underlying tension that permeated the room. Cal hadn't said a word since we sat down. Ashley snuggled into her robe, almost disappearing beneath the pink fluff. It was the same one she'd dressed Micah in during his makeover. I hid a smile at the memory.

It was amazing how quickly I'd become comfortable with the boys, though I'd known Teddy for so long, he was more than a brother. That sparked a thought I'd wanted to ask Cal about — and while we were putting on a faux show for Ashley's sake, I let myself indulge my curiosity. It had always been my biggest failing. Well, that and my antisocial tendencies.

"How's Danny doing with your ex?"

I aimed for a casual tone. Cal choked on his steak, looking at me with wounded eyes as he gasped for air.

"Really? You're asking me *now?*"

I shrugged, unable to hide a small smile. *Distraction achieved.* We could all use a little humour at this point. Cal was still coughing when Ashley thumped him on the back with enthusiasm. He flinched and moved away.

"Should have kept the ice packs on."

"Nag, nag." Guilty eyes found mine. Cal ducked, hacking at his food. Instead, he answered my earlier question, "I think they're going well?"

He turned away, coughing into his hand. I wasn't quite convinced, though pain sliced through his face with each of Ashley's whacks. This wasn't quite the diversion I'd planned. I leaned over, filling her small hands with ponies.

"Ash, if you're not going to eat, why don't you play ponies while I clean up? There might be something on TV."

She sent me a bright smile paired with a huge hug, disappearing to the floor. I marvelled at the resilience a child had to move past traumatic events, which I clung to every emotional morsel. More ponies appeared on the huge screen Cal had set up in the lounge.

Leaving Cal to finish his meal in peace, I collected plates still half-filled with food. He snagged mine as I went by, dumping the contents onto his own. I smiled, carting the rest back to the sink. Cal appeared a moment later with an empty plate.

"That was fast. Big day?" It was so wrong to be talking about things as mundane as work when there was the most dangerous man in the world stalking us. I flitted back to the messages on my phone, the floor dropping out from beneath me. I clung to the sink, but fortunately, Cal didn't seem to notice. He shrugged my comment off, sorting through the dishwasher as though nothing was amiss.

Ashley sprawled on the floor, her head nodding. We'd had dinner, played, read...it all seemed so normal when outside these walls, for us, the world was anything but.

"What are we going to do?"

The words slipped out, and I wished I could take them back.

"How about we talk about that after she's in bed?" His tone was light as he nodded towards Ashley.

"I think she might be ready to go now. Do you mind if I read to her?"

He shook his head. I gently pressed on his shoulder, and with a sigh, he allowed me to minister to his back. The ice packs had almost refrozen during dinner.

"Just want my shirt off again," he grumbled, his movements much slower than before as he removed the garment. My mouth was open to retort when I caught the speculative look he sent my way.

Ignoring him, I moved the ice packs around on his back, trying to cover areas that hadn't been treated yet. It was like a crazy game of Tetris.

"I've reset the microwave. Don't move too much, or it will all come sliding down."

I re-balanced the packs with a pat. Cal's hand shot out, closing light around my wrist. It was just enough to stop me. Goosebumps pebbled my arm.

"Thank you, Mila."

I nodded, unable to summon a smile, and went to put Ashley to bed.

I knew she was a little old for it, but she still enjoyed being read to. We'd gone most of the way through the unicorn quest when her eyes fluttered closed. I stayed a few minutes longer, then crept out of the room, flicking the light off.

Cal was still leaning on the bench, texting on his phone. I knew he had moved to get it, and couldn't help fussing. Water beaded on his back. I wiped it away, and swapped the carrots in their saturated cloth for a bag of frozen peas instead, wrapping them in a dry towel.

When he turned his head, the dark look in his eyes unnerved me. My anger from before had dissipated, leaving only room for a bone-deep dose of exhaustion. I tried my hardest to drag it back up, but beneath his hard gaze, my courage failed.

"I don't want to fight with you," I said quietly. "Not after everything that has happened today."

Cal's phone hit the bench with a light smack. Apparently, his anger was right at the surface. I shook my head, moving away. All I wanted to do was sleep, and forget today had happened. Even though that wasn't entirely possible, I was happy to keep pretending.

Cal's arms caged me against the bench so quickly I hadn't realised he had moved. I pressed a listless hand to his chest, but as usual, it made absolutely no difference.

"Can we do this tomorrow? Cal...I'm so tired."

His fingers caught beneath my chin, raising my face to his. I couldn't be bothered to resist him. His eyes bore into mine, a burning intensity, directed at me. It came as a surprise, but I wasn't afraid, not like I had been back at the house. This time, I knew who he was.

"I will never use you as *bait*," he spat the last word, his fingers firm on my chin.

He rose to his full height, towering over me. Ice packs slapped the tiles as he released me, but didn't step back, out of my space. Half-naked, he was a sight — ridges of muscle covering his stomach, travelling down to the vee of his hips. I swallowed, refocusing on his face.

"I would never hurt you. Or her — though believe me, I've had plenty of *good cops*," he snorted, "tell me I should use her to drive him mad. But I won't stoop that fucking low. I'm not *him*."

Something hard lay in his face. Cords of sinew tightened at his neck, his chest broad and sculpted. I raised one hand to touch him, to trace the lines that made him so fine, then slapped it back to the counter. His gaze heated, igniting something deep inside me.

"Keep looking, Mila." His voice was rough, deep. His breath hit my lips, and I had to repress the urge to react. My eyes closed for a second, and with effort, I snapped them open.

"No! You don't get to do this to me, again and again. Cal, please. I was terrified this afternoon. I wanted nothing more than you home so I could feel safe." His fingers grazed my cheek, and I closed my eyes again, willing myself not to cry, the weight of the day draining my sudden burst of energy.

"I won't let him hurt you. I promise, Mila. There's nothing here I can't control. You are safe," he punctuated each word. I opened my eyes, looking straight into him. His voice dropped to a whisper, "You are safe with me."

I so desperately wanted to believe that.

"Cal," I whispered, shaking my head in an attempt to clear it, "You can't control him. That's always been it, isn't it? He wins because he isn't predictable. Please, if you're wrong...don't let us be your mistake."

His thumb brushed my lips.

"Damnit, Mila." He was far too close. "You– you're right." He stepped back, breaking the contact. He ran a hand over his head. "I have four cops downstairs, one in the foyer up here." He nodded to the door. "There are three cars patrolling, and Black will do the night shift for the next few days. It leaves us one man shy, but he wanted to make sure you're safe. He's happy to sleep here during the day, if you want, though I was thinking of working from home, as well."

I shook my head.

"No."

He peered at me cautiously.

"No...what?"

"No. Don't stay here, cooped up. Do your job. We're just...distractions." The corner of his mouth curled upwards. My heart lightening, I swatted his arm. "Not that sort."

He stepped back into me, hands sliding from my waist to my ribs, his thumbs brushing beneath my breasts. "You know you are." He kneed my legs apart, stepping between them. I let my fingers run the length of his arm.

"We shouldn't," I murmured.

"Mila." His fingers curled into my hair, tracing patterns on my shoulder. "Stop telling me what I shouldn't do. I like your type of distraction."

He caught the back of my neck, tilting my head up. I stared into those eyes and wanted very much what he was offering. Desperation warred with exhaustion. His breath hot on my lips, he dragged his other hand down my ribs. I wanted this, but it still felt like a bribe. And I wasn't sure I trusted him to not play us over his need to catch Logan.

Eyes wide, I slammed my hands to his chest, pushing him back as I slipped away from the bench.

"We stop this now. I can't trust that you won't use us to get what you want — what you've been fighting for. I can't trust you," I whispered, tears pricking my eyes.

His face shut down in an instant, wiped clean of all emotion. Cal surveyed me with cold eyes, and I shivered. If this was the man that hunted Wayde Logan, I'd hate to be between them when it all came crashing down.

"I'll be in the study. Knock, if you want me." His voice was distant, but his gaze sharp, and the double entendre wasn't lost on me. I watched him stride away, wondering if I hadn't made a huge mistake.

With him only a room away, I was more alone than ever.

CHAPTER NINETEEN

MILA

I stayed up for a few hours, not remotely tired, but sickened to my core. Fear of Logan for Ashley and I, paired with the worry I'd destroyed everything Cal and I had built up, haunted me. On the floor, my phone buzzed, but I couldn't bring myself to pick it up. I knew there would be more messages, and I couldn't face them right now.

I closed my eyes, leaning my head on the back of the sofa. I didn't want to go into Cal's room, sleep in his bed. It would just remind me of what I'd turned down, because of fear.

He fucks with your mind.

Cal's words turned over and over, echoing inside my head. I pressed the heels of my hands into my eyes, trying to repress the tears that threatened. Eventually, with all the lights still on, I managed to fall asleep.

His eyes were cold, staring into my soul. Tiny cries tore the air around us, alone in a dark place. *This isn't real; he's not here.* I knew it was a dream — which was unusual, as I rarely remembered mine at all. And I never knew when I was in one, usually. But the knowledge *he had wasn't* here, helped. Even so, I was stuck — staring at those eyes, my whole body spasming in fear. Hands on my arms tightened. Is this what it would feel like when he found me? Fear overcoming every sense, wanting to vomit, but frozen, unable to move, to escape.

Itsadream, itsadream, itsadream.

The hands squeezed, shaking a little. I looked down, breathing cold, morning air. Hands were still wrapped around my arms, and my mind jammed.

He's here, he's here, he's here.

A scream built inside me; beginning to tear free when a hand clamped down over my mouth, pinning me to the lounge. I launched out in flail of arms and legs, desperate to get up, to get free. Dimly, I heard a groan as my hand connected with something solid.

I focussed on Cal's worried face as he leaned over me, holding my wrists gently in one hand.

"Mila, honey, it's me. It's not– it's just me." His voice was barely a whisper, and I looked around in the pale light of the early morning. Tugging my wrists from his grasp, I concentrated on Cal. He let go, still hovering over me.

"You were dreaming." I snorted. *Thanks for stating the obvious.* "Nightmare?"

I nodded, wiping tears from my cheeks. Last night's or this morning's? I couldn't be sure.

"Logan?"

I nodded again, sitting up. Cal backed away, still watching me. A blanket covered the floor beneath the lounge.

"Did you sleep on the floor? You should have had the bed. Your bed." My voice was raspy and dry. Cal passed me his water bottle.

"I didn't want to leave you alone. In case..." He didn't finish the sentence. I nodded, wrapping my arms around myself.

"Honey, are you okay?"

I shook my head wordlessly, tiny shivers beginning in my hands, soon wracking my entire body. Cal slid his arms beneath my legs, sitting with me curled in his lap. He pressed my head to his shoulder and held on, even when the tears started anew.

"I'm sorry, Mila. Last night was just...we didn't end that well. I'm sorry, honey."

Eventually, the tremors stopped. My cheeks were damp, and I looked at the mess I'd made of his shirt, mortified I'd completely lost it in front of him. I wriggled and tried to get up.

"I'm so, so sorry." This morning seemed to be all about apologies. I pushed against him, but he refused to let me go.

"Cal, we shouldn't be–"

"I don't give a fuck what we should and shouldn't be doing right now. You're not going anywhere." He swung his long legs across the sofa, bringing me with him. Our legs tangled together, one hand firmly pressed on my lower back. The other he reached between us, shucking his shirt off over his head, wincing only a little, and pulled me back down to him.

In the pre-dawn, the light was soft. I was reminded of him outside my house, keeping watch while I slept. I rested my head on his chest, the scent and warmth of him surrounding me.

It seemed perfectly normal to be pressed against a half-naked man, even though I knew it shouldn't. Should it? I closed my eyes, listening to his heart beat its strong, steady rhythm.

We lay quietly for a long while, my eyes heavy, and I began to yawn, ready to doze off, comfortable and warm as I was. *Safe.* It was one of the first things I'd said to Cal; that he made me feel safe. I trawled through everything in my head and found it was still true. Maybe we would be okay together, after all.

"Thank you. For sleeping near me. Thank you for keeping us safe."

Light brightened as the sun broke above the horizon, setting the room aglow, even through the drawn blinds. His skin was more golden than ever; like he was made by the sun. He regarded me steadily, one hand splayed between my shoulders, making tiny circles there with his fingers.

Cal was silent for so long the nerves began to jump in my stomach again. I wiggled, wanting to sit up but he stayed me with one hand flat on my lower back, holding me against him.

"Don't do that," he hissed between clenched teeth, "unless you want to find yourself in my bed damned fast."

I caught my lip between my teeth, wondering. My fingers trailed the rigid muscles of his abs, up along his rib cage. He was perfectly still beneath me, barely breathing. I

stretched long against him. He wasn't going to hurt me —
this man was a protector. And he wanted to protect me.

I was okay with that.

My palm pressed over his heart. I counted the beats,
still not looking at him, afraid I'd set something off that
would change this moment. His breathing deepened, hands
sliding beneath my jumper along my bare skin beneath.

My breath caught, I slowly raised my gaze to meet
his.

CAL

I saw she'd accepted me the moment she raised her
head, lips red and swollen where she'd been biting them. My
hands explored her skin beneath her black sweater. I wanted
to rip it off her, press her bare skin against mine. I needed to
claim this woman, but I also knew she needed me to take it
slow – though the other night had been anything but. Still, if
I rushed her, Mila would run – from me, from the safety of
the apartment.

And I needed to be at work in an hour.

My hands almost encompassed her entire back; she was so tiny. I drew her up my chest, so her mouth was level with mine. Her breath puffed gently against my lips. I didn't lean into her to kiss her, though I wanted badly to roll her onto her back, open the blinds so I could explore every damned inch of her skin, every curve.

This needed to be her choice. My restraint taughtened — if she kept staring at me for much longer with those half-lidded eyes, blush staining her cheeks as she stared at my mouth, I wouldn't be taking anything slow.

Mercifully, she leaned in, pressing her lips to mine. I closed my eyes, lost in the smell of her, the softness of her skin beneath my hands. Her tongue flicked against my lips, and I groaned, pulling her flush against me. I let her open my mouth with hers, let her have the control, moving to her rhythm.

She wiggled her hips, palms planted on my arms as she stretched the length of me. It took everything I had not to make good on my promise. I slid my hand down her back, curling my fingers around her ass.

A mewling sound started in her throat, making me so hard it was painful. The material of her pants was thin, and I could feel the heat of her through it.

"Mila," I growled as she moved again, squeezing her ass — it fit so perfectly in my hand. "Honey, just be still for a moment."

Her eyes widened in understanding as she took in my deep breaths, the rapid pace of my heart beneath her hand. I slipped my other hand between her shoulder blades, pressing her down to me. Her mouth found mine again, and I kissed her slowly, every inch of me reaching to control my need to flip her, and fuck her senseless.

Tiny footsteps padded into the lounge, and a high voice greeted us.

"Cal, look what I found! It's an old–" Ashley's voice cut off. Mila jumped off me, smoothing her clothes. Ashley eyed us with wisdom beyond her years, a mass of dirty blonde hair standing out around her head, like a halo. I grabbed my shirt, pulling it back over my head.

"Are you two together? 'Cause that would be fun. Then I wouldn't have to move again, right? I could live here. With you." She hopped onto the sofa between us as we inched away from each other, making room. "Just like having a real mum and dad in my two favourite people. Can we have the TV on, please, Cal?"

Mila looked at me over her head; both of us completely speechless. I slipped my arm across the back of the sofa, encompassing both of my girls, and squeezed Mila's shoulder. She found my hand with hers, lacing our fingers together.

Only last night I'd wondered if she'd ever let me hold her again. I fumbled for the remote with my other hand, cheery morning cartoons filling the room.

Mila leaned her head back on my arm, hair mussed, colour still staining her cheeks. She looked gorgeous as all hell.

I tipped my head up, closing my eyes so no one would see the tears welling there.

We stayed that way — the three of us perched on the lounge together — until my phone rang, jarring us out of our comfort zone. I picked it up, sliding out from under my girls to take the call.

"Boss, we've got to move the girl." Black's voice held an edge of exhaustion.

"What? Why?"

"Liam called. He's got a house sorted; we're to come and pick her up. She'll be with a family counsellor and her old foster mother. It's a safe house, off the grid. Micah will do a twenty-four-hour rotation with me. Hole up there for a bit, work from this new place."

"That's mad! What the hell is Liam thinking? She's bloody safe here."

"I know, man, but the legalities of her living with you, if something happened...you'd lose your job. Not worth the risk."

"But worth the risk of moving her? I don't like this."

"I'll be there in ten with these two dickheads. We'll leave someone to guard Mila, take the trucks and head off in three different directions. That's the plan, as far as I know."

"Black. Why the hell didn't Liam call me directly?"

"Dunno, man. Be there soon."

I hung up, turning to the girls. Mila was right behind me, frowning.

"What's going on?"

I sighed, running a hand over my head.

"Liam's moving Ashley." Mila's mouth opened in protest, her beautiful eyes widening. I shushed her quickly. "We don't have a lot of time. There's a secure house with her old foster mother and a counsellor. It's off the grid. We need to pack her and move her, right now. No arguments, okay?"

Mila looked like she wanted to argue very much, but gave me one last, hard look, and turned on her heel, calling out cheerfully to Ashley. The woman was an actress. We

were blessed because this sort of thing was my weakness —
too job focussed, not gentle enough. I gave a wry grin.

I tapped my phone on my leg, unhappy with how this
had played out. Bugger it; I'd have to call Liam. Something
just didn't ring right about this, and I wouldn't risk Ashley on
a whim.

I pressed call on Liam's number. I counted the rings
by habit, pacing in a tight circle. He picked up right before it
would have gone to voicemail.

"Cal!" he sounded surprised to hear from me. "How
are you doing?"

"Good, Liam. Listen, you've called Black this
morning, right?"

There was a pause before he answered.

"Yes. I have. What's up?"

"Just wanted to check your orders. Seemed a bit ah,
out of character?"

"Stick with the plan. It's an open line, and I'm not
risking this, Cal. Your team will be there soon. It's to protect
you and...all of you. Right?"

"You're absolutely sure this is necessary?" I was
loathed to say more. Liam was right — it was an unsecured

line. My paranoia was getting in the way of my work. Damn Logan and his mind games. I ran a hand over my face.

"Yes. I'll be back in three days. Look after everyone. You'll be fine." Liam hung up.

I'd see him in the morning.

MILA

I hung around the door, fussing with Ashley's backpack. Ponies and pyjamas were stuffed haphazardly inside. I could swear there were more things in there than she'd arrived with. Jamming them in in a hurry had been a challenge without alerting the poor girl. She hadn't wanted to leave Cal and me — something I wholeheartedly agreed with — though Jenny had been the draw card.

As soon as she found out she'd see her foster mother again, she was happy to go. I breathed with relief on that one — having her crying and screaming as she left would have torn my heart out. Traumatising her further than she already was, wasn't on the top of my list.

After only a few days living with her, I was more attached to her than I had already been. The boys arrived in their typical fashion — en masse — and left the same way. Ashley had jammed herself in between Micah and Danny. Teddy crushed me in a huge hug, immediately interrogating me.

Warm eyes assessed me as he put me back down.

"Are you okay here? He hasn't gone apeshit on you again, right?"

Teddy shot a contemptuous glare at Cal. I was surprised, knowing they were so close. I put a hand on his arm — it was so big my fingers didn't stretch halfway around it.

"I'm fine," I reassured him, though he didn't look convinced. "Cal is taking care of me. And he hasn't scared me...well, too much. No!" I shook my head, bringing Teddy's attention back to me, "I had a nightmare this morning. He slept on the floor to make sure I was okay."

I clamped my mouth shut before I could say anything more. If Teddy was already protective over me, hearing that his work buddy had gotten hot and heavy with one of his best friends wasn't going to help the situation at all.

He nodded slowly.

"You look after you, okay? I'm going to go with Ashley, make sure she gets settled in. Danny will stay here — in the apartment if you're okay with that; outside the door, if you're not. Are you comfortable with him?"

Considering my experience with him was as one of Ashley's makeover projects and knowing he had punched Cal because he was dating his ex, I couldn't really say. But he seemed friendly enough, and I knew he would be safe if he was one of Cal's hand-picked team.

He trusted the younger man — I was pretty sure he saw himself there, a few years back. Plus, it seemed rather rude to shunt someone who was looking after you outside the door for the day. I smiled at Teddy, nodding.

"Sure, that's fine. He's fine inside the apartment. Right?" Cal approached us.

"What's happening?"

"You okay for Danny to stay inside the apartment with Mila?"

Cal turned to me. "Are you?"

"Sure."

"Okay, that's settled then." Cal turned to Teddy. "We're going to take the three trucks. They'll still stand out, but we can use Micah's monster as a diversion. We'll leave now, and meet there in thirty-five minutes. If anyone is late, call it in." He turned to me, slipping an arm around my waist.

Under Teddy's watchful gaze, Cal drew me to him, leaving no room for me to pull away, and kissed me soundly in front of the whole room. When he raised his head, I was breathing deeply, every inch of me aching to touch him.

Danny and Micah gave whoops, swinging Ashley in the air. Teddy watched us in silence, the air heavy as he weighed Cal's worth. Finally, he nodded. I looked up at Cal, who stared back, calm-faced but blazing eyes. I wrapped my arms around him, not caring who saw.

"Please be careful. With her *and* you, too."

"I will be. I'll be back tonight, for you."

He said the words into my hair, sending shivers through me. He kissed me once more and with a rushed hug from Ashley, they were gone.

Danny grinned at me awkwardly, playing on his phone. The door rattled, and I jumped. Cal's head popped back in, reaching to program the alarm. He waved, disappearing behind the closed door.

I wiggled my toes on the carpet, suddenly claustrophobic. Not even allowed to open the blinds — I understood why not, but still, it grated on me. For a girl with an open, old house and a big backyard, being cooped up in an apartment was bad enough. Not being able to see the sun was worse.

"Would you like a cup of coffee, Danny?"

He grimaced, waving his drink bottle at me. I assumed it had some sort of protein shake in it. The boys appeared to be mad on them. I stood at the edge of the kitchen counter, unsure of what to do next. My fingers drummed on a stack of A4 paper Cal had placed there this morning. Three graphite pencils sat on top of the pile.

I looked over at Danny, ridiculously seated at the small table, overflowing the chair, which I thought might collapse at any moment. An idea grew in my mind.

"Hey, Danny. Would you mind if I drew you?"

Eight hours later, I had a much smaller stack of paper in front of me, though sheets filled with random parts of Danny's anatomy were scattered about the apartment. I followed him from table to sofa as he charged his phone. Mine still lay under the lounge, and I wasn't game to pick it up yet. The stupid thing was probably flat. I knew I should charge it, in case Cal called or messaged but I was still too afraid to look at it. Finally, I gritted my teeth and decided it was time.

I pulled Danny's phone off charge, scooping mine up to plug it in. Opening the screen, I tried to ignore all the messages scrolling through as I entered my password. I clutched it for a moment, then handed it to Danny.

"Can you please clear the messages? The ones at the top of the list, please?" I couldn't look at them. I knew I'd be sick if I did.

"Sure, babe. You want me to block the number? Mind if I send these to myself? I'll keep them as evidence for you." I nodded. Danny did as I'd asked and passed the phone back. He flicked through the Netflix menu, settling on a sci-fi series I hadn't heard of before.

No messages from Cal. Disappointed, I cleared my other messages and email for something to do.

"Can I make you food? Anything?"

In the end, I think he agreed to shut me up, and I stopped casting around for something to say.

Instead, I filled him up with as much as he would eat — which, for a young man in his twenties, I guessed, he was as fit as he could be.

"How many hours do you spend at the gym?" I asked as he devoured the third bowl of tuna and rice. He shrugged.

"Hour in the morning, hour in the evening. And I like to fight your boy, too. He's damned fast. You don't take your eyes off him." He grinned, "not if you don't want your ass handed to you."

It was odd to hear Cal referred to as my boy, but seeing as he had kissed me in front of everyone this

293

morning, I supposed it was a natural conclusion. It still sat a little uncomfortably, nerves tingling with a sort of desperate hope that things would work out okay, now we'd announced ourselves to the world.

I fidgeted around in the fridge, trying to work out what I could make for dinner. Just cal and I. Butterflies rioted in my stomach at the thought. Need warred with common sense in my head.

I absently selected chicken, grabbing some parsley and cucumber from the crisper. I scored harissa paste in the pantry and started to make a marinade. The parsley I would turn into tabbouleh, maybe find some more vegetables for a salad later on. Danny poked his head over the breakfast bar.

"Looks good. Boss said he'll be back in an hour. Mila, any chance you have enough of that to share for tonight? Just to take home. Mandy is coming round, and– look, I can't cook. My Mumma, she can cook for anyone, but I'm no kitchen bitch. Oops, sorry. No offence."

"None taken. There's a box in the fridge ready to go. A big one. But you have to cook it; I've left instructions on the lid."

Danny leaned over the bench, giving me a one-armed hug. "You're the best, Mila."

"I try."

Danny cleared his throat, leaning on the counter. "So...." I stopped rubbing my batch of chicken, waiting. "Cal. He, uh, seems okay with me seeing Mandy, right? I mean, she's his ex. It probably wasn't my smartest move."

I nodded in agreement.

"Probably."

"Has he– has he said anything?" Danny shuffled, uncomfortable. "I mean, he is okay with it, right?"

I gave him a reassuring smile. "I think so, Danny. It hasn't really come up, we've been a bit..." I gestured at the apartment, bereft of ponies, though the glitter remained. I suddenly missed Ashley very much. "He's not angry with you. Well, there was that punch."

The enormous cop had the grace to look sheepish.

"Well, yeah, I mean..." He coughed into his hand. I resumed rubbing spices into the chicken pieces I'd trimmed. "I shouldn't have. But...Mandy said some things, and I believed her. You know."

I didn't, of course, but I let it go. I covered the chicken in its bowl with plastic wrap and washed up so I could make the salad. The parsley was fresh and aromatic — one of my favourite herbs to cook with. Danny leaned expectantly on the counter.

"Danny, have a think for a second. You're dating your boss' ex — recent ex from what I hear? You're worried he's still in love with her; I honestly don't think so, but hey, I could be deluding myself. And she's probably made up some sob stories to get your attention and sympathy, maybe? You felt all protective of her?"

Danny nodded, running his hand over his head in a familiar gesture.

"Yeah..."

"She just wants to know you're putting her first." I raised my hands quickly, "Which, of course, you do, *but* she's also probably still sore about the break-up. Just be wary she isn't on a rebound, and don't let her come between you and your job, okay, Danny? You have the most amazing team in the world. The four of you have something really special — don't waste that."

I felt like a mother hen tutoring a student, but Danny looked happier. He leaned over for another hug.

"Five."

"Huh?"

"There's five of us. You're right; it is Cal's team. He selects us, motivates us, keeps us going when we're bored, or frustrated. But Liam — he's something else. Ex-military. He's hard. And shit scary. But he's a leader — all of us, we'd follow him anywhere. You'll like him. He and Cal are good mates."

"I'm glad you have each other. That's a huge thing, Danny. You might not find a team like this anywhere else."

"Thanks, Mila. Really."

"It's okay." The parsley was finished, and I added some mint in, alongside chopped peppers. I kept tomatoes aside for the chicken salad.

"What made you want to be a cop?"

Danny looked sideways at me.

"What made you want to be an artist?"

I stopped cutting and looked up at him sharply. His eyes twinkled, and I realised the façade he put on was just that. A brawny outer was a solid cover for a much smarter man hiding behind what others couldn't see past.

"Those smarts must be handy in your job, hey?" I heard his snort as he huffed air out. I looked up quickly, knowing I was bordering on pushy now. "Whoever the girl is you're with, make sure she's at least as clever as you."

Danny caught my eye, and a smile flickered at the corners of his mouth. The door rattled, and he was out of his seat, gun drawn and cocked — I recognised the sound — before I had blinked. Every time I saw these boys in action, I realised the incredible level of training and tenacity they had. As a unit, their capability increased tenfold. I was beginning to realise just how lethal Logan must be to evade Cal's team for so long.

Cal sauntered in, flicked the alarm off, and flipped the bird to Danny.

"I called you, asshole. Not my problem if you don't pick up your phone."

"It'll be your problem if I put a fucking bullet in your head."

"Nah, you'll miss me too much."

Danny hugged him, calling to me over his shoulder. "Mila, you got that chicken, babe?"

I was already passing him boxes which he collected under one arm.

"Instructions are on the post-it on top. Low heat, so it doesn't burn. The salad is made, and there's dressing on it already, so don't add anything else. Serve it with all the greens on the bottom, cooked chicken on top, and scatter some of the salad over it. Oh, and get a Semillon. Like this," I held up a bottle of Jacob's Creek Reserve.

Danny engulfed me in a two-armed hug, and I disappeared beneath a wall of muscle. I patted his back, waiting to be released so I could breathe.

"You'll be fine." I kissed his cheek. "Good luck."

"Thanks, Mila. See you tomorrow. Bye, dude."

The door clicked behind him. Cal locked it all up, frowning at the alarm. He tapped it impatiently, then pulled the cover off.

I put everything in the fridge, pulling out plates and cutlery. I guessed we wouldn't eat until later, but knowing how intense their days were, I wanted to have food for him ready when he needed it.

It might have sounded old fashioned, but at least cooking was something I was confident in. Cal appeared from the hallway leading to the foyer as I was cleaning up.

"Damned alarm is fu– buggered, again. Are you okay to have the repair guy back tomorrow? Danny is happy to do the extra shift."

I nodded, though something small inside my stomach crumpled. He'd had time to message Danny, but not me? I shook my head. I was being silly; these boys had work to do.

"How did Ashley settle in?"

Cal leaned on the counter, almost exactly where Danny had been standing earlier.

"Famously. As soon as she saw Jenny, she was good. They really missed each other."

I forced a smile, truly glad Ashley had been reunited with her foster mum, but it didn't make missing her easier.

"I think I'll leave the glitter in the carpet for a bit," Cal said the words casually, but his gaze was on me. I chewed my bottom lip, shocked when tears sprang into my eyes. I turned away to hide them.

"Thank you," I murmured, hovering near the fridge. "Would you like a drink? I know it's been a huge day…"

Cal moved fast, pressing one hand on the fridge door to shut it, the other snagging my waist, so my back was to the kitchen wall. His gaze was intense, sending tiny shocks through me. His hand on my waist slid up to my rib cage, squeezing gently.

"I think I'll have you instead." His words were soft, but his voice was harsh. He laid his forearm above my head, closing the space between us with his physical presence.

I looked up into his eyes, letting him see me — all of me; nervous, scared, and wanting.

He leaned down, brushing my mouth in a touch so light it was barely there. He trailed his lips across my cheeks, down the side of my neck. Gooseflesh raised everywhere he touched me, shivers chasing them across my skin. Cal paused, drawing back. A small noise escaped my throat, and he smiled, though the look in his eyes was hard, setting my heart racing.

"Mila, will you let me do this my way?"

It was said as a whisper, asking permission. *Trust me.* I nodded, barely able to catch my breath. The fire in his eyes darkened, and I couldn't look away. He collected my wrists in one hand and raised them over my head. His hold was gentle, nothing forced, or fast, as I'd expected. Instead, waiting for him to touch me was agonising.

I desperately wanted him to kiss me, but every time I leaned towards him, he moved away, teasing my skin with the lightest kisses, his thumbs rubbing tiny circles over my wrists, across my palms.

I writhed against him, and he pressed his knee between my legs, holding my gaze. He pressed up, hard, and I whimpered, sensation enveloping me until I was gasping. He pressed his knee higher, and I remember the night he'd had me on the counter, his fingers between my lips. His gaze never wavered, never released me. I arched, wanting his hands on me, his mouth on mine.

His knee pressed higher, sliding me up the wall until my toes barely touched the floor. Balancing against him left pressure on my core where my jeans pressed against the sensitive flesh there.

I breathed hard through my nose, eyes fluttering for a moment as I scrambled not to lose myself so fast.

"Cal,' I whispered. "Please–"

His mouth crashed down, tongue sweeping across my lips, demanding access. I couldn't hold back wanting him, curving my neck to let him kiss me deeper. His tongue slid inside, flicking, playful, pressing his knee against me in a rhythm that was all him. I moaned, every inch of me liquid.

I stopped fighting to stand; letting him take my weight. He drew back from my mouth, eyes on mine again, and I knew I wouldn't have mercy from this man, not tonight. His knee pressed again, and again, and I gasped as my whole body tightened, arching against the wall.

I tugged against his hands, and they loosened, but not letting go, either. His thumb rubbed my palm in tiny circles. Knowing that he would let me go if I asked was more than I could bear. I tipped my head back, and his lips were on the sensitive skin around my throat, licking, kissing, sucking as I teetered on the edge, and fell into the abyss.

His arms were wrapped around me, and he murmured sweet things against my mouth, dragging his tongue against mine. Barely aware, I responded to him, reaching up to pull him closer, needing to feel him against me. He licked my bottom lip, hands fisting in my hair as he nipped the sensitive skin of my collarbone. I gasped, and he drew back, eyes dark. A sinful smile graced his lips.

"You said you had dinner ready?"

CHAPTER TWENTY

CAL

Mila stumbled across the kitchen on unsteady legs. Something inside me loved torturing her, knowing she desperately needed me to fuck her, but I couldn't stop the tease. I was an asshole, and I knew it.

Just watching her heated my blood to boiling point; my hold on her had been light, more to let her know what I wanted than forcefully restraining her. I sipped the beer she'd opened for me, leaning against the wall, still warm from the heat of her pressed against it.

I enjoyed watching her struggle. I wanted to draw this out so that by the time I was ready to take her, she would have lost all control, be completely raw and just *her*.

It took her two tries to pull the fridge door open.
Collecting herself with deep breaths, she extracted what
she'd made.

Spicy scents filled my apartment, my stomach
rumbling. Mila heated the food and served it. She stood still
at the bench, gripping it hard, and every damned part of me
roused at the sight of her so vulnerable, but still so strong.

I love this woman.

The thought took me completely by surprise, and I
took another swallow of beer to keep anything from showing
on my face. Tonight was about *her*. We could worry about
how I felt tomorrow.

Dark hair tumbled over her shoulder where it had
fallen loose and tangled in itself. I slid my arms to either side
of her, taking the plates from under her hands, careful to
limit the amount of contact my skin had with hers.
Anticipation was the key to this woman; I was certain. For
her to let go completely and just *feel*, she needed to stop
thinking.

Control was something I had studied for a long time; I
knew it intimately. I placed the plates on the table she had
set, appreciating the effort she'd put into tonight. I was glad
to know she wanted to try to make this work as much as I
did — and I wanted to give her all the reasons in the world to
stay.

I drew out a chair, gesturing for her to sit. She dropped gracefully, and I pressed the chair in beneath her, bending to brush my lips over the side of her neck, lifting the dark mass of her hair to expose her skin. Placing a glass of wine in front of her, I let my fingertips trail her cheek. She sighed as I sat opposite her, and we ate silently for a few moments. Dinner was amazing. I loved that she cooked as well — better — than I did.

"This is amazing, Mila." I caught her eye, and she blushed, fidgeting. "Tell me Danny was good to you today." I smiled, "But not that good."

Mila shook her head.

"No, he respects you too much for that."

I raised an eyebrow. The man was shacked up with my ex, had punched me in the face with no warning a few days ago. Which still irritated me. For all that, I couldn't deny he worked his ass off for me.

Mila laughed, waving her fork.

"I know, I know. Your ex though — that's different than, well, different to us?"

She stared down at her plate, discomfort radiating from suddenly tense shoulders. I reached over, stroking the fingers that clutched her fork in a death grip. I gently pried them open, surprised the thing didn't bend under the force she exerted.

"You're right, Mila. They're nothing like us." I squeezed her hand for a moment more, sliding my hand over hers. She smiled, light sparkling in her eyes.

God, but she was so beautiful.

It took me a second to realise I was staring and finished my own food.

"Tell me about your day."

She stumbled on the words. I realised it had been a long time — if ever — that she'd had a partner to ask her. She blushed harder when she asked me how my work had gone.

"Lot of paperwork, settled the girls into the house. I think they're happy there. Ashley is certainly glad to have Jenny back, though she misses you."

I skimmed around the topic of Logan, not wanting his shadow in the room with us. Mila collected our plates as soon as I had scraped the last of the sauce from mine.

"That was delicious. Thank you."

I tried to take the plates from her, beginning to rise, but she pressed her knee atop my thigh, pushing down.

"Stay, please. I'll be back in a moment."

She returned swiftly with two small glasses filled with dark mousse, topped with a small bud of fluffy cream and some mint leaves. I grinned, happy she'd raided my potted herbs. Sweet and earthy scents wafted over the table.

"Tell me."

"Dark mocha mousse with mint and Chantilly cream."

"You're amazing."

Mila passed me a thin, long-handled spoon she must have dug out from the bottom of the cutlery drawer or somewhere else in my apartment. Her eyes were on me as I tried the dessert. The flavours were perfect, and I suspected dark chocolate might be a weakness of hers.

I could see the nerves building in her and wanted to sweep them all away. Hooking my foot around her ankle, I gave a little tug. Her shoulders relaxed until she finished her dessert. Mila flipped her hair over her shoulder and rose before I could say anything, stopping beside me. I relaxed, not wanting to scare her, but I wanted to see what she would do. She leaned over me, one hand on my shoulder, pressing her fingers into the cotton of my shirt.

Her lips found mine, brushing across my mouth. Hesitant fingers slid to the buttons of my shirt. I let her undo each one, not daring to move.

When she reached my waist, I shifted back slowly, letting her tug my shirt from the waist of my pants. My hands itched to touch her, but I held back, giving her the reins.

She traced down my stomach, curving her tiny hands around the muscle there, her touch so light it was fucking torture. She struggled with the button on my pants, and though I loved seeing her flustered, I placed my hands over hers, easing her through the movements. Her hands slipped inside, fingers curling around me, so timid. Her breath brushed over the length of me, and I fought back a groan.

Who was it meant to be tortured with anticipation here?

I gripped the edge of my chair with one hand, fighting the urge to bury my hands in her hair. She looked up at me with big eyes as her mouth touched the head of my cock, tongue flicking out, around. I closed my eyes, straining against a building need to bury myself inside her.

I laid a light hand on her hair, pressing down only the minutest amount. She engulfed me with her mouth. I groaned, hand fisting her hair as she slid her tongue along me in a steady rhythm. Her hands weren't idle, sliding into my pants to cup me as she licked every inch. It was torture and heaven at the same moment.

And she looked at me the entire time.

Her hands and mouth built an increasing rhythm. I cupped my hand beneath her jaw, urging her up, but she didn't move, those huge, luminous eyes on me as I lost myself in them. I came with a groan, straining against her.

Slowing my breathing, I looked down at the incredible woman kneeling before me. She hadn't moved, leaning her cheek on my thigh. Her skin was soft beneath my touch. I loosened my hand from her hair, not pulling it free just yet. Those eyes widened, still watching. I never broke her gaze, pressing her wine glass into her hands.

She sipped, tilting the glass up. A drop slid from the corner of her mouth, trailing down her cheek. I brushed it back between her lips, her teeth nipping my fingers playfully. She rose, placing the glass on the table, hips loose and swaying.

I lifted her, standing in one fluid motion. She gasped, gripping my shoulders, her dark hair tumbling around us. Her legs wrapped around me as I claimed her mouth, pulling her down to me. Our tongues met, stroking and teasing as I walked us into my bedroom, my hands fighting to find bare skin. I desperately needed to feel her flesh against mine.

Flicking the light on, I slid her down the length of me, letting her go only to shuck my shirt onto the floor, grabbing a condom out of my pocket before I kicked my pants free. Naked, I stalked the few steps to her, my hands on her waist, lifting her thin jumper over her head. Her lips parted, eyes sweeping over me. I slid my hands down her sides to her waist, pushing beneath the yoga pants she wore so they puddled around her ankles.

Every inch of her was curved perfectly. Tiny and petite, I felt as though she'd disappear in my arms. Mila reached back, unclasping her bra, so it fell from her shoulders. I raked my gaze from her perfect ankles to her swollen lips, then she was in my arms, tongue tangling with mine. I lifted her to my hips, then spun her in my arms, so she was facing the en-suite mirror.

I lifted one of her legs to stand flat on the wooden bed end, hooking her other leg around my calf. I trailed my fingers along the delicate flesh of her thigh, stroking where it curved around me, holding her up with only my arm around her waist.

"Watch," I murmured into her hair, sliding my hand over her throat, dipping down to the curves of her breasts. Sucking and licking her neck, she rewarded me with the tiny mewling sounds I loved. Tiny circles around her nipples drew breathy moans from her lips, and I ached to thrust into her, but not yet. I wanted her senseless with need, first.

When I finally ran the pads of my fingers over the sensitive tips of her nipples, I nipped her neck. She cried out, arching. Her nails dug into my arms, desire ripping through me at her reaction.

My hands dropped lower, trailing down her beautiful body, over soft skin to the apex of her thighs. I stroked around her clit, never entering her as I delved lower, her thighs slick with arousal. Her tiny hands gripped my wrists tightly, pulling me closer against her. I thrust two fingers straight into her, knowing she was ready. Her head dropped back onto my shoulder; lips open in a silent *O*. I nudged her up, flicking my tongue along the bottom on her earlobe, down her neck.

"Look, Mila. Watch. I want you to see yourself come."

It was an order, and she responded immediately, watching my hands on her skin. The foil packet crinkled as I tore it open. I shifted, lifting her onto me, so I pressed against her entrance. I took it slow, though I needed her as much as she did me. She gripped my arms hard, gasping as I rolled her nipple between my fingers, tugging just a little.

I eased her down onto me, squeezing my fingers into the pale flesh of her thigh with my other hand. She clung to my arm, gasping, whimpering, allowing me to hold her up. I gave her a moment to get used to the feeling, the way she clenched around me almost driving me over the edge. I kissed along her jaw, the corner of her mouth.

"Mila, this won't last long." My voice came out harsh and rough. She shook her head, catching my gaze in the mirror as she slid her hands behind my neck, my skin stinging a little where her nails dug in.

"Hard, Cal. Please."

It was the way she begged that wrecked me. I found her hips with both hands, slamming into her with no more thought than that I needed to fuck this woman as if my life depended upon it. She screamed, arching against me. My arms wound around her, needing to feel every inch of her pressed against me.

She clenched around me as I thrust deep, riding the wave of my own orgasm as hers overtook her, and we crashed to the floor in a tangle of slicked limbs.

CHAPTER TWENTY-ONE

MILA

I awoke curled around Cal, splayed across his chest. His arms wrapped around me, our legs intertwined. I couldn't tell where he started, and I ended. Content, I enjoyed his warmth, the peace that came with that moment in half-sleep before wakefulness hits. I stretched languidly, arching and sliding along his skin, both of us still slick with sweat.

Cal's fingers trailed along my spine, stroking up and down in smooth motions. I leaned up, kissing his jaw without untangling myself from him. He just felt so good. I snuggled into him, never wanting to move again.

"Morning."

"Morning," I mumbled drowsily into his shoulder. "Don't you dare move today."

A laugh rumbled in Cal's chest. His hands knotted in my hair for a moment, then relaxed.

"Honey, I have to go into work today."

"Stay. Please?"

His fingers slid through my hair, massaging in slow circles. "I have to go in. But..." His hand dropped lower, catching my legs and drawing them up, so I straddled his hips. I sat up, smiling lazily, enjoying the desire in his eyes. He hardened beneath me, pressing against my sensitive flesh.

He reached into a draw beneath his nightstand, removing a foil packet. I unrolled the condom, covering the length of him. A wicked smile curled my lips, and I hid behind my hair as I slid onto him with a breathy moan, still slick from our lovemaking the night before. He fit perfectly, hitting all the right places, throbbing inside me. I whimpered, and his hands squeezed my hips.

"Gentle, honey. If you're too sore..."

I shook my head, rolling my hips. Cal hissed breath through his teeth, thrusting up into me, hard. My thighs squeezed his hips, and I ran my hands down his stomach, exploring. Tracing the sea dragon where it curled around his arm, peeking over his shoulder, his golden skin was aglow beneath the sunrise. Planes of defined muscles stretched across his chest.

I slipped my fingers down the groove in the centre of his abdomen. He watched with hooded eyes, tracking my progress. Reaching around to hold my ass, he moved with me, a growl rumbling deep inside him. My thighs tensed. I moaned, unable to hold back, my entire core clenching. His hands squeezed hard, pressing into the sensitive corner inside my hips, slamming me down.

A strangled cry tore from my throat. Cal's hand wound into my hair, pulling me down to him, kissing me deeply. A growl built in his chest, his movements sleek and fast. His mouth ripped from mine, his hands wrapping around me until I was drowning in his scent. I stared into his eyes when he shuddered, taking me with him a second time.

Sometime later, Cal slid out from beneath me, leaving me in a puddle of unresponsive limbs in the centre of his enormous bed. I sank into the pillows, not bothering with the sheet. He paused, at the edge of the bed, fingers trailing along my calf. His smile was sin, and I stretched beneath his gaze.

His eyes darkened, and I thought he might kneel back on the bed. Anticipation coiled inside me. I didn't dare move, not wanting the moment to end. One corner of his mouth curled and with a last look that sent desire straight through me, he headed for the shower.

I exhaled, both disappointed and glad he hadn't come back — something to look forward to for tonight. I smiled at the thought, recalling his hands on me, what he could do with that mouth. Forget the looks; the man was a god in bed, as well as out of it.

If Cal was getting ready for work, that meant Danny would be here soon. I groaned. In that case, clothes were a necessity. Flapping around on the bed, I couldn't locate anything I'd worn the night before.

One of Cal's shirts was on the floor. I slipped it over my head. The cotton hem stopped mid-thigh, and I turned up the sleeves a few times. Arms wrapped around my waist, and I leaned back against a familiar, warm chest.

Cal curved around me until I was completely wrapped in him. His fingers caught my chin, drawing my head back, and his lips found mine. His kiss was searing hot, sending tingles to my toes. I ached deep inside for him, returning his kisses with equal fervour.

His fingers trailed down my neck, closing gently, but firmly around my throat, tilting my head further back. It was an incredibly arousing feeling, to trust him, to let go of everything. I slipped my arms around his neck, giving him complete control. He drew back, eyes glinting as he released me. I protested, but he caught my hand, pulling me to him for a last kiss.

"Tonight." His eyes glowed with the promise of his words. I shivered as he towed me to the kitchen. "Coffee."

Danny buzzed halfway through breakfast. Cal checked his watch and swore. His gaze swept over me, eyes sparkling with mischief as he pressed the button to let Danny up.

"Honey, I'd go change, unless you want Danny to see more of you than normal. I don't mind if he's fucking my ex, but you...that's a different story."

I looked down, realising how much the shirt showed. Leaping off the stool, I raced into the bedroom to change. When I came back out, Danny was eating my breakfast, and Cal was nowhere to be seen. My stomach dropped, a sudden ache blooming low in my belly.

Danny caught my eye, nodding to the balcony.

"He's taking a call."

My breath released, a long exhale. I worried about him out there, though I knew he was more worried for me than for himself. Surely Logan would take any chance to get rid of him. Though Cal had said he screwed with people's mind — I could definitely vouch for that, and most of Cal's unit too, I was sure.

Cal slid the glass sliding door back, then pulled the blinds closed behind him. Light became muted, like a cave. I wanted to be outside quite badly at that moment, feel the sun on my skin. How long would I be hiding away like this?

Cal pulled me into him, brushing his lips over mine. I rose up on my toes, pressing my lips harder against his, wanting more. He slipped his hand into my hair, holding me up, his tongue invading my mouth until all I could feel and think of was him.

Danny muttered behind us, and I could swear I heard "get a room." Cal grinned against my lips, gently letting me off my toes, his arms winding around me.

"Stay here; be safe," he murmured into my hair. I nodded, my hands curled in the fabric of his shirt.

"You, too."

Cal let me go, looking over his shoulder to Danny.

"That bloody alarm is busted again. I've told Steph; she says the boyfriend will be around later this afternoon to fix it again." Cal paused, his hand squeezing my arm, though his stance remained relaxed. "Be wary of him, alright? He's stirred some shit up, and I know Mila was uncomfortable with him last time. When I meet him, he's going to have to impress me with some fast talking." Shaking his head, Cal sent me a tight grin.

I nodded, relieved he'd listened last time. He dropped a quick kiss on my head, grabbing his phone and keys from the breakfast bar.

"Take it easy today, man. I'm going to need you soon." Cal gave the younger cop an easy smile. Danny grinned widely, holding out for a fist bump.

It was quiet when Cal left. Maybe he had some books I could read? I turned to ask Danny if he knew if Cal had books around and found him watching me, a lopsided grin on his face.

"What?"

"You know he's falling for you, right? I haven't seen him like this in years. Since, well, before Mandy."

Caught off guard, I shook my head.

"We've only known each other for a week or two..."

"Yeah, but you've been living in each other's back pockets for the last week, and stressful situations put you in a mindset you don't usually have. Speeds shi– stuff up."

I realised I knew nothing about Cal's relationship with Mandy. "Um, why did they break up?"

"He hasn't told you?"

I shook my head. Danny sighed, his eyes on the floor.

"He walked in early one afternoon, thinking he'd surprise her with a romantic night together. Found her in his bed with another guy."

I winced.

"That really sucks. And you're okay with that...going out with this girl?"

Danny shrugged.

"My relationships don't last long. She's a bit of fun, for now."

"Oh." That seemed sad, but I didn't want to be rude. Danny was worthy of more than a cheating ex-girlfriend of his friend's. A thought occurred to me.

"Wait, was the other guy *you*?"

"What? No!" Danny backed away, caught between shock and laughter. "You think I'd still be alive if it had been me? Hell, Cal had the guy brought up on charges just to throw him in a jail cell for the night."

I laughed — it was something I could see Cal doing. I sobered at the thought — he must have been furious, as well as heartbroken. Danny fidgeted beside me.

"Are you still hungry?"

The huge cop nodded enthusiastically. I made up some more eggs and toast, refilling my coffee. His plate emptied quickly. I offered more, but he shook his head.

"Nah, shouldn't eat too much of the boss' food, seeing as I'm boning his– damn, sorry."

I smiled, loving that the boy had no filter. Crass and bulky, I knew he hid behind the facade. Anyone who underestimated him would be unwise — and I was pretty sure he used the look to his advantage in his work.

"I'm so sorry you've been stuck here with me for the last two days. You must be bored out of your brains."

"It's a break. I go home, not tired for the day, work out, go to bed. Anyway, you get Black for the next three days." Danny grinned.

"It'll be great to see him again. Not that you're not good company!" I hastened to reassure him, but he shrugged it off.

"You've known him for a long time, yeah?"

"He was my minder — at first — but now he's more like a big brother. My only family, for the last few years."

Danny nodded, swivelling to face me.

"You've got family now, babe. Anytime you need us, even if Cal isn't around, we'll be there for you."

I swallowed back tension that closed up my throat.

"Thank you," I whispered, tears stinging the corners of my eyes.

Danny gave me a crooked grin, holding out his arms. I hugged him back, grateful for what I'd gained in the last few days.

"No sweat, girl. We got you. And we'll get that asshole, too."

I stood back, looking at him, thinking of the four of them — five, if I added in the unknown Liam. The strength they had together as a unit, how they covered each other's weaknesses, even when they didn't get along. There was a rare loyalty there. Danny was right — they were family, tight-knit and formidable together.

"Yes, I rather think you will."

Danny had eaten most of the fridge out by lunchtime. I made a note to message Cal to pick up groceries. I cringed, asking him to do things I'd always done for myself, in my own home. Home. That I was calling his place my home — even if it was temporary — was a huge step for me.

You'll be alone when it all falls apart.

322

I shushed my inner voice, tired of not living my life. Tired of hiding from everything out there. I thought of Cal, smiling and scrabbled for my phone where it had skittered beneath the lounge. It would be flat, and I had no idea where the charger was, either. Cal probably had one in his study. I stretched as far as I could, digging across the carpet when suddenly the lounge was gone.

I looked up in surprise. Danny held the whole thing off the ground, amusement written on his face.

"Mila, I know these guns are big, babe, but could you grab the phone? This thing is a bit of an awkward lift."

I grabbed my phone, scuttling backwards as he eased the lounge back to where it had been before. The buzzer rang for the door. Danny strode over to answer it, while I lifted pillows, looking for my charger. Maybe I'd left it in Cal's truck? Surely he'd have another one. I headed for Cal's study.

"Mila, I'll be back in a minute, have to let Steph's boyfriend up." He grimaced at me theatrically. I waved him away, intent on my hunt.

I hesitated at the door to Cal's study. He'd cleaned it out, he said, but I didn't want to step into the room with so many eyes staring at me. It had been truly horrifying, but after I'd calmed down, I'd understood what Cal had meant when he said it was his obsession.

Turning the handle, I drew in a quick breath and flicked on the light. It was the only room without windows in the apartment. No cold eyes glared down at me, this time. Cal had held to his promise. Relieved, the trust I had for him rebuilt with every moment.

I dug around behind the pair of screens and mass cords hanging down the back of the desk, checking one adapter, then another. Something white glinted at me, and I lunged for it. A clatter told me I'd knocked it beneath the desk and I groaned, kneeling down. The charger sat in a neat pile of cords and notes stored in stacks beneath Cal's desk.

I grabbed it, wandering back to the kitchen, and plugged it in. Messages pinged, and I scrolled through, deleting as many as I could quickly in threads without looking at them. The ones from Teddy and Cal I kept and sent a quick one about groceries.

My phone buzzed again, and I looked at it with hesitation. When I saw Cal's name pop up, my heart gave a little leap.

Cal: Sure, honey. Will do. You left your keys in my truck...mind if I get your paints and things from your house before I head home?

Me: Please. You're a miracle worker.

Cal sent a smiley back. I grinned — my paints. The man was a god. My phone pinged again, and I picked it up, grabbing my mug for another cuppa. But it wasn't Cal. A new unknown number filled the screen, but I knew right away who they were from.

You look so beautiful today.

I blinked, but the words wouldn't go away. My hands shook as they flicked the kettle on, filling the apartment with white noise.

Too pretty.

I blinked again, wishing I could unsee it. My eyes were glued to the screen. A tiny sliver of logic in the back of my mind wondered where Danny was.

The floors below are empty. I might come up.

Coffee splattered the floor, ceramic tinkling on the tiles.

Why don't you open the blinds? I want to see more of you.

Stepping out of the steaming puddle of coffee, I grabbed a bottle of chartreuse. The incandescent green liquid sloshed into the bottom of a new mug. I slammed the lot back, my lips numbing almost instantly.

Cal. I need to call Cal.

I fumbled with my phone, shaking hands stabbing desperately at numbers. Stepping around the mess on the kitchen floor, promising myself I would clean it up later. I couldn't get the numbers right, and slowed on the third try, praying I wouldn't lock myself out of my phone. The door opened, and I headed up the hall.

"Danny, thank god. We need to call Cal–"

I stopped, looking up as I finally unlocked my phone, thumb hesitating over the call button. The alarm repairman stood in the doorway in his blue uniform, key in hand. I frowned, then remembered Danny had gone to get him. Some semblance of reality broke through my fogged mind.

"Oh, I'm sorry. Cal said the alarm was faulty again. Are you okay to fix it?" My attempt at normalcy came out reasonably believable, and I was proud of myself.

He just stood in the doorway, unmoving. This guy had always given me the creeps. And surely he shouldn't be up here alone. The facade of normalcy began to break away. He didn't utter a word, just stared with those piercing eyes. I retreated, one foot behind the other, thumb pulsing a staccato on the call button.

He walked down the corridor toward me, leaving the door open. I gestured to it, but he was in front of me before I could fully form a sentence.

"Shouldn't you–" I looked around him. A dark form that shouldn't be there was crumpled on the carpet, just outside the door. I craned over his shoulder, my stomach lurching with the knowledge that all this was terribly wrong.

His hand shot out, closing relentlessly around my throat. Pain shot through me; my mind blanked as air trapped in my chest. My phone spun to the floor, cracking. I gasped, but his grip afforded me no air. He tilted his head, still not speaking as he watched me choke. I scrabbled at his hands, slapping at them, then his face, scratching and hitting. He didn't blink.

Logic kicked into my numbed brain. I was being attacked in Cal's apartment, and no one knew.

No one was coming.

My vision began to cloud, and I frantically tried to suck in air, but his grip was too tight. Nothing got through. His hand opened suddenly, releasing me, and I collapsed to the floor. Gasping and coughing, I flailed about, trying to stand, but nothing responded right.

Air filled my lungs for just a second before his boot caught me hard in the ribs, knocking the little remaining from my lungs. Something cracked, my vision flashing white.

"Danny," I gasped, as the world trembled around me.

"Took a decent shot of ketamine to put that dog down — horse tranq. Your boy is too trusting. Not too smart, though." His voice was snide, laced with derision. "Not about to kill a cop. There'd be more than Liam's pathetic task force on our asses."

I closed my eyes for a second and struggled to open them again. Stay awake. My head was fuzzy as I worked through what he had said. I stared past my attacker's feet to Danny, crumpled on the carpet outside.

At least he's alive.

He kicked me again, and I choked on a scream. The toe of his boot flipped me over, and I lay on my back, half gasping for breath through the pain radiating in my side. Surprised I wasn't panicking more; another prod helped clear that up — the excruciating pain in my chest held it at bay. It was the numbness that worked its way along my legs that terrified me most.

Stay awake, stay awake, stay awake.

Air fought with the swollen flesh in my throat, heaving, until I thought I would vomit. The idea of choking to death on Cal's apartment floor sent ice through me. His head tilted again, and those hard eyes I'd found so creepy last time surveyed me, assessing.

"I know he wants you, but honestly, I don't see it."

He dismissed me sharply, hand on a gun at his hip beneath his open jacket. I hadn't noticed it before. I sucked in air through my nose, trying to get past the pain. It was impossible to breathe on my back. I tried to roll over, but his boot pressed down on my chest, grinding my back into the floor.

His hand came but left the gun.

"I don't think I'll need this."

His foot pressed down, bit by bit, on my chest. I screamed. Cracks echoed in my head, white-hot pain blanketing my vision. When the room came back into focus, I stared up, terrified by the smile crept over his face. The smile transformed his face — his eyes, his mouth, everything, to someone I knew, to someone who had haunted me for five years.

This was Wayde Logan's little brother.

He pressed down harder, and something else cracked, tearing in my side. Agony lanced across my back, stealing precious breaths.

Finally, black clouded in, and I stopped fighting.

CHAPTER TWENTY-TWO

CAL

Ashley had taken to her new home with Jenny quite well. She was too used to being shunted from place to place as foster parents discovered what it meant to have a child in their custody under constant police protection and regular surveillance. The selfishness of it saddened and enraged me at the same time.

No breaking laws, unless it was the occasional parking ticket. It never failed to amaze me how many people thought they could get away with illegal shit, even minor stuff. Growing weed in a house with foster kids was definitely on my *no* list. It was only a short step from that to dealing, or trafficking something bigger when they wanted an increase in their cash flow, and there was no way in hell I was letting

Ashley be exposed to that. She'd had enough tragedy in her short life as it was.

"Bye, Cal!"

Tiny hands wrapped around my waist. Smiling at Jenny, I hoped I could protect them the way they expected. I damned myself for letting Logan into my head as I patted Ashley's hair, a pang slicing through my heart.

She released me, and I walked back to my truck with Black.

"Are you good here for another night, anything you need? I can get patrols." I'd have to play politics with the departments upstairs. It might cost me my sanity, but I'd do it for Ashley.

"Yeah, man. We're good. Girls are fine. Don't worry about the extras. The more people who know, grunts around us making mistakes, the faster Logan will find her. What about my girl, you looking after her?"

I raised an eyebrow, hand on the truck door.

"Your girl."

I let the statement hang flat in the air. Black looked at me, arms folded. His biceps bulged past the sleeves of his black Under Armour tee. He and Micah were so broad in the chest and shoulders they needed custom makes.

"Yeah, Dane, *my* girl. She was mine to protect long before you ever came on the scene."

Anger coursed through me. I pushed one hand into the pocket of my jeans, trying not to clench the door handle with the other. I wasn't into chest prodding, but I also couldn't let this one slide.

"If you'd let me know what you were doing, I could have been looking after her long before this."

Black snorted. "Yeah, I know what your brand of *looking after* her entails."

I glared at him, letting my anger settle into something cold.

Control.

"Are you fucking done?" The words hissed from between my teeth. Pissed with myself that I'd let him get to me, I waited for the reaction I knew was coming.

Black stepped into me. He was only half a head shorter than me, and I refused to back down.

"You take care of her. And if I hear anything like what Mandy is spinning, I won't care that you're my fucking boss. Clear?"

"Are you seriously listening to something my *ex* is saying to one of my boys?"

333

"Yeah. 'Cause if you pull any of that with Mila, we're done."

I stared back, incredulous. I couldn't believe that after all we'd been through as a team, for three years as *partners,* it was an ex-girlfriend I should have had the brains not to hook up with in the first place that breached such a rift in my team.

"Message received. I guess I'm off to collect paints from her house, so she has something to do while she's cooped up in mine." I forced a grin, working on de-escalation. "Tried to work out what to buy, but I was out of my depth."

"She's into oils at the moment. Likes spring colours, anything bright. Preferably blue base." Black stepped back, having made his point. His arms were still folded, though his expression wasn't as hard. But I couldn't call it *soft* either. I exhaled sharply, pulling the truck door open.

"That kid that fucked up so bad a few years back — he's still in there. Don't let all that distract you from this." Black waved back at the house where Jenny and Ashley had disappeared. "This has to end."

I ran a hand over my head.

"Man, we've been looking for him for five fucking long years. I–I can't even see an end at this point."

Black's hand landed on my shoulder. "Yeah, it's a long game. But we need to find this fucker before he finds *them*."

"Yeah." I echoed. "See you tomorrow."

I got into the truck, easing slowly up the long drive through trees to where it emerged onto a dirt road. I was halfway down the road when it hit me. Mila had mentioned she worked with oils on our first date, at the chocolatier. It seemed an age ago, not a few weeks. There was a gas station just outside the small town, and I stopped to wash the truck down before driving back out to the city. I'd made cleaning the trucks a requirement — that way any of Logan's crew were less likely to know where we'd hidden the girls.

The drive back to the city took me a good hour. I clenched the steering wheel, thinking of what Black had said. Great pep talk. I snorted, mulling on it. He was right, though. I did need to put my ego aside — and I hated that Mandy was impacting my team.

We hadn't had any new leads. The brother — Joey — hadn't turned up anywhere. The only thought that still ran around in my head was Central. Logan hadn't been able to get what he was after there — even though he'd gotten away then, it had always been on the cards that he might come back to finish it.

Like me, he wasn't a good loser.

The question was, how much of a chance was there that he was back to finish that job this time? I was still surprised we'd spotted Joey — why the little bastard didn't stay away was beyond me. Pride could be a useful tool, and then there was Ashley and Mila, of course. He might come back for either one of them — or both.

The thought itched in my head until I couldn't think straight. Losing either one of them would kill me. Especially Mila. She'd gotten under my skin faster than any woman had before.

Waking up with her on my chest this morning was the most incredible thing. Hand tangled in sleep-mussed hair; she'd looked so soft and relaxed, as though the night before had pushed away all the worries of the last week. She'd been so beautiful I'd thought my heart would burst.

Hell, after just two weeks, was it possible I was falling in love with the woman?

I expected the thought to freak me out, but it didn't. I let it sit for a moment, waiting for the panic that usually accompanied it, but this time it wasn't terrifying. She'd been living in my house for only a few days, and I didn't want to imagine how vacant it would be without her there.

With a sudden urge to speak to her, I flicked my phone over, spotting her missed call. Great minds, and all...I pressed call. One ring, two...I tapped my fingers on the steering wheel. At seven rings, it went to voicemail. I left a quick message, cutting myself short before I babbled to her inbox.

Fortunately, her house was on this side of the city. I pulled up out the front faster than I'd expected. I assessed the entry as I walked up the drive, but nothing seemed amiss. The door was locked this time, and the windows were shut.

Everything was as we had left it. I wandered around the back, after remembering everything was stored in the cupboard on the back veranda. I didn't need to go into the house — if it was still all safely locked up, then I was happy to leave it that way.

It occurred to me that I should have asked if she wanted more clothes while I was here. I fired off a short message, checking my phone, but she hadn't called back.

The tiny key turned in the cupboard lock, and the door popped open. I grabbed an armful of canvases of various sizes and decided to come back for the rest of the paints and brushes. The canvases took up half the tray. How Mila fit them all in her bubble car, I had no idea.

Returning to the cupboard, I found boxes of paints. "Oils," Black had said. I read label after label until I found the right ones and picked out ten bright colours, plus a black and white. I added some brushes to the box, a plate I suspected she mixed the paint on, a collection of rags, and a small bottle of turpentine mineral spirits to clean everything with. The box was a bit overcrowded, but hopefully, it would be enough.

Honestly, I just wanted the girl to be happy, which wasn't easy when she was stuck in my apartment. Maybe I should have moved her when I moved Ashley, but the risk was huge. And I hadn't wanted her to go, selfish as it was. I rolled my shoulders, standing.

My legs cramped from crouching while I sorted out what Mila would need. I stretched, looking through the glass doors to the kitchen. Nothing inside was out of place; Black and I had done a thorough clean up after the place had been trashed.

I was about to head for the truck when something caught my eye. The outside lock was scratched, one deep slice where it looked as though someone had tried to jimmy it and been too rough. Whatever they'd used had gouged the metal.

I didn't touch the lock in case I marred any fingerprints, but nudged the door with my foot. It opened easily, and I cursed myself as an idiot for not checking it when I'd arrived. Hand on the gun at the small of my back, I slid through the doorway.

I was one step inside the house when I realised I'd made a second error, and this one was going to cost me dearly. Motion reflected in the glass door as I stepped through, far too fast for me to react to. The blow caught me on the back of the head, the floor rushing up to meet me.

CHAPTER TWENTY-THREE

CAL

My head ached when I woke up kissing the wooden floorboards of Mila's veranda. I was outside the doors; whoever had brained me must have dragged me back out. Very considerate.

I groaned, trying to rise to my knees. My hand came away bloody when I touched the back of my head. I cursed myself for being so stupid. That's what I got for focusing on the girl, not the job.

Time and a place, Dane.

Staggering out the drive, I was relieved to see my truck still there. Even better, the tyres hadn't been slashed. Nausea rose in my throat as I clambered in, starting it in a hurry. I felt around in the footwells of the back seat and came up with some old gym gear. Leaning on it between the back of my head and the headrest provided some compression on the wound.

So fucking stupid.

The road swam in front of me. I straightened and made a call that terrified me. Danny's phone rang out, as did Mila's. Again. The next call was to Liam, who swore so loudly, my head thumped harder.

"Liam, tone it down. Head's a bit tender right now."

Liam stopped yelling.

"Shit, Cal. Get your ass to the hospital. I'll take care of the rest."

Like hell, I was going to let someone else look after me when my girls were being hunted by a murderous psychopath.

"I'm fine," I lied, trying not to throw up on the dash. "I'm heading to my place. See what's happened there. I can't raise Danny."

Worry gnawed the pit of my stomach. I couldn't decide which was worse: the pain, or the fear of not knowing if they were all safe. Danny never left his phone unattended. Hell, the man would answer my call if he was hooking up — he had actually done that once, much to my disgust.

Which meant he was in some serious shit.

Never had the gate to my apartment block been so slow. In the end, I ditched the truck out front, tearing my keys and access cards from the ignition. I couldn't race the elevator, though. Seven flights were too far and not fast enough, even for me.

Finally, the doors pinged open, and I saw what every cop fears — one of my boys on the ground. I checked him, already calling an ambulance, messaging Liam as soon as I was done.

Relieved to find a pulse, I rolled Danny gently over, supporting his neck, and made sure he could breathe. I checked his head, then his neck, and found the smallest hint of blood. It was no more than a pinprick, and I would have bet a month's wages he'd been knocked out with tranquiliser. No sane man kills a cop. They'd have more attention than ever, something Logan would never risk, and I knew it had to be him.

We weren't dealing with a sane man.

I drew my gun — the second time in a day — and approached my apartment with caution. If I sustained another head injury, I wouldn't be able to help Mila, or anyone else. I scanned every room, finding the broken mug in the kitchen, the bottle of chartreuse on the counter. Danny never drank on the job, which left a very frightened woman who drank to drown her fear.

My woman.

My head throbbed as I grabbed some basic painkillers and a fresh compression, returning to the foyer to wait for the paramedics. Liam turned up at the same time, Micah close behind. Black wasn't answering his phone, and Micah took off, trailed by a line of regular patrol vehicles.

I watched as Danny was loaded into the ambulance, and let a paramedic fuss over my head.

"Where will he be?"

Liam's fingers flew over his phone, impeccably dressed in grey suit pants and a cotton shirt that would have cost my week's wages. He worked ridiculously fast; everyone we needed as back up would be on standby in under a minute. When he looked at me, his gaze was hard — his infamous *how the hell did this get fucked up so fast* glare.

I shook my head, the world swimming again.

"I don't know."

Liam crouched in front of me, speaking over my head.

"Is he okay?"

"He's got a concussion and–"

"I'm fine. *Fine,* Liam. You're not going without me."

Liam straightened, distant and cold as he processed my ability to spin shit.

"Going where."

"Central. It's always been on the cards. That's where he'll hit, and he's taking everyone with him."

MILA

I was back in the bank: the same faded carpet, the familiar bank of teller's stations lining the back wall. I snorted at the thought of Cal's Jeep dangling through the front window and gasped for breath at the motion.

An ache deep inside sliced my heart, wishing desperately Cal and Teddy were here with me now. As I took in my surroundings, my mind began to pick out subtle differences; different time of day than from my last memory of this place, warm light shone through the windows in the late afternoon sun. The row of offices a little more tired, a little dingier than before. After the first robbery, I had never returned.

The bank was nearly closed, and over half of the employees had already left for the day. The few who remained had been given a free pass — apparently, Wayde Logan wasn't interested in hostages this time. I was surprised — the man had no concept of mercy. Or maybe he just didn't want any witnesses.

This time, I sat on the hardwood floor, alone, propped against the wall.

Logan paced a worn strip of carpet in front of me, his little brother — *Joey* — leaned on the counter above me. He kept nudging me with his boot, smiling as the added shock of pain lanced through me. At least it prevented me from passing out.

I tried to keep the shakes that wracked my body from becoming evident, clutching my elbows tight to my sides, regardless of the pain. A sick, knowing smirk from Joey sent my ideals back into delusional land.

Logan's long fingers snapped against his thigh as he paced, turning at the end of the wooden partition where the vault was located. Two of his men stood there; one facing the vault, the other the front of the bank.

It hadn't taken them long to access the vault this time — after five years of planning, whatever Logan expected to retrieve, he'd have to be organised. The little box was presented to him, the silver key already in its lock. I wondered where they had retrieved it from, but realised it didn't matter. He'd been steps ahead the whole time.

My mind filled with worry for Cal. I had a sudden longing for him to crash a car into the bank again, but I also wanted the man I loved as far away from this madman as he could possibly be. He'd cost me my peace for five years — I wasn't going to let him take Cal, too.

I'd only just found him.

The box popped open, revealing an old piece of paper — parchment. Browned and curled at the edges, I stared. *This* was what Logan had been after the whole time?

My mind blanked for just a moment. He paused in front of me, rotating on the toe of his black leather shoe to face me. He knelt, bringing those cold, hard eyes that had terrified me level with mine.

I retreated as far from him as I could — which wasn't much, as the wall was right behind me. My head butted into it, adding an extra dimension of pain to my already wavering world.

Paper crinkled in his hands, brittle, and I wondered if it might snap with age. I gave a half laugh at the thought of it dissolving before he could read it, earning myself a deadly glare that quickly sobered me.

"Linage. Here, you see?" Logan pointed out family names linking to future progeny, marriages and deaths listed on the side. I could barely make out the faded dates — sometime in the early nineteenth century. I shook my head, not understanding. Pain ripped through my chest, and I swayed. His hand brushed my cheek, but I was too disoriented to fully register the contact.

Logan smiled as he spoke, as though we were discussing a shopping list, nothing more.

"Five men robbed the Bank of Australia on George Street, Sydney, in 1828. And here — John Dingle — you see? My heritage. Ashley's. I wanted her to have this, to show her who she is, where she comes from. Like a family business."

A satisfied look settled on his face, reminiscent of pride. My mouth was open, and I couldn't bring myself to close it. All the years of trauma, counselling, seeing Karen dead on the floor of this building — all of it — was for this.

"You're insane." The words slipped from my lips, terror ripping my heart as he paused. Everything in him stilled. The urge to vomit hit me. I looked down, nausea swimming in my stomach, but he curled a finger around my chin, lifting my face back to his. My throat screamed at the movement, and I could barely swallow. Logan tilted my head side to side, and I blinked back tears that sprang to my eyes, taking shallow breaths because that hurt too.

"My brother did a job on you. Did you fight him, my love? Ah, I like your strength. Never mind, I will punish him later."

Joey snorted, turning away. Logan stroked my jaw gently. It was so reminiscent of the way Cal had touched me last night but so twisted my stomach clenched again. *Cal.* God, I hoped he was safe. Bile rose in my throat. Logan's lips curled into a sneer, drawing me up the wall, closer to him. So close, I could feel his breath on my skin as he spoke.

"Don't worry, *honey*, I have made sure he won't bother us. Possibly ever again."

Hearing Cal's endearment coming from *this* man, made me sicker. Then the innuendo crashed through my hazed mind. I choked on the pain in my chest, slapping his hand away, flailing at him. Raising my arms brought pure, white pain rioting through my chest. I hit the wall behind me, sliding a little as I almost passed out.

The brightness in my eyes dimmed, a tunnel of darkness eating the edges of my vision until I could only focus on the man before me. His hands trailed from my shoulders to my waist, eyes reflecting greed and lust.

"Come with me, Mila. There is something you need to see." He lifted me to my feet, hand wrapped around my arm as he propelled me to the windows overlooking the street front.

Logan stopped. He slid the hand holding his pistol beneath my chin, tilting my head. I stared out the window, confused by the lack of police. Surely the bank workers would have reported the break-in by now? Unless...new tears welled. I gasped in short breaths.

'You're here, and maybe *he* will be too. Then I can kill him in front of you, so all you have left is me," he whispered the words softly in my ear. A warped lover's caress, promising a new darkness. His lips brushing my cheek, down my neck. My eyes squeezed shut, tears running from the corners. He licked one away, pressing a kiss there. My brain numbed, I curled over his arm, retching on the floor.

Cal. Be safe.

The tears flowed faster. Breaths shuddered in, but not enough air reached my lungs. My head swam, and I braced myself as best I could without touching him.

"It's okay, love, you'll be okay with me," he crooned the words as though I were a naughty child begging forgiveness.

I would never beg this man for anything.

I inhaled sharply through my nose as he propelled me toward the door to the bank office, calling instructions to his brother that I missed completely, terror building as the door came closer. I desperately didn't want to be alone with him. Tremors wracked my limbs, and he rubbed my arm, kicking the door open. It moved slowly, and I saw the room wasn't empty.

My relief was short-lived when I recognised the occupants. Jenny knelt on the floor, her wrists zip-tied in front of her. Teddy took up most of the small floor space, slumped in an enormous pile on the ground, unmoving. I cried out, yanking from Logan's grasp despite the pain, feeling around Teddy's head and chest for a heartbeat, a pulse, anything. Hot breath hit my palm when I placed it over his mouth.

I sagged on the floor, my arms around him as far as they could go, which really, wasn't much, and let the pain from my movements consume me. Sniffling, a smile broke through my haze for a moment. I looked at Jenny, checking she was okay — well, as okay as she could be. She gave a small nod, but I read desperation in her eyes.

I wanted to give her reassurance, but with Logan behind me, every word would be false. Cal had called him unpredictable; now I understood why he was still free. To catch this man, they needed to be in his head. But insanity like his couldn't be predicted. Hands reached around my waist, pulling me from Teddy.

I shook my head despite the pain, which was giving way to a numbness that scared me. Logan turned me around, and this time I faced him though my heart pounded with abject fear.

He smiled gently.

"You are so beautiful when you smile. I've been watching you for so long now. It was such a wonderful surprise when Dane moved you in with him, where I could see you day and night." My brow furrowed, trying to make sense of his words. His hands on my waist squeezed what little breath I had left from me. "Though I wasn't able to watch him touch you. Joey did. He seemed to get some...enjoyment from it." His mouth twisted with disgust. I echoed the sentiment. Then I shook my head.

"You were able to see us?" It came out as a thin whisper. I couldn't scream to save myself.

"But of course, love. I have been watching the Great Dane now for many months, oh, since that wonderful alarm he had put in was wired up." Logan smirked. "He really should have been there, watching. It would have made putting surveillance equipment into his apartment much more difficult." He drew me closer. "I do so love a challenge."

His eyes raked me, grip around my waist still tight as my knees buckled. He had watched everything, seen everything I had done, every moment with Cal...Logan stared at me, silent, as all the pieces clicked into place. If I thought I'd felt ill before, it was nothing compared to this.

"Why do you hate him so much?" The words croaked from between my lips before I could haul them back in. Logan canted his head, considering.

"He took what I loved most. Hid her, stole her away from me. But I found her, and watched him have the time with her that should have been *mine*."

Ashley. His tone grew hoarse as he spoke of her, and I truly believed that he must love his daughter. But his definition of love was worlds apart from mine. Everything he encountered, it seemed his emotions were heightened, skewed: Cal, Ashley, his heritage...me. We were his obsessions.

Logan kept talking. I focused on him, but in the back of my mind, I tried to work out where she was. Ashley had to be here, somewhere. I cursed myself for not asking before — would he hurt me if I asked now? My own fear became a backseat affair as I panicked about her.

And he blamed *Cal* for the loss of his child? Anger roared through me, five years of sleeplessness, nightmare, therapy, not being able to step outside my own door for fear he would see me...it raged in my chest, a storm of emotion that overrode the pain.

"But, *you* left her behind that day! You bloody drove off and left her! Do you have any idea how many foster homes she's been in, how many sets of parents? I always wondered if you would come back to claim her, terrified of it, but you never did, you fucking bastard!" My voice hoarse, tearing at the edges, I punctuated the last word with a resounding slap across his face, then doubled over as the burst of rage left me, spent. I remembered who I was screaming at, what he could do to me, to the people behind me in this room that I loved, but the words wouldn't stop.

I couldn't straighten, so I looked up instead.

"You forgot her."

His eyes flashed, the first emotion I had ever seen cross them. He gripped my jaw hard, dragging me up. I screamed with the movement, his fingers long enough they pressed against my cheeks and temple. He squeezed, just enough to make it painful, holding me so I couldn't escape those dead eyes.

Logan leaned into me, taking up every inch of my space. My skin prickled, alarms screaming in my head as the numbness worked its way into my mind. I tried to wrench free of him, but he was everywhere. His mouth smashed against mine. I was so surprised I just stood there.

He drew back, fingers gentle on my skin. I froze in shock. What the hell had just happened? There was blood on his lips, and when I touched mine, they throbbed.

"You will make the most beautiful mother for our child. I knew I chose right in you, Mila. You are perfect for us."

"What?"

He smiled, but there was no light in his hard eyes.

"I need a mother for Ashley, since hers so inconveniently died at the wrong time. You will fill that place. She trusts you, even loves you...though you chose the wrong man as a father figure for her." Something cruel crossed his face, and he nodded. "Yes, there will be recompense for that. But still, you'll make a fine mother."

I gaped. He was madder than I thought.

"You're a mad motherfucker," Teddy groaned, rolling over. Heavy cuffs secured his arms. He patted his head with them. "He'll kill you for that, you know," he said conversationally, nodding toward me. "What the fuck did you shoot me with?"

"Horse tranquiliser." Joey appeared in the doorway. "Less than your mate at the apartment. Three fucking shots." He shook his head in awe, turning to his brother. "They're here."

Logan smiled, a truly terrible thing. Wait, they were here? Who? Hope blossomed in my heart but died in the same instant.

"The charges are set?"

"Yeah."

"Then let's move." He towed me to the back door of the office that led into a secure alleyway behind the bank, where security would empty the deposit boxes and vault.

I shook my head, frantic, my eyes catching Teddy's. He gave a small smile which rent my heart.

He was saying goodbye.

I screamed hoarsely, my throat tearing. Wrenching away from Logan, who watched in amusement, rage built in me, and I couldn't stop screaming. Raspy, wretched shrieks that barely made any noise at all.

So much for grace under fire.

Though it felt like it nearly killed me, I turned to Joey, swinging as hard as I could. Pain shot up my arm, almost winding me, but I didn't care if I had broken something else. He took a step back against the doorway, a hand to his jaw, glaring through narrowed eyes.

"You little–"

A blow caught him on the chin, and he dropped. I spun dizzily, thinking it was Cal, but Logan still observed me with those cold eyes.

"He shouldn't have hurt you."

He dragged me to the back door, shoving me through it. A black SUV stood a few meters away, idling. Through the open front door, I could see Ashley, bound and gagged, strapped into a too-small child's restraint fitted to the backseat.

Tears tracked her puffy face, and I knew then I had to be stronger for her. The engine purred low, but it wasn't the only vehicle in the alley. Blocking the end of the entire thing was an enormous blue truck, with an equally huge cop standing in front of it.

Micah.

My heart burst, and he gave a minute nod when he saw me. He raised a weapon I had never seen before, but it certainly matched the bulk of him and his truck. Anyone who could stand next to that thing and not be dwarfed was a giant indeed.

Logan stepped out the doorway behind me, his grip like iron on my arm. I wrenched at him, kicking and thrashing as much as I could without succumbing to the pain radiating across my chest, but he just laughed until he saw Micah — who aimed the weapon at us. I hoped if he fired it, it wouldn't kill all of us. Then I remembered what Logan had said.

"He's set explosives in the bank!"

I practically screeched the words down the alley. They bounced off the brick walls in tinny echoes, giving volume to my hoarse but forceful croak. Micah's mouth moved, speaking into a small headset. My breath came easier, knowing the boys were here.

Now they knew what they were up against.

Logan clearly came to the same conclusion, yanking me back through the bank door. I stumbled and slammed into the ground. His pristine, leather shoe found the same rib his brother had snapped, and he pressed down, slowly, increasing the pressure every second. Darkness threatened my vision. I fought it, desperate not to pass out here with Logan standing over me.

A single figure filled the doorway of the office; tall and golden, weapon zeroed on Logan. An intensity I'd never seen filled Cal's face, sending a zing of hope through me. His eyes flicked to me, and I smiled as much as I could, but my vision wavered. As my eyes closed, all I wanted was for him to be safe.

CAL

Seeing Mila crumpled on the floor, Logan's foot on her chest, nearly undid me. Her smile, small but strong, brought me back into focus. Blood smeared her lips, matching a red stain on Logan's. He'd touched her. My stomach plummeted. What else had he done to her? Her eyes drifted shut, and I knew I was going to kill the bastard.

Micah's voice grumbled in my ears, something about explosives in the bank. Great, another thing to worry about. Logan smiled, aiming his handgun at Mila. Cold dread filled me, and I gripped my weapon tighter.

She blinked from the floor. I was relieved she hadn't passed out completely.

"Put it down, Logan. You've got nothing left."

"Nothing? You call this," he gestured at Mila, "nothing? And my daughter, is she nothing, too? Though she should be, to you."

I wanted to snarl, but I refused to lose it with this man — he was far too dangerous. That, and I cared too much about the woman on the floor to risk giving into my emotions. From the triumphant glint in his eyes, Logan knew it, too. I cursed myself inwardly for being so obvious, but kept my face a blank mask, channelling everything Liam had ever taught me.

"You — I have no idea what you want with her, but sure as hell aiming a gun at a woman tells me your intent."

Logan's eyes filled with loathing, pure and encompassing. I noted it — hatred was a tool I could use against him, and I'd need everything he could give me.

"What I want with her? Oh, the same thing as you, I imagine."

He smirked, staring at me with emotionless eyes. It was eerie how fast he could switch from hatred to nothingness, just an empty shell — Wayde Logan at his most dangerous, right there.

His brother stirred at my feet. I knelt, never taking my sights off Logan, and punched him in the jaw with one hand. He lay still as I slowly straightened. The smirk was back on Logan's face.

"My little brother enjoyed watching your antics last night." Anger sparked in his eyes, though his tone never bellied it. "I, on the other hand, did not."

I narrowed my gaze. He was far too confident, too relaxed for the situation. And where the fuck was Micah? The man should have been blowing the back off the bank by now. Liam shouldn't be far away, either. He'd skirted the edge of the bank, coordinating with local police from the outside. But he'd get jack of that soon enough, I knew. Despite the politician he'd become, Liam couldn't keep out of the action for long.

Then I registered what Logan had implied; the thought of either of them watching us — watching *her* — made my blood boil, as the final pieces began to fall into place. There would be time for a good dose of self-loathing later, but right now, I refused to allow him to goad me.

The building rocked, and I smiled, but there was no engine revving outside. Instead, it was Logan who reflected victory in his eyes. Damn it. Maybe the fuses weren't just *inside* the bank, after all.

I couldn't afford another mistake.

Mila shifted beneath him, and he removed his foot from her body. I watched her take strangled breaths in my peripheral vision, pressure building in my lungs. She was hurt — quite badly from those shallow breaths and the lines on her usually soft face — and I couldn't even go to her.

Logan cocked his head, as though reading my mind.

"My little brother may have broken something in her." His smile was wide, the bait so sweet. I inhaled through my nose, readjusting my sights.

Micah's voice whispered in my ear. I shifted slightly, blocking Black's bulk as much as I could, though Jenny was too far to my right to cover. Micah called in again, and I suppressed the grin that wanted to sneak onto my face.

"All clear, boss."

I couldn't fire on Logan without risking Mila, and I still didn't have a clue how he was setting off the charges, or where the damned things were. For all I knew, I could kill him, and the room would disintegrate around us. My only consolation was that Micah had Ashley safe and well away by now.

Logan watched me, disdain written on his face.

That's right, you bastard. Underestimate me.

"Playing the hero again, are we?"

My eyes flicked to Mila. She lay still, her chest rising in quick, shallow breaths. I had to approach this carefully, or she would be...I couldn't finish the thought. The time to wait for Logan to make mistakes was well past.

"Your brother watched us last night? Dirty bastard." I let the words flow casually, placing little importance on them. Logan's lips thinned; his grip shifting, just a little. Strike — first time. We were on.

"You couldn't stand to watch? Pity, you missed a decent show." I smirked. "She's fucking gorgeous when she comes."

Mila's eyes widened as she stared hard at me, no doubt wondering what the hell I was doing.

I slid across the room, a minuscule movement. Logan's eyes tracked me; his attention completely off Mila, though he still aimed the pistol at her.

"Must be hard to watch a woman you adore be defiled by another man," I murmured the words, relaxing my shoulders with effort, recalling the way I'd felt when I'd walked in to find Mandy in my bed with another man in my damned bed. I'd make Logan feel that, tenfold. The back of my neck felt cool, damp. I hoped to god I wasn't losing blood.

C'mon, bite, you bastard.

Logan snorted, though the muscles around his eyes ticked.

"The Great Dane, rutting like the dog he is for everyone to see. You bore me."

That he had spoken at all meant I was getting to him. I cocked my head, drawing his eyes back to me, and waited.

Don't speak first.

"My brother has some...despicable habits. Useful though, that the violence ran to his side, not mine." His eyes lingered on his brother's still form, and I was surprised to see thinly-veiled disgust there. Maybe they weren't as close as I'd thought, though his reference to violence was confusing — I knew he'd killed. Perhaps it was something in the way he saw himself...I stored the information away to look at in the aftermath.

"He liked what he saw, I presume." I smiled with no humour, showing teeth.

Logan nodded jerkily but said nothing.

"Did he show you her face as I had her come against the wall," I edged closer, "when she served me through dinner...all the way? I've never felt anything so fucking incredible as her lips wrapped around my cock." My mouth was dry, and I swallowed, leaning back a little too far. The ground was spongy beneath my feet.

Mila's eyes were as wide as could be, and I knew things with her would never be the same, but for all it was worth, I was trying to keep the girl I loved alive. And I did love her, with every damned part of me, including the part obsessed with Logan. His obsession was her — his weakness. But no more.

A growl emanated from Logan, and I knew I'd won. I tightened my grip as he began to turn my way. Blackness swam at the edge of my vision, nausea rising in my stomach. I tried to focus on the man before me, but I could barely recognise his face, though I'd hunted through thousands of hours of footage to be here, now.

Logan's smile was wide, gloating, as he directed his weapon my way. The moment dropped out from under me, my head colliding with the floor. A retort echoed distantly, and I waited for the pain.

The floor was cold against my cheek. Fluid pooled beneath me, but the ripping sensation of being shot didn't come. I blinked, pushing up as far as I could — mere inches from the floor. Just enough to look at Mila. It pissed me off that I hadn't been able to save her.

Mila's fingers curled around the butt of Joey's gun, arms raised. It must have cost her everything to take it — pain taughtened her face, the set of her shoulders, and I promised myself I would give her every damn thing she needed to forget today. The lump at her side was Logan, doubled over. Blood ran freely from his shoulder.

I scrambled for his gun, fingers just brushing the metal edges, rolling fast. The world spun down to a tunnel, with Logan at the end of it. My disorientation lasted a moment, then I had his gun in my hand. Logan raised his head, eyes terrible.

My finger tightened on the trigger, remembering all the things he'd done, but he wasn't looking at me — his gaze was fixed on Mila. Anger rolled over me, my breath coming fast. That bastard–

"Put it down, Cal." Liam's voice was soft and calm, right behind me.

I didn't blink.

"You got him?"

"Yeah."

I relaxed, lying back, and let the world spin around me. Liam edged through the back door of the bank, sights on Logan. The hint of a smile played on his lips.

I only saw it because I knew him so well. The last time I had seen him with that victorious look was the night Selena had slapped some random in a pub who had hit on her. Liam just sat back and watched, raising his glass when the unwanted paramour had teetered in front of her, then collapsed to the floor while his mates laughed.

That same damned smile, knowing she was his, though he was yet to truly claim her. But it was coming. We were family.

The man always had our backs; we all knew that.

Logan stayed down while Liam cuffed him. I edged toward Mila across the carpet, but one look from Liam held me back. I stayed put. The floor was amazingly comfortable. Mila smiled faintly, creeping forward, lips framing words I couldn't hear. I was out before she reached me.

Mila fussed with the ambulance crew, refusing bandages and finally taking an ice pack for the bruising to her throat to placate the paramedics attending her. She was a small but formidable opponent and eventually won over the ambulance crew, assuring them she was alright.

The small group watched with concern as she tried not to cradle her ribs crossing the road to me. They moved on to greener pastures — namely Ashley, who couldn't argue her way out of the situation.

Mila found me where I sat on the steps of an ambulance, crouching to look into my eyes with a worried face.

"You're okay? He-I-when you passed out..."

I huffed a laugh at the woman who sported at least one broken rib but refused to go to the hospital to have it treated. I wanted her to go, but at the same time, admired her tenacity.

My kind of woman.

I pulled her gently onto my lap, surprising her with a kiss.

"I'm *fine*," I murmured in her ear, "just like you."

She blushed beautifully, lacing her fingers through mine. Her dark hair fell forward to obscure her face. I brushed it back, studying the line of her brow, the way her lashes almost touched her cheeks when she looked down to the ground.

"Are you okay?" It seemed like a silly question, but I had to ask. She nodded, placing a hand to her ribs. "You should go with them." I knew she was hurting.

Mila shook her head, pressing into me.

"I'm sorry about what I said back there, in the bank. I had to get his attention off you– I could only fire when he was–"

"I understand, Cal." She shushed me with two fingers over my lips, shaking her head. I kissed her fingers, leaning forward to press my forehead to hers.

"Plus, I'm proud of you." Her head lifted, surprise in her eyes.

"Whatever for?"

"For being able to take that shot. For not freezing. You beat it." More than any of us, she had beat *him*, broken through the fear. The position I'd put her in, letting Logan into the space I'd thought was safe — safe enough to keep her in my home long past when she should have left — consumed me. "I'm sorry," I whispered, worried I'd broken something between us that might never heal.

Mila smiled. "It's okay, Cal. I'm here."

Those two words filled my heart. I wound my arms around her, never wanting to let her go. Something niggled in my mind.

"Afterwards, you said something, when you were crawling across the carpet. I think I passed out," I smiled at her, apologetic. "What was it?"

Her face was unreadable as she looked at me. She leaned down, which must have been excruciating, brushing her lips against my ear.

"I love you." It was a quick, breathy whisper, but I could replay those words over forever. She lowered her head to my shoulder, just resting, but I needed to see her face.

"Mila, I–"

Her fingers pressed over my lips, cutting off my words, but I got my wish. She looked into my eyes, so deep I prayed she'd never leave. She shook her head.

"You don't need to say it." She lowered her head, but I caught her chin with my fingers.

"Yes, I do." I ran my fingers over her cheek, tangling them in her hair. "I love you, Mila." Her eyes closed, and she let out a long breath. I pulled her to me, stealing her air with the gentlest of kisses.

Cops and paramedics bustled around us, bystanders kept at bay behind yellow tape that cordoned off the area.

Liam stood with a pair of federal police, notable for their suits amongst a crowd of uniforms. He waved me over.

I grimaced, hating the political aspect to come, glad it was Liam that dealt with the bureaucracy, not me.

Very gently, I placed Mila on the step I'd been using as a seat. It was warm, at least, and protected from the chill breeze that evening afforded us. She clutched a water bottle. I motioned at an ambo on the way to Liam, requesting a blanket and some company for her.

She'd need to be checked, regardless of how determined she was, though I'd be damned if she'd go without me. I gave the paramedic a few extra instructions before I approached the Suits, noting that I'd counted Liam as one of them. I cringed internally, face austere.

Would I become one of them within a few years? My career had been fast-tracked to get me to where I needed to be to hunt Logan. Now it was done, where was I headed? I needed a new direction, and while the future of the team was uncertain, I had a feeling my personal life led to Mila.

I threw her a grin back over my shoulder. Paramedics accosted her, surrounding her in a small group. She grimaced, holding her arms out while an ambo prodded her ribs. A wince crossed her face, and the crowd descended on her. I walked away smiling, knowing she was cared for in my absence.

How I felt for her had crept up on me. I grinned as I walked over to Liam, though it faded as I faced the glares from the local bureaucrats. God, I hated this part.

The chatter ceased as I joined the group. For a moment, it was only eye contact and staring each other down. They might call me the Great Dane, but it was the little yappy bastards you needed to watch out for.

Liam stood still and relaxed, but I knew from the slope of his shoulders he was on edge. I resolved not to add to his stress, though I never broke eye contact with the two smaller men. Finally, one coughed, breaking the awkward silence.

"So, you finally caught him, eh? Took you long enough."

I tried to rein in my glare, but it wouldn't hold. The other man smirked at me as if knowing my struggle.

"The Great Dane. My congratulations. What are you going to do, now that you've caught your bank robber?" It was said with disdain.

Wayde Logan was a hell of a lot more than a bank robber, but I wasn't going to say that. I opened my mouth to retort, the slightly balding man's eyes gleaming beneath the street lights. Liam puffed out a cloud of steam.

"Smith, he'll be after your job if you keep spinning shit like that."

"He'll never get my job," the small man sneered, teeth gleaming.

Liam nodded genially, smiling.

"Then I guess he'll have to have mine."

There was silence in our small circle. I tried not to gape at Liam; what the hell was he playing at? The other two regarded him in something like shock. I had the impression of laughter being well reserved. They both nodded to Liam, ignoring me, and walked away. I turned to my boss and friend.

"What the hell are you doing?"

Liam slowly turned to face me, relaxed at face value, though I could feel the energy radiating from him; it was what made him so formidable. I thought of the way he looked at Selena, how strong and energetic she was. They would be a power couple if Liam ever got himself together enough to ask her out.

"I've always groomed you for my job, Cal. You know that." His tone was slightly rebuking, though I didn't resent him for it.

"I know that, but not now, not this early—"

"You've just come off the back of a major win. If you want it, now is the time."

I just stared.

"What will you do?" I was at a loss to ask anything else.

"I was thinking of retiring."

"You can't retire. You're not even forty, for god's sake."

Liam shrugged.

"With the help I've had from Selena's father in setting up investments, I don't need to be here. The job is yours; if you want it."

The world stopped for me. This was the dream job I'd been chasing for years, what I'd worked towards while hunting Logan. But the team was at a loose end; if we wanted to stay together as a unit, we'd have to fight for it, and hard. I couldn't do that from a chair upstairs, stuffed into meetings all day with a bunch of suits. I wasn't one of them, not yet.

"Thanks for the vote of confidence. But...it's not the right time yet, for me. I still have these guys to look after." I nodded to the small cluster where Danny, Micah and Black stood. Jenny hovered next to Black, and he slipped an arm around her shoulders beneath my gaze. Danny held an ice pack to his head. He would be daunting, in future, with more focus on the job.

"Professional development course. Should be one coming up in a few weeks."

Liam had read my mind. Danny caught my eye, and I smiled wryly in return, considering. I nodded at him and turned back to Liam. He surveyed me thoughtfully and gave a small nod.

"When you're ready then."

I knew it was me he was talking about, not Danny. Liam departed with a small smile, aiming for the suits, ready to go into battle again. It hit me with a jolt that he hadn't expected me to accept; he was setting me up for a future in his role. Now he'd announced the succession publicly there would be eyes on me — and the team. We needed to choose our next job carefully.

Everyone would be watching what we did next.

Logan was escorted from the building — cuffed — to an unmarked car. No special treatment or press for this man, he enjoyed it too much. His lip lifted in a snarl. I smiled inwardly; he was still trying to get a rise from me. I turned my back to him, walking slowly over to my team.

Mila stood on the other side of Black, flanked by the boys. I knew Black was happy in his role but wasn't sure about the younger two. Micah had some serious skills, and his own toys — the man was a weapon in himself. Danny, on the other hand, needed to specialise.

A professional development course would secure him a future if he wanted it badly enough. He wasn't stupid, by any means. He had issues with authority — his fling with Mandy showed that — but it wouldn't last.

Once he was free of distraction, I could channel his energies into something more long term. Liam had done me a favour, tracking my career and guiding me when I needed it. I couldn't do any less for my team.

Mila stepped away from Black, straight into my arms. I drew her gently into me, looking at them all over her head. Danny fidgeted, sliding from one foot to the other. I wondered how much of the conversation with Liam had been overheard.

"What's next, boss? You still hanging out with us plebs?"

I grinned, tugging Mila into my shoulder. Damn, but the woman felt good there.

"You lot are stuck with me for a while yet. We've had a huge victory today; you all worked your asses off for it. Probably have the pick of whatever job you want right now," I said the words casually, letting the idea hang in the air. I'd handpicked this team, but I didn't want anyone staying if they needed to be elsewhere. One by one, they shook their heads.

Finally, Black nodded to me.

"You heard the man. What's next?"

If you *loved* Cal & Mila's story, please head to amazon to
leave a review for Collision:

www.books2read.com/Collision-LQP

ACKNOWLEDGEMENTS

This book has been so, so much fun to write, and I can't wait to share all the boy's stories with you! But there's a LOT more to putting a book together than just putting words on a page — or screen. This one started during NanoWriMo — a month of the year when writers madly attack their keyboards. Thanks to the Nano team, Blue Blooded Brothers was born.

Mr. A - thanks for supporting me with a growing collection of gorgeous notebooks and diaries. It keeps the walls (mostly) free of scribbles.

The Australian police community I've spoken to for information on task force structure, undercover work and general police culture, you guys have been amazing! Thank you and honestly, most of it made it in - in one form or another!

To Jacinta, for writing ridiculous good (but fun!) fanfic with me on a public forum. Your crazy keeps mine sane.

Jem - thanks for pushing back the demons. No mean feat. And for some amazing feedback.

My beta & ARC teams - you guys make all the difference! Thank you for picking apart my book, and stitching my ego back together afterwards.

My amazing editor - thanks for the countless hours you put into bringing Cal and Mila to life and teaching me something new every week.

And to you, the reader - I write for you. Thanks for getting this far into my story. I hope you loved my boys, imperfect as they are. Their stories (and their HEAs) are coming.

Sofia xx

ABOUT THE AUTHOR

Sofia is a romantic suspense author from Brisbane, Australia. She started writing romances when she couldn't find the books she wanted on the shelves in her local bookstore and became addicted to storytelling. She exists on a diet of coffee and champagne and routinely kills her collection of tortured orchids.

Join Sofia's newsletter:

https://mailchi.mp/5fda6750cad0/sofiaavesnewsletter

Find her on Amazon:

www.amazon.com/author/sofiaaves

Stalk Sofia in her reader group:

https://www.facebook.com/groups/365889224364512/?ref=share

Politics and Paperwork

A Blue Blooded Brothers Novella

Liam is constantly swamped beneath the politics of managing an elite task force. Now, given more downtime than he can handle, the ex-special ops sniper flounders to find purpose outside the strict rigours of his working day.

Selena has been Liam's best friend for nearly fifteen years. Elegant and intelligent, and a partner in her own law firm, she's helped Liam through difficult cases, as well as the aftermath of PTSD. Watching Liam drown in day-to-day life, Selena ups the stakes with a little flirting to restore life to the man she adores.

When a series of vandalisms target Selena, Liam is determined to keep the captivating solicitor safe, so long as she lets him. Intent on playing her game by his own rules, Liam risks an uncertain future for the woman he's always loved.

Liam and Selena's story will continue in RECKONING.

Keep reading for a sneak peek of Danny's story in
BLINDSIDED, Book 2 in the Blue Blooded Brothers
series...

BLINDSIDED

CHAPTER ONE

DANNY

Mandy chattered away as she texted, her bosom swaying provocatively. *Did bosoms sway*, I wondered, watching them bounce around beneath her skin-tight top. Perky nipples pressed against the stretchy, orange material, making it quite clear she wasn't wearing a bra. Again. Which should have been mesmerising.

But it wasn't.

A little niggle in the back of my mind suggested it was something I should have noticed before we left my apartment this morning. I'd thrown on a muscle tee and a pair of running shorts — standard weekend fare, though it was the middle of the week.

What the hell was wrong with me? I loved boobs. And legs, and a good butt. Mandy had all of those, but suddenly, it had all stopped working for me. Which meant one thing.

It was over.

I scratched the back of my head, stretching back against my chair, keen to put as much distance as possible between my girlfriend and me. Blue eyeshadow from last night smudged her eyebrow on one side. It gave her a slightly clownish look when she briefly raised her eyes to me, still talking before she returned to her screen.

How many of the hours we'd spent together had she been on the damned thing? Thinking back, the only time I'd looked at her face had been in bed — and that was only half the time.

I nodded, trying to keep up with the rambling diatribe that shifted from friend to friend and who they were currently doing — it varied, day-to-day. Studying her, fingers jabbing at her phone, limp curls flipping and bobbing around her face, a sudden pang gripped my stone heart. If I walked away now, I'd leave her in a pile of tears, in a coffee shop.

In public.

It was potentially social anathema, and I didn't want to be an asshole to her. She was cute, and we'd had fun. But now...I groaned a little, understanding how Cal must have felt. Another groan left my throat as my situation fully hit me. I was about to dump my *boss' ex.*

Who I'd been fucking for the last three months — admittedly, it had lasted longer than either of us had ever anticipated. And I'd punched my boss, in the face, when he hadn't expected it. He suggested I'd needed to reassess my life — which was when I'd walked away. In the last case we'd worked together, I'd made a lot of mistakes — including letting *his* girlfriend get kidnapped on my watch. I winced at the thought.

I stared out the window where the café overlooked the lake and the park centred around it. Joggers flitted past, flustered uni students with bunches of dogs dragging them from tree to tree. Near the edge of the water, a lone figure ran at a steady pace.

Long, shapely legs covered in black workout tights and a white crop displayed a toned, tanned figure. She was running at a decent pace too, as it looked fast from where I sat. I knew the café was situated a decent distance from the lake. I knew because that was *my* circuit.

Something sharp poked me. I looked down to see a pointed, glitter-covered nail poking my bicep.

"Ouch? I asked with a mild rebuke. Mandy gave a sexy smile, or what I supposed was meant to pass as one, as she was still wearing last night's makeup.

"Whatcha thinkin' about?" she drawled, though she wasn't from the south. Or west. Or America, for that matter. Aussies may have some interesting accents and slang, but we never drawl. From what I'd gathered, Mandy had always lived in cities and never strayed far from her high-priced hairdresser or nail technician.

I nearly snorted. Rule one in the boyfriend book, if there was such a thing, is *never* ask a man what he's thinking. Bad juju right there. I glanced out the window, but the runner I'd been watching was long gone.

Stalker, much?

Peering around the thick window frame, I jumped when I was poked again, this time banging my head on the glass.

"Ow." I clutched the same spot as before, looking back at Mandy. She sat there, attempting to look sexy — or sweet, I couldn't tell which — dull hair hanging limply around her face with those razor-sharp talons that had cost me half a week's wages, and I said it. Honestly, it was meant to come out kinder, as a compliment, something.

But really, I was as brutal as they come.

Still rubbing my head where I'd banged it on the window, the words just slipped out.

"Mandy, I can't do this anymore."

It was like she'd been waiting for it. Tears on tap, they erupted from her in waves. I tried to reach out — pat her, wasn't that what you did when faced with emotional trauma? Remnants of mascara quickly tracked her cheeks until she resembled a washed-out panda.

Tears always put me on my back foot. Widow's tears, even parent's, I could deal with. Anything to do with the job. But not personal ones. And when you'd fucked a girl seven different ways on your couch —and hers — things got classed as pretty personal.

She slapped her hand flat on the table, glaring at me as she knocked over her coffee, then scrambling to dry her claws on her skimpy top. She whacked me with her dripping phone on her way out the door. The place was silent, and I realised everyone was looking my way. Social anathema? Only for me. She'd gotten away with that one scot-free. Hell, she could probably blog it, and make a mint.

My throat burned with self-disgust, which quickly moved to self-loathing. I gave it a few more seconds before I made my move, just to put a little distance between us, hoping to god I wouldn't find her waiting at my truck.

Rising, I tossed money on the table, taking care to slip a few extra notes down. The waitresses had to deal with the fallout from this morning's domestic disaster — pretty much the story of my life.

I nodded sharply to the patrons at the next table. A tiny lady hidden beneath a swath of purple curls glared at me, and I made my exit in haste.

I was still shaking my head when the elevator doors pinged open to the office. Slightly dazed, I was halfway through the bland reception area when I realised the place was absolutely silent. Steph wasn't at the reception desk. Peering into the fishbowl that represented our Incident Room and general office area, I noticed a frazzled head of red hair in front of Cal's desk. Steph was rigid — whether with anger or shock, I couldn't tell.

After the mess with her last boyfriend — who turned out to be the younger brother of a murderous lunatic — it was unsurprising to see her at Cal's desk. What was surprising, was that he'd taken several weeks to get around to firing her.

Maybe my boss was a good guy at heart, after all. Or maybe Mila had softened him up. I fervently hoped for Steph's sake that it was the latter. She hadn't done anything wrong, really — no more than having poor taste in her love life — Cal and I were both guilty of that.

The elevator doors pinged behind me again but I was too busy trying to read Cal's lips — though he was half turned away from me — to notice the only other occupant in the room.

"That's not going to end well."

My head snapped sideways at the feminine voice. Blonde hair flowed to a white business suit and a pair of the longest, tanned legs I'd seen in ages. Still dressed in the singlet and running shorts I'd donned early this morning, I felt distinctly underdressed. A hand was proffered at waist level.

"Ally Sinclair. You must be Danny." A warm smile accompanied brilliant blue eyes. I snapped my mouth shut before I drooled on her.

"I am." My brain kicked into gear. "Uh...what are you doing up here?"

"I'm her replacement."

"What?"

Her smile dimmed a little, possibly with her assessment of my IQ, but that wasn't a problem.

"I'm the new receptionist."

"Cal hired you before he sacked Steph?" Internally, I cringed but kept my face smooth as my eyes slid between the two women. Though only a thin wall of glass separated them, they were worlds apart.

Way to run off your mouth, Danny. You're out of practice.

"Liam sent me down." She shifted a small box in her arms. I took the hint and liberated it while she shook her arms out. The box was heavier than I'd expected.

"What have you got in here, a bowling ball?"

"Conscience of the men upstairs," she bantered, the sparkle back in her eye. I laughed, placing the box on Steph's — *Ally's* — desk.

"Surely they wouldn't all fit in something so small."

"Coffee machine and thirty pieces of silver." Startled at her humour, I laughed again.

"Time and a place, Danny." Cal's piercing gaze caught me as he escorted a despondent Steph through the office, making me feel like a school kid waiting outside the principal's office. Her head dropped as she collected her handbag, not making eye contact with any of us.

I wanted to make her feel better, but what do you say to the girl who got your boss' girlfriend tortured? Cal looked briefly at Ally with a small nod as he passed, his hand between Steph's shoulder blades as he propelled her into the elevator.

"He'll be back in a moment." I gestured to the office. "Want a tour?"

Ally frowned after Cal as the doors closed behind them. "He shouldn't be touching her." Her voice was soft, but her tone brittle. I noted it for later, unable to help myself.

Always watching, never stopping.

It was the curse of any — decent — undercover cop. Even in the office, or at home, I couldn't just switch it off. Always on edge, waiting for them — or me — to make a mistake. It wasn't logical or rational. But it was part of me - and something in our new receptionist was bringing out the old paranoia. Time to test the waters.

"Well, you know what she did, right?" I turned away but watched Ally's in the reflection of the fishbowl.

"Ooh, no. Tell me." A swishing sound drew my attention to those long, slender legs swinging over the edge of the desk. She tilted her head back, perched on the desk, a speculative look in those bright eyes as she surveyed me.

I gave Ally an easy smile, leaning my back to the desk next to her, not answering. If Liam hadn't told her, then she didn't need to know. I relaxed, close enough to be in her space, but not touching her. Especially not after that comment aimed at Cal.

I might not always get along with the man, but he was my boss, and he'd earned my respect more than once in recent months.

I just hoped I could earn his back.

"What'd you do to catch Liam's eye? Guy's a machine," I commented, not looking at her. She gave a soft snort.

"He works hard," she acknowledged, but there was a pause in her voice I didn't like. Something seemed off about this girl who had just walked into our office, and how she got here. I needed to know more.

"But...?" I pushed. She shrugged, flipping blonde strands over her shoulder.

"I don't know. Just... He's got an agenda." She shrugged it off, flipping her sheet of straight blonde hair over her shoulder in a practised move.

The stairwell door creaked. I turned to look straight at Ally as Cal walked back into the office, running a hand over his shaved head. A clear face and clear eyes stared back at me. I knew that look, because it was mine, every time I was in a situation with work. My mask.

"He does. Us." I pushed off the desk, waiting for Cal. "You alright, boss?"

Cal nodded, shadows shifting beneath his skin as energy seemed to leave him, though it wasn't yet midday.

"That never gets easier." He threw a forced a grin at me, and turned to Ally. "Thanks for coming down so quickly."

Ally smiled, never moving from her spot on the desk.

"Thanks for having me in here. This one's mine?" She stroked the desk beneath her. Cal followed her hands, gaze sharpening.

Not the right guy to flirt with, not now.

Especially after having to have *the talk* with one of his staff. My estimation of our new receptionist was sinking with each moment. Cal nodded in her direction, and she simpered at his attention. I hid a grin, knowing what was coming.

Hell, I was becoming as jaded as Cal and Liam. Was it possible I was growing up? I snorted. Never going to happen.

"After what I've just had to do, let's keep everything professional and above board, shall we?" Cal raised an eyebrow at our new receptionist until her head bowed under his sharp gaze. She hopped off the desk, fiddling with the box of things she'd brought with her. Cal's eye caught mine. "Got a job for you."

I nodded. "Thanks," I nodded to Ally, "good luck."

"You, too." She smiled thinly, but I couldn't help thinking there was more to what she wasn't saying.

Cal squeezed my shoulder, and I headed into the incident room. Four terminals took up the space, with a blank wall at the far end, and a new sheet of blackboard wallpaper spread across it. Cal had taken the old one down right after our last case and given us all time off.

It had been a hell of a case, and we'd earned the downtime. All of us. I rubbed my neck where I'd been jabbed with horse tranq and woke up after all the action had been done with. I winced — we'd all gotten complacent, but I'd let my guard down.

I couldn't afford to let it happen again.

I flicked my terminal on, slumping in my chair. I always felt odd sitting at the tiny desk, too bulky for it, by far. Not as bad as Micah — the man dwarfed everything he touched. The glassed door to the office rattled as Cal came in. I sat up straight. I wanted to be part of his unit, but unless I could give him something more than I had in the last case, I wouldn't last long. Elite meant being elite — the best — *all the time*. I needed to up my game.

"She seems nice," I nodded to Ally setting up her desk on the other side of the glass. Books emerged from the box, followed by a stationary caddy with lots of sparkly accoutrements. At least there wasn't anything fluffy in there.

"Keep your eyes in your head, Danny. Haven't you got enough to deal with on that front, right now?" Cal glared at me. Not the best start. It took me a minute to work out what he was talking about.

"Whoa– Dude, we broke up. And I'm not after an office affair. Too bloody messy." I held up both hands in mock defence, grinning to de-escalate. "Besides, you said you had something for me?" The thought of a new job revved me up. Nothing worse for a cop than boredom.

"Good." Cal hefted a file from his desk. The thing looked like a bible, post-its and tags dangling from all sides. He canted his head and tossed the file to me. I caught it — just.

"What's this?" Cal nodded, and I opened the cover, looking at a much younger picture of myself. "Cal?"

"You're up for professional development. I've booked you in with a coach. You start tomorrow, and it will run as long as it needs to."

"No."

"No?"

I closed the file.

"You're wasting both my time and yours. Put me in undercover or get me a hacking job. Somewhere I can be useful." I waved the file. A pink post-it fluttered to my feet and settled on industrial-grade carpet. "Do something, more than just sitting around."

Cal grinned. "You sound like Liam."

That caught me off guard.

"What about Liam?"

"He's on leave until further notice.'" Cal grimaced, "Until we get a new caseload. Something decent. I'm working on it, but he's...not taking downtime well. Selena's babysitting him."

"Ouch."

"So, until then...you're on PD. The coach is–"

"I told you, I'm not doing this." I could barely keep the desperation out of my voice. "Just put me somewhere I can do something. Please." My voice had a whining quality I instantly hated.

"You need this," Cal held up a hand, "to specialise. You can't work undercover forever, and you need a career path if you want to stay here." His gaze connected with mine, and I slumped back into my chair.

And there it was. What I couldn't get past. If I wanted to stay on the team, it was Cal's way, or I wasn't on the team.

A few months ago, I'd decided to sleep with Cal's — my boss's — ex. Very recent ex, who was now *my* recent ex. If that wasn't enough, I'd decided to top it off by sucker-punching the arrogant bastard. He hadn't deserved it, not really — my own insecurities shone through, chafing about authority when I thought I could do Cal's job better than him.

Cal pulled out the chair at Micah's desk opposite me, scooting forward.

"Danny, you're the smartest guy on this team. Hell, you're always going to be the smartest guy in the room, apart from maybe Liam." I smirked at that. "I know you work hard at looking like an idiot—"

"Gee, thanks, boss—"

"*But*, you need direction. So, let's find where you're going. All the info for your coaching is in there. You just have to turn up tomorrow. Plus, Liam insists."

Awesome. If Liam had his hand in this, there was no way I was getting out of it. I rose, gripping the file, so it bent in the middle despite how thick it was. Cal leaned back, looking up at me, but didn't stand.

"Is this the part where I say I'll have your job?" I gritted my teeth before I said anything I'd regret. "Guess I'll see you when you have real work for me."

I strode out of the office, making sure the door didn't bang on my way out. I'd lost my temper and Cal had seen it — again. Damn it, I needed to get a handle on this. Glad I'd worn my running shorts in — the gym wouldn't cut the edge off my energy, but a few laps around the lake might.

"Leaving so soon?" Ally popped up from behind her desk, a tangle of phone and computer cords in her hands. I gave her the same easy grin from before, slipping comfortably back into my mask. Shoulders relaxed, stride turning to a strut. *Hide everything.*

"Gotta keep the guns big." I flexed, and she giggled. It was a pathetic routine, but at least I didn't have to go into the argument I'd just had with my boss. Besides, it was in me to flirt just because I knew it would irritate Cal further. I winked. "See you 'round."

"Bye, Danny." She waved as I got into the elevator, her facade as fake as mine, I was sure.

Danny's story continues in BLINDSIDED.

www.books2read.com/Blindsided/BBB2

Read Liam & Selena's story in Politics & Paperwork

www.books2read.com/PoliticsandPaperwork

www.ingramcontent.com/pod-product-compliance
Lightning Source LLC
Chambersburg PA
CBHW030702190726
48286CB00001B/130